Sir Michael's Mayhem

Susan M. Baganz

This is a work of fiction. Names, characters, places, and incidents either are the product of the author's imagination or are used fictitiously, and any resemblance to actual persons living or dead, business establishments, events, or locales, is entirely coincidental.

Sir Michael's Mayhem

Contact Information: titleadmin@pelicanbookgroup.com

Scripture quotations, unless otherwise indicated are taken from the King James translation, public domain.

Cover Art by *Nicola Martinez*

Prism is a division of Pelican Ventures, LLC
www.pelicanbookgroup.com PO Box 1738 *Aztec, NM * 87410

White Rose Publishing Circle and Rosebud logo is a trademark of Pelican Ventures, LLC

Publishing History
Prism Edition, 2018
Electronic Edition ISBN 978-1-5223-9778-6
Paperback Edition ISBN 978-1-5223-9780-9
Published in the United States of America

Dedication

To those who fight valiantly against
a darkness few understand.
You are not alone. May you find that
God is our hope in the stormy seas of life.

BOOKS BY SUSAN M. BAGANZ

Black Diamond Regency Romantic Suspense

The Baron's Blunder (Prequel) novella

The Virtuous Viscount (Book 1)

Lord Phillip's Folly (Book 2)

Sir Michael's Mayhem (Book 3)

Lord Harrow's Heart (coming soon)

The Captain's Conquest (coming soon)

Orchard Hill Contemporary Romances

Pesto & Potholes

Salsa & Speed Bumps

Feta & Freeways

Root Beer & Roadblocks

Bratwurst & Bridges…

and others coming soon!)

Historical Christmas Novella

Fragile Blessings

Gabriel's Gift

Short Story Compilation

Little Bits O' Love

Author's Note

During the tempestuous years between 1800-1820 or the more specific "Regency" years of 1811 to 1820, it was common for the upper classes, especially the men, to drink various forms of alcohol as part of their daily life. A glass of port wine was often savored by the men after the evening meal. French brandy was considered superior and highly coveted even though England was at war with France. In these stories, my characters do at times drink, and sometimes even to excess with serious consequences for their overindulgence. This is not in any way a recommendation on the part of the author or Pelican Book Group to advocate the drinking of alcohol or to abuse any substance. Laudanum is actually an opiate that was often prescribed medicinally (although many did become addicted to the drug). The use of these in the story are merely an attempt to use this period in history and its notorious excesses as a backdrop where appropriate.

Lord, will he ever open his eyes to see me? Help me, Lord. And protect him from those who seek to end his life.
~Miss Katrina Shepherd

Mischief:
ῥαδιουργία rhaıdiŏurgia krad-ee-oorg-ee'-
a recklessness, i.e. (by extension) malignity, mischief
(Strong's Exhaustive Concordance)

O full of all subtlety and all mischief, thou child of the devil, thou enemy of all righteousness, wilt thou not cease to pervert the right ways of the Lord?
~Acts 13:10

1

Late Winter London 1811

Sir Michael Tidley scanned the crowd for his contact. Who had Lord Hughes sent? He'd been wandering around the fringes of the ballroom in hopes of finding the person. He spun on his heel, bumping into a petite, nondescript woman dressed in grey. Most likely a companion. The contents of the drink she carried spilled down the front of his unmentionables and her dress. Insipid red wine designated for the ladies.

"I beg your pardon, miss." He pulled out a handkerchief to blot in vain at the stain on his buff pantaloons and the dark spots on her gray skirt.

"'Tis no matter, sir." Her expression revealed neither embarrassment nor dismay over the incident. "I will procure another ratafia for Lady Orion." She curtsied before him almost bumping heads as he rose up from his task. She fearlessly met his gaze.

"Allow me to fetch a glass to Lady Orion and make your excuses while you retire to repair the damage," he offered.

"That will not be necessary."

"I insist." He reached for the now empty glass in her hand and she relinquished it without further protest. "Where is she seated?"

"Over on the far west side of the ballroom, under the painting of *A Midsummer Night's Dream*. The one showing Puck up to his mischief." And with that she disappeared into the crowd.

Michael's valet would not appreciate the work ahead in getting the stains out of his pantaloons. He approached the refreshment table to refill the glass and glided through the crowd to Lady Orion as she held court with the lions of the *ton*. He bowed before her. "Lady Orion, I had the misfortune to cause an accident, so pardon my appearance. Your companion has gone to try to clean up, but will return shortly." He gave his most charming grin as he handed over the drink.

Lady Orion stared up at Sir Tidley, holding his gaze, almost as if she could peer into his soul. Michael sensed a challenge from the older matron, whom he equally feared and respected. He ignored the nagging feeling that she saw more than he preferred.

"My companion will likely find her way home rather than be seen. You say the accident was not due to her clumsiness?"

"Most certainly, m'lady. Would I lie to you?"

"I believe you might tell me whatever truth you deemed appropriate and suitable for your present need." She gave a little huff with that pronouncement, and the ladies nearby tittered as they eavesdropped.

Michael chuckled. "I shall depart to tend to my own wardrobe. Good evening, ladies."

As he walked off Lady Orion's exclamation to the other women caught his ears. "Now there's a man too charming for his own good. Too bad about his parentage." He cringed as he slipped through the crowd to an empty parlour.

He searched his pockets. Had someone managed

to get the promised message to him? He found the note in his right front coat pocket, pulled it out, and glanced at it. He scanned the contents and memorized the information before he crumpled it up and threw it into the fireplace, waiting to make sure it completely burned. The door to the patio that led to the gardens opened soundlessly, and Sir Michael became one with the night.

~*~

Katrina slipped into the mews after her collision with Sir Tidley. Stopping by the wall of the stable she held her hand to her chest to steady her heart. That man never ceased to set it racing. He failed to recognize her and hadn't asked her name as proper introductions were not possible at that juncture. She sighed. Would he find the paper? Did he realize the danger he faced? She shook her head. He probably didn't. Lord Hughes requested she only pass the note and not involve herself further. It proved he didn't understand just who he was dealing with.

Foolish men.

Pushing away from the wall she melted into the bleak alley to the Orion townhouse. Sneaking up the servants' stairs she located her room and changed from one disguise to another before departing. Armed with a pistol in her reticule and a knife sheathed to her right thigh, she hoped that she would not be too late to be of any assistance to Sir Tidley. She hailed a hackney and gave directions to the seedier side of London.

~*~

Sir Michael had changed into common labourer attire before striding into the Ox and Rooster, a pub filled with drunk and rowdy labourers. The odor wasn't any better here than at the ball, except he didn't have to choke on the perfumes used to cover up the stench of sweat, dirt, and spilled lager. His face was smudged with a bit of dirt. He hoped this meeting would be as helpful as Lord Hughes indicated it might be.

The aroma of fresh baked bread and beef stew was barely discernable. His mouth watered. He left the ball before the supper dance, but often these little pubs had the superior food. He found a seat at a small table, placed an order, and leaned back against the wall to wait while he sipped the dark brew set in front of him by a buxom maid with a sly wink. He shook his head. He gave up that game many years ago and had no desire to add a woman into the thick of the intrigue he was involved in. Women made things messy.

He sipped his ale and savored the bitter aftertaste. True, his friends Marcus and Phillip found wives they adored and whom he admired. But their lives were not as complicated. On the surface he seemed like the simplest of fellows living a carefree existence. He chuckled to himself over the irony of it all.

He kept an eye on the working class as they moved about the room. But for an accident of birth and a mother who chose to face scandal to keep her illegitimate son, this could have been his life. He respected the labourers who did an honest day's work and lived with anxiety over where their next meal might come from, or how they would provide for a wife and children. Most of those wouldn't be here tonight. This evening it would be the single men—the lonely and discontented. He sensed it in the air. The smell of danger hovered on the edge of the convivial chaos around him.

His soup arrived. He paid the tab immediately in case of trouble. The hair prickled at the back of his neck, alerting him that someone watched. He pretended ignorance and leaned forward to plunge the home-cooked bun into the savory soup and let the juice dribble down his chin. He grinned. How long had it been since he'd allowed himself to do that? Sometimes playing dress up for these missions permitted him little pleasures that walking amongst the *ton* couldn't. He wiped the soup away with his sleeve and picked up a spoon to dig in with relish. As he scraped the bottom of the stoneware bowl, a man with his cap pulled low, dirty clothes, and unshaven appearance, sat across from him.

His table was quickly surrounded by more men with similar attire, missing teeth, and unshaven faces. The lout across the table leaned forward, and the smell of stale ale assailed Michael's nostrils. He fought not to make a face and hoped this was his contact.

"Yur not from 'roun here." The man started out with a menacing tone and leaned back against his chair to wait.

"I 'eard tell this was the best ale and stew this side of the Thames." Michael tried hard to ape the accent of the lower classes. It had never been his strong suit. Although he spoke several languages, the dialect of the street often escaped him.

"You lookin' for some un?" The man picked his teeth with a knife.

The men around him shifted from foot to foot. The noise in the room dulled.

"Mayhap." Michael raised his glass to take a sip of ale, his eyes never leaving the man across the table. All senses were heightened.

"We don' like strangers hir." This came from a man behind him whose hand now rested on Michael's shoulder. Michael remained calm. *Where was his contact?* The man continued, "Nother gent made the same mistake, not an hur past."

"Really?" Michael tensed involuntarily. So his contact had been intercepted.

"He ain't gonna be tellin' anyone 'bout this place anytime soon." This came from a third man.

Michael wondered how he might escape. Three to one he might handle, but the room was packed and he'd prefer to avoid an all-out brawl if he could.

The door opened from the outside bringing in a gush of fresh air and the scent of impending rain. An attractive, petite blonde stood in the doorway. All the men turned to stare. She smiled shyly as she searched the room. Spying Michael, she ran to his table, propelled herself into his lap, wrapped her arm around his neck, dislodging the hand of the man behind the chair.

"Dear, I am sorry to have 'arped at ye after all ye done for me. Take me back. I canna live without ye." The voice was loud enough for all to hear, and she hugged his neck and laid her head next to his ear. "Follow my lead, I'll get you out of this," she whispered.

Michael grinned as he pulled the young woman's face in front of his own and leaned forward for a kiss.

The men around the table hooted and hollered. The woman in his arms melted into him before pulling away. "Ye forgive me and you'll come 'ome?"

Michael nodded.

She threw her arms around him and hugged him tight before leaning back again and jumping off his lap. She grabbed his hand and raised him to his feet. Michael was not a tall man, inches shorter than the ruffians around him. But this woman was smaller still.

He gave the men a grin and a shrug. "Lover's spat, ey, men? Guess I gotta go. 'Twas an interestin' evenin'."

The woman tugged Michael through the crowd. Once outside and still holding his hand, she dragged him down the alley at a run, veering down another and another almost as if through a maze.

Finally, he pulled back, stopping her. "Wait a minute. Where are you taking me?"

"To safety. Your contact was unconscious behind the inn." Her breathing was labored, and she doubled over to catch her breath.

"You saved my life. Thank you. Will you be all right?" His own chest was heaving from the adrenaline rush and the mad dash through the streets and alleys.

"Shhhh, footsteps." The blonde hissed as she pushed Michael up against the wall and leaned into him for a kiss.

His arms naturally went around her body as he bent his head to hers. Someone turned the corner and headed their way. They kissed more passionately, and the blonde made some noises indicating she was finding this a satisfactory performance. While Michael was frustrated at the failed meeting, he enjoyed the interlude with this little armful. This woman's kisses branded his soul. He would have a hard time forgetting her when they parted ways. Fanciful thinking for a spy.

The man stopped not far from them, watching.

The woman broke off the kiss and leaned her forehead against his chest, trying to catch her breath.

"This ain't no peep show. Go away!" Michael growled at the stranger, who then turned and left. The coast was clear. "Who are you?" Michael asked.

"No one of importance," she replied.

"Please. A name."

"Mouse," she whispered.

Michael held her at arm's length, getting only the vague impression of a petite build, a heart shaped face, unruly blonde hair, and the garb of a lower-class servant.

"Where can I find you?" he asked.

"You can't." She glanced up and down the alley, disengaging from his embrace. Her voice was softly musical, with a huskiness to it that indicated she'd been as affected by their kisses as he was. "Go home. If I need to, I will contact you. You should be safe enough now. I'm sorry your meeting didn't work out as you'd hoped." With that, she took off at a run.

Michael belatedly pushed off the wall to give chase. The woman skirted and tossed garbage in his way before vanishing. Michael didn't recognize this part of the city. He walked several blocks before finding a hackney to catch a ride home. He flipped the driver an extra coin for the fare and made his way to his living quarters.

Tristan, his batman, greeted him when he entered his room. Michael threw his hat on a chair, followed by the ratty coat he wore. He began to undo the buttons of his shirt.

"No success?" Tristan asked cautiously, as if sensing Michael's darkened mood. He came forward to take the discarded clothing away. Tristan possessed reddish hair that curled and was kept short. He'd been with Michael during the war and returned more recently to help him in his secret work. His blue eyes saw way too much.

"My contact was intercepted before I arrived. I barely got out intact myself."

"Oh? A woman?"

Michael's gaze flew to his servant, who was putting his dancing shoes aside. "Why do you think there would be a woman involved?"

"Blonde hair on your coat and lip color on your cheek might be my first few clues. Your foul temper being my last one. Usually, a woman causes that."

Michael gave a bark of laughter. "You're impudent, Tristan. But you are also observant and correct. A woman saved my skin tonight, and I don't even know her name or how to find her again."

"Impressive chit, huh?"

Sir Michael wagged his eyebrows, "Well, she sure does something with a kiss that I've never experienced before."

"You want her for a mistress?"

"I didn't say that."

"You implied it. Lust has no place in the games we are engaged in. 'Women are dangerous and distract from our mission. Avoid them like the plague.' I believe those were your words on that subject only a few nights ago."

"Quite true."

"So why is this one different enough to warrant reconsidering your stance?"

"Reconsidering my stance?" Michael's eyes narrowed as he searched his valet's innocent looking face. He pulled off his labourer-style boots.

"You expressed a desire in seeking this chit out, didn't you?"

"I did. She helped me significantly tonight. I would only want to thank her properly and ensure she made it safely home."

"Noble thoughts, indeed." Tristan's voice dripped with sarcasm.

Michael reached out to bat a hand at his servant and partner in espionage. "Leave off. I've had a rough night."

"You had a run in with some reddish liquid."

"Actually, I collided with a companion to Lady Orion, who carried a glass of ratafia."

"Well, that makes it so much better, doesn't it? Those stains will be far more understanding of my attempts to remove them since a young lady was involved." Tristan ducked as a boot sailed over his head. "You need to work on your throwing arm. Even in bowling you were never very good at the pitch." Tristan grabbed the boot and its pair and headed to the adjoining room before any more items could be tossed his way.

Sir Michael rubbed a hand over his face and went to the mirror above the dresser on the far side of the room. He grabbed a cloth and dampened it to remove the lip color from his lips and cheek. Dropping the fabric, he placed both hands on the dresser and stared at himself. He appeared older than his eight and twenty years. Frown lines had grown between his eyes and on his forehead. Crinkles from laughter bracketed his eyes and mouth. Tints of silver began to show in his sideburns he kept shorter than his peers.

Peers? There was really no peer for him, was

there? He possessed friends, true. But being born on the wrong side of the blanket left him in a social no man's land most of the time. A comfortable income, but no property. A mother from the *beau monde* tinted with scandal and a father whose name she took with her to the grave. T'was the reason he engaged in the risky business of espionage. He needn't worry about providing an heir to some trumped up lineage. He had no real family name to live up to, although his grandfather begrudgingly gave him his. Because of that, loneliness warred with despair. He didn't want to die, but he didn't fear it either. It didn't really matter to him either way.

His friends, Marcus, and Phillip, made it clear it did matter. They were under the firm belief that were he to die without Jesus, he would be damned to hell for eternity. Maybe so. Wasn't hell really here on earth anyway? Where people exchanged power for money and lives for land? Where deceit and betrayal were stock and trade of almost every man? Maybe that's why he liked Marcus, Phillip, and Theo. They were honest. They didn't let class or an accident of birth hinder their expressions of concern for his life. He dropped his head and moved away to find the brandy decanter. He poured a drink and gazed into the warm, bronzed liquid.

A small creature jumped from the bed to the table to Michael's shoulders and sniffed at the drink before turning to lick Michael's face.

"Well met, Fidget. Keeping out of mischief, are you? Tristan didn't complain about you tonight at least." This was met with some quick clicking noises from the brown, white, and black ferret that scampered down his arm, jumping back to the bed. The rodent turned in a circle three times, almost as if chasing his fluffy tail, before curling up and focusing his beady black eyes on Michael.

Michael grinned before glancing at his drink. The image of another face sprang to mind, that of a delectable young woman who courageously and mysteriously saved his skin tonight.

What color were her eyes? He hadn't been able to tell. Why would her kisses affect him so? He'd kissed many women through the years. Some to gain information, or to merely stave off the loneliness that crouched at the door of his heart. He shook his head. *Mouse*. What kind of name was that? He chuckled to himself and took a swallow of the brandy, allowing it to burn all the way down and savoring every inch. Ironic that his code name was 'Cat,' so named because of his reputation for stealth and nocturnal work. Was Mouse a code name? She was aware of the meeting and his contact's injury. She arrived to save him. Had Lord Hughes involved her in this case somehow?

Anger welled up inside. He drank the rest of his drink and picking up Fidget, Michael threw back the covers to his bed. He set the ferret down next to his pillow. First thing in the morning Michael would be pounding on the doors of the Ministry of Defense at Whitehall to demand an audience and find out what was going on. He didn't need a woman interfering in his work.

Soon the ferret was wrapped around his head. Well, thought Michael, at least someone loved him, even if it was only an elongated, fuzzy rat.

~*~

Katrina sneaked up the servants' stairs for the second time that night. With the blonde wig in a bag by her side, she managed to gain entry to her room, unnoticed. Something she seemed to be able to accomplish too easily. The space was cold and she rushed through changing and washing the rouge and lip color off her face. As the towel brushed her lips, she recalled Sir Michael's kisses. How many years had she longed and waited for him to notice her as a woman? For him to kiss and desire her. Tonight, it appeared she got her wish, but he didn't even realize it was her. Only a nameless woman who catapulted herself into his lap. The heat of a blush rose up her neck at the memory of her audacity in throwing herself at him at the Ox and Rooster.

It was only acting. Even on his part. Wasn't it? Perhaps not. From what she understood, there were certain signs a man was interested. She took note of that at the table and in the alley. But men could be physically attracted to almost anyone, so that meant nothing. It was merely physical. So why had that first kiss seemed so magical to her? Was it just the danger of the moment and the thrill of being observed and passing off her role with such success?

Maybe if being a companion didn't work out after this case was resolved, she should try the stage. She grinned as she brushed out her hair and braided it. She climbed into bed and hugged her pillow close, recalling the sense of security and passion she experienced in Michael's arms. Things he would never offer a mere companion by the name of Katrina Shepherd. Still, a heart in love didn't always listen to reason, did it?

~*~

The next morning Katrina made herself scarce, begging off being alongside her employer for the round of visitors sure to come. She sat by a window doing mending and with a view to the street to observe who visited. When Sir Tidley arrived, she grinned. He would not discover her identity yet.

2

Sir Michael was escorted into a lavish drawing room and bent over Lady Orion's hand. "My lady, as stunning as always, you would make the sun jealous."

"Cheeky devil," she riposted, as she patted the seat next to her, indicating he should sit. She was dressed in yellow, the dress and style were obviously meant for a much younger woman. Still, she grinned at him appreciatively. "Sir Tidley, what brings you to my door this fine day?"

"I came to inquire after your companion. To ensure she did not suffer any harm as a result of our collision last night."

"I regret to say she is not home to visitors today, but when we spoke earlier, she seemed none the worse for wear. I cannot speak for her wardrobe, but with what I pay her she can probably purchase a new dress or make one up herself. I don't understand her penchant for grey. She appears mousy in that color with her hair."

"Mousy?"

"Well, you met her, didn't you?"

"Only for a brief moment, my lady."

"So you were not formally introduced, and she fled before any more conversation could take place as a proper lady of virtue should."

Michael nodded and grinned. Proper would

definitely be an apt description of the young lady he'd collided with. Images of another young woman, not quite so proper, inserted themselves at the forefront of his mind, and he reluctantly shoved thoughts of her aside to focus on the older matron before him. "You're correct."

"I always am, Sir Tidley, and you would do well to never forget that. Now, where was I? Oh, yes. Mousy. Wears gray all the time. Muddy brown hair pulled back so tight it makes me hurt to look at her. Quiet. So quiet I rarely realize she's around until she's almost upon me. I cannot complain, she is related and definitely works hard to earn her room and board here. I indulge in some of those novels once in a while to pass the time, with her lovely, soft voice reading them to me. I am glad that I agreed to take her in."

"She sounds like the perfect companion for you."

Lady Orion's eyes narrowed and she tapped her right forefinger against her lips. "I was going to ask you how your friend, Lord Remington, and his lovely Viscountess are doing. It seems an age since they've been in town."

"It is early in the season, and I expect them within the month. They are at Rose Hill. Their daughter is a few months old now, so I expect they will all descend to town together. Marcus has work to do in Parliament."

"And what about Lord Westcombe? Now that marriage was a fishy business that seems to have come out smelling quite nice." She preened. Had she anything to do with all that?

"He arrived a week hence with Lady Westcombe and their son."

"And Lord Harrow, he was also a part of your

convivial group, wasn't he?"

"He was, but is currently in the country. I am not certain when to expect him."

"So, there is no one to ensure you stay out of trouble?" Lady Orion winked. "I'll need to keep an eye on you."

Sir Michael grinned. "You go right ahead. As a man of leisure, I can assure you that trouble is my middle name."

Lady Orion chuckled and rapped his knuckles gently with her fan. "You are a scamp. I hope you will do me the honor of visiting again." She rose and so did Sir Tidley, who gave a bow and departed as his fifteen minutes of allotted time had elapsed.

~*~

Katrina placed her sewing on her lap. Michael took the reins of his horse and leapt into the saddle in one flawless movement. She sighed as he rode away, so lost in thought she did not hear Lady Orion enter the room.

"So, Miss Shepherd, you observed Sir Tidley? Were you embarrassed to meet him after your clumsiness last night?" Lady Orion sat down in a chair across from her.

Katrina grew warm as she picked up her mending again and tried to focus on making the nice even stitches that were required of a lady of quality. "I suppose so."

"He inquired after you." Lady Orion's comment was met with silence as Katrina focused on her stitches. "He would be a good catch. Given your father's reputation, you'll never garner a titled gentleman, and you are a bit older than most women going through their season, but at five and twenty, you would be a suitable age for a man such as Sir Michael."

Katrina's heart sped up. She accidently struck herself with the needle. "Oh!" She pulled the finger up and stuck it in her mouth, before glancing at her employer with wide eyes.

"He does impact your sensibilities. Good. And why not? He is a fine figure of a man, even if of shorter stature. He has noble blood in his veins as well, but that should be of no importance to you." This was said with an air of finality, but before Lady Orion rose she added, "Make him work for it." With that parting salvo, she left Katrina in peace.

Make him work for it? He doesn't even realize I'm alive. Katrina ignored the pain in her heart, sighed, and resumed her work.

~*~

Michael presented himself at the Ministry of Defense at Whitehall and was forced to cool his heels in the anteroom. He wondered if it was a deliberate ploy to keep him on edge. After a half an hour, he was escorted into Lord Hughes's inner sanctum.

"Sir Tidley." Lord Hughes sat at his desk scattered with papers. He didn't glance up, but motioned with his fountain pen for Michael to sit, and continued writing for a few minutes.

Michael chose to stand with his arms crossed in front of his chest, waiting.

Finally, Lord Hughes raised his white-haired head. Seeing Michael's stance, he leaned back in his chair. "Out with it."

"The contact failed."

"You got the message?"

"I'm not sure how, but yes, I did."

"Good, good. I'm delighted about that. The messenger was new, and it was a test. Glad to see it went flawlessly." He grinned broadly.

"Flawlessly? Apparently the informant I was to dine with met with violence. Did he survive?" Michael's tone was quiet with a hint of menace.

"He'll recover. That was unfortunate, but it was the location he chose, so he will live with his choice."

"And what of the girl?"

"Girl?"

"The young woman who helped me escape that same fate."

"I didn't send a girl. Describe her to me."

"Petite, blonde, heavy rouge and a great…" Michael coughed, "imagination."

Lord Hughes supported his elbows on the arms of his chair with his fingers steepled in front of his face. He tapped his nose a few times. "Did she give you a name?"

"Mouse."

Lord Hughes's eyebrows rose.

"You know of her then, but you didn't send her?" Michael frowned. "Yet she was aware of the mission."

Lord Hughes pulled his hands away from his face. "She acted on her own initiative, and trust me, she will receive a severe tongue lashing—after I thank her for saving you. Since when did you need a partner, Michael?"

"I don't. I might have escaped on my own with minimal harm, but she appeared and took over. I want her stopped. I'm fine with Tristan. I most especially do not need a meddlesome chit butting her head into my business."

"You mean the government's business?"

"Of course," Michael sighed. "But what next? I can't decipher without that code. We are running out of time."

"What if I told you that Mouse may be the very person to help you?"

"I would say you are lying."

Lord Hughes stood up and leaned forward on the desk. "I bet this young woman could run circles around you with this one."

"I gave up gambling, Lord Hughes. You can keep your girl. I'll figure this out on my own."

"No, you will follow orders. Tonight, at half past midnight, Mouse will be at your home to assist you. But I warn you, Michael. She is quality, and I will not have her reputation compromised. Act the gentleman." He paused. "And accept her help."

Sir Michael swallowed hard and ground out "Yes, my lord" between gritted teeth. A muscle in his jaw moved furiously as he contained his anger. "Will that be all?"

"No. Protect those documents. Until we get them deciphered, we cannot risk them being stolen."

"You doubt my ability to perform my job?" Michael's left eyebrow rose slightly.

"I never doubted your ability, Michael. But don't underestimate your enemy." With that, Lord Hughes resumed his seat. He picked up his quill , dipped it in the ink and continued his writing.

Taking this as a dismissal, Michael departed.

~*~

Katrina received a missive later that afternoon. She made her excuses to Lady Orion, grabbed a dark cloak with a hood to shield her face, left the property through the mews, and walked three blocks before finding a hackney. She arrived at the Ministry of Defense and was without delay escorted into Lord Hughes's office. She seated herself, with her hands tightly folded in her lap and her back rigid, not touching the chair.

Lord Hughes considered her for a few moments. "You disobeyed orders, Katrina."

She held her gaze steady. She would not be cowed by this great man.

"However, I cannot be too angry since you saved the life of one of my most valuable agents."

She gave a terse nod.

"At half-past midnight present yourself at Sir Tidley's to help him with a document. Do you really believe you can decipher it?"

"Based on notes from my father's journal, yes."

"You seem certain that your father was not a traitor. Lives could be at stake if you are wrong, including yours and Sir Michael's."

"I am unafraid," Katrina said.

"He still doesn't realize who you are?" Lord Hughes asked.

"No."

"Working side by side, how long do you think you can conceal your identity? You cannot afford to be discovered or Lord Remington will interfere. He won't stand for a female family member engaging in these kinds of activities. You understand the risk I am taking by giving into your whim here?" His forehead wrinkled. He reached up with his left hand to pinch the bridge of his nose. "I worry for you, Katrina."

"I can take care of myself. You have no need to fear." Katrina gave this assertion while trying to hide a shiver that unexpectedly coursed through her.

"Go, then. This evening. Keep me apprised." Lord Hughes went back to sorting some papers on his desk.

Katrina rose, left, and returned home. When she got to the safety of her room she gave a subdued "Yes!" She didn't want Lady Orion to know the reason for her happiness.

~*~

Sir Tidley arrived home to find Tristan cleaning up a mess in the dining room.

"Tris, have we been invaded once again, or did Fidget do this?" Michael leaned against the doorway with his arms folded and a frown on his face as he surveyed the broken dishes and silverware strewn about. The ferret was nowhere to be seen.

"It would appear we were intruded upon, sir." Tristan rose to a standing position. "Twice in less than twenty-four hours. I question the safety of staying here this evening."

"Is this one of your premonitions?" Michael raised his right eyebrow as he gazed at his former batman.

Tristan nodded, his eyes darkened. "I cannot explain it, but I believe it would behoove us to move to rooms at the Savoy."

"The Savoy? Have we risen up in the world, Tristan? I'm not saying I cannot afford such luxury, but the Savoy?"

"Taking the papers, you would have extra

security. It would be harder for them to find you. I doubt my ability to keep you safe here given the stakes and the perseverance of our enemy." With that, Tristan returned to a crouch to clean up more broken pieces of china.

Michael pushed away from the wall and crouched down next to his servant. "It will be as you wish. How soon can you make ready?"

Tristan glanced to the side to meet Michael's eyes. "I could have your most important items out within the hour. If anyone is watching the house they will be none the wiser."

"That sounds reasonable. I will meet you there in a little while. Hire a maid to come and put this all to rights tomorrow."

Tristan nodded, and both men rose to their feet. The servant left the room, and Sir Tidley gained access to his study. Reaching his desk that so recently had been searched, a surge of anger coursed through him. Somehow his secret had been compromised. Someone searched for the document for now, but how long before they came after him? The previous evening had been a wake-up call. He scribbled off a note to Lord Hughes to pass information to Mouse regarding the change of location for the meeting.

He grinned. How would this Mouse gain entrance to his rooms at the Savoy? He almost relished seeing how she would get past all the security there. And yet, he anticipated spending time with the blonde who haunted his dreams last night with her breathtaking kisses. Michael licked his lips. Lord Hughes was wrong, the Mouse was far from a lady and while he was a gentleman with a task to accomplish, he didn't understand why he couldn't enjoy himself a little.

~*~

Michael fell asleep in a comfortable chair in front of a warm fireplace in his luxuriously appointed suite at the Savoy with Fidget curled up on his lap. He waited for Mouse to come and the papers were secure. He sent Tristan out to guard the townhouse again, and discover if there were any further attempts at a break in. He almost hoped there was, as it would justify the expense of his temporary digs.

Tristan burst into the room at quarter past one. His reddish hair was mussed and the man was out of breath.

"Tris, what happened?" Michael yawned as he rose and shook his head to clear the sleep from his brain. Fidget jumped to the floor, bared his teeth, and clicked at Michael before stalking off to the bedroom to find a more secure nest. Michael glanced at the clock. "Mouse never showed up."

Tristan was bent over with his hands on his knees, gasping for air, but raised his head. "You were broken into again. Several men. A huge fight broke out. Came as fast as I could."

"After you catch your breath, we will go survey the damage." Michael went to change into clothes more suited for an evening that held the possibility of dirty work, and the two men departed. Michael hailed a hackney, and they arrived a block away from the townhouse, alighted and reached the home through the alley and garden. Surprisingly, the back door was secure. Michael opened it with a key, and they stealthily entered using only the moonlight illuminating through the windows to guide them.

Gaining the study, Michael cautiously peered in to find three bodies scattered about in odd positions. One had been knifed, but still lived. Tristan tied him up. The other two were dead. No information would be obtained through them. They slowly moved through other rooms on the ground floor before taking the steps to the next level.

The master bedroom door was ajar. Michael cautiously approached. This would be the first time the intruders invaded his personal space. Two more men lay dead. One shot and one with a judiciously applied short knife. A third was underneath the knifed man, but unconscious. Working together they removed the dead body. Michael motioned to Tristan to pick up the smaller man to take him downstairs. The man had suffered a gunshot wound to the left shoulder. Hopefully, he would live to be interrogated.

Michael surveyed the damage to his room and followed Tristan down the stairs. The injured man was placed on the couch. Michael motioned to him as he spoke to Tristan. "Check out that wound."

Tristan peeled off the dirty brown coat and suddenly stopped. "Sir?"

"What is it, Tris?"

"The gent here."

"Yes?"

"Isn't a gent."

"Excuse me?"

"'Tis a woman, sir."

Michael rushed over to the divan and glanced down at the individual lying there. The coat had been pulled halfway off, but there were definitely the curves of a woman showing against the white shirt that was exposed. Blood saturated the shoulder area. Michael knelt down next to the furniture and placed a hand up to the face. Smooth skin, smudged with dirt. He tugged the hat off the head. Brown hair pulled back but starting to escape the confines of the pins loosened from the hat being removed and the struggle she had undergone. He glanced back to the face. *Who was she?* This was no mere burglar. He was sure of it. He carefully searched all the pockets. Nothing. Michael checked for a pulse. It was weak.

Slowly the trussed-up man became conscious. He moaned and weakly struggled against the ropes that bound him to the chair. Tristan went over to check on him. The young woman's wound still bled. Michael removed the loose cravat and pressed it against her shoulder, applying gentle pressure to staunch the flow. His mind raced through his options. He couldn't take her back to the Savoy but obviously, she needed immediate medical attention. He didn't dare strip her here, but if the clothing were not removed soon, it would be plastered to the wound fostering infection. Where could he take her and not arouse suspicion? Lord Hughes was also a single gentleman, having been recently widowed. Not a good option.

Tristan appeared by his side, glancing down at the girl. "The man won't give his contact. He was hired by a middle man. He said that this—person—surprised them and fought them all. She is not a part of their group, and they had no idea where she came from or why she was here. It appears she was a fierce little warrior."

There was admiration in his valet's voice. Was this Mouse? Perhaps the message failed to reach her about the changed location? Michael ran a hand over his face in frustration. Lord Hughes would flog him if anything happened to this agent. He glanced again at her pale face, the perfect eyebrows, and the long lashes fanning her cheeks. Lips that would appear better formed into a smile. It wasn't an extraordinary face. It was, however, perfect and heart-shaped and he wondered who this master of disguise was. He reached over and opened up one eye that stared blankly at him. Hazel. Her eyes were hazel. Well, at least he'd satisfied his curiosity about that.

Lord Westcombe and his bride were in town. Beth would make sure Mouse was safe, wouldn't she? There weren't many other choices. "Call a hackney, Tris. We need to get her to the Westcombes's."

Tristan betrayed no surprise and immediately left the room. Michael took some extra rope, and tied the cravat around the shoulder and under the arm to hold it in place. He gently put his arms under her neck and knees and lifted her. She was surprisingly slight. She gave a soft moan of pain at being moved.

"You's ain't leavin' me?" the tied-up man asked.

Michael stopped and glanced back. "Someone will return to take care of you." He made his way out the door and down the steps of the townhouse to the waiting carriage and with Tristan's help, entered, still holding the young woman in his arms.

Tristan gave directions to the Westcombe house and climbed in.

Arriving at the darkened residence, Tristan went to the door and banged loud as Michael stood behind him holding the injured woman. Soon the butler was there and Tristan and Sir Michael were escorted into the foyer.

"A room, my good man. There is an injured woman here. Tris, go fetch a doctor please." Michael began to make his way up the stairs with his armful and made his way to the room he used when he visited. The butler followed after him, in his night rail, quite flustered. Michael entered the room and lay his charge on the large canopied bed.

"Michael, by all that is holy, what are you doing here at this hour?" Phillip rushed into the room tying a robe around himself.

"I cannot fully explain right now, but I have an injured woman here. I'm obligated to provide care. Tris has fetched a doctor. She's been shot. The bullet needs to come out."

Phillip came up to the bed.

The woman's hair was completely loose now. Her tresses fanned across the pillow to one side and flowed down the side of the bed.

"Kat?" Phillip whispered.

"What?" How could Phillip be aware of his code name?

"Miss Katrina Shepherd. How did she end up getting shot, Michael? Marcus will have your hide for this. I would not want to be in your shoes." Phillip patted Michael on the shoulder. "I'll get Beth. With the baby, she doesn't get much sleep anyway. You'll need her." With that, he left the room.

Michael stared down at the woman lying unconscious before him. He stared hard at her features. Kat? Could it really be her? How? He reached for her left hand. There was a scar there from pinky to wrist from a fall she took from a tree when they were younger. He reached up and pulled her hair back so he could see behind her right ear. Birthmark. Phillip was right. It was Miss Katrina Shepherd. If she also happened to be Mouse, he was in trouble from every angle.

Beth rushed into the room with a purple robe flowing around her tall, lithe body and soft red hair flowing down her back. "Michael! Phillip says you brought us an injured young woman?"

Michael reached out to grab Beth's hands and planted a kiss on her cheek. "I did. I couldn't think of where else to take her where she could get the care she needed and preserve her reputation."

"You did the right thing. Phillip said her name was Katrina." Beth gently pushed Michael aside to untie the rope and peel back the cravat. "Oh. My. Michael, you need to leave. I will take care of getting these clothes off her so the doctor can extract that bullet. I believe Phillip will meet you in the study downstairs." She glanced over at him. He was a few inches shorter than her. "Don't worry. I will take good care of her."

Michael nodded and looked again at the woman in the bed. Kat was Mouse. A childhood playmate and cousin to Viscount Remington. He was in deep trouble. What else could he expect when a woman was involved? He nodded to Beth. "Thank you." He left to find Phillip.

3

A fire blazed in the library by the time Michael reached it. Phillip had changed clothes, but his hair was still mussed up. Marriage had changed his fastidious friend. Before that, one would never catch his friend with a hair out of place. He blushed as he remembered that his friend was a married man. Maybe he'd come at an inconvenient time?

"What were you thinking, Michael? Katrina? I know she's pluck to the backbone and was always getting into trouble, but I thought Marcus said she was staying with a relative?"

Michael went to the sideboard, poured a brandy, and took a sip. What excuse did he have? How could he have been so blind? Katrina had been a burr in his saddle since he was a young man. Following the boys everywhere, constantly getting into trouble that he usually needed to rescue her from. And gazing at him with those adoring eyes. Calf love. He resented that as a university graduate full of himself, but he would never have wanted her hurt.

"Michael?"

"I didn't realize it was her, Phillip. Until you said it, I didn't recognize her. I don't know how she came to be in this situation." Well, at least that much was true. Until he spoke with Lord Hughes. He assumed that estimable man knew what was going on. Michael'd been tricked and was not happy about the surprise.

"Can you tell me what you do know?" Phillip asked quietly.

"Not really."

"Are you in trouble, Michael?"

"Possibly."

"I would help you if I could."

"I'm not sure that will be possible."

"You keep your own counsel. You always have. I often suspected there is much you withhold from your friends."

Michael's eyes grew wide.

"All right, so maybe I got it right this time. Whatever you are involved in, I will do what I can to assist you. I suppose we need to send a message to Marcus in the morning. He was due to arrive in a few weeks anyway. He may want to come sooner."

"I would rather we didn't," Michael said as he walked over to the window to stare out at the dark early morning. It was close to three now.

"We can't wait too long. Marcus takes his responsibilities as head of his family seriously. He would be displeased to find Miss Shepherd in such a state." Phillip went to the sideboard, poured a drink, and took a sip.

"Do you think this doesn't bother me? What was she doing in London anyway? Why wasn't she home?" There was something missing that he ought to know but couldn't put his finger on.

"You don't remember? Her father died under suspicious circumstances around a year ago."

"Wasn't it ruled an accidental death?" Michael asked.

"Was it murder or suicide? His name was smeared and tarnished with unanswered questions. Marcus reported that Katrina was devastated to lose her father, which is only natural but she also vehemently defended him. There were whispers he was a traitor to the crown."

"Impossible. Mr. Shepherd was an outstanding man. I cannot picture him as a traitor."

"Nor could most who truly knew him, but rumors take on a life of their own."

"Miss Shepherd must have been doubly devastated."

"She was. If I remember correctly, Marcus invited her to live at Rose Hill, promising her a season. Her father's ill health the past few years kept her by his side, and she is no longer as young as most debutantes."

"I'm assuming she refused. She always was a stubborn little thing." Michael grinned as memories of a younger girl standing up to him and throwing down challenges came to his mind. "I haven't seen her in probably seven years, Phillip. When did she grow into a lady? I truly didn't recognize her." Michael sipped his drink as he watched his friend. He let the warmth settle in his mouth before swallowing, closing his eyes as he savored the heat moving down through his chest.

"Be honest, Michael. She always favored you. I was always a bit jealous. She was such a spirited little thing and tried so hard to fit in with our gang. But it was you she trailed after. I even wondered at one time if she would have ended up being a good wife for you someday."

Michael set his glass down with a bang. "Recant that."

Phillip chuckled. "Or what? Will you pummel me in my own home because an injured young woman threatens your bachelor status in my imagination?"

"No. I've no need of a wife. I remember her following me around like a puppy dog. A cute, friendly pet."

"What did you always call her?"

"Mouse."

"That's right! You nicknamed her mouse because she would be so quiet and sneak up on you, but when you caught her she would squeak."

Michael smiled at the memory. *Mouse*. Why didn't he make the connection? How dense was he? He obviously was not on top of his game anymore. Maybe after this case, he would retire from the espionage business. He was weary of the intrigue anyway. With any luck, he would die doing his job and not need to deal with the loneliness of the future stretching before him. If it happened before Marcus got a hold of him, all the better.

"Phillip, can we keep this silent for now? I need to find out how Katrina got where she was. I need more information before we contact Marcus."

"But someone will surely be worried about her."

Michael sighed and set his glass down. "I need to investigate. I will return shortly to see how she fares."

"I'll have a room made up for you."

"Thanks, Phillip, but that is not necessary. I've rooms at the Savoy for the night. I will return in a little while."

~*~

Michael gained entrance to the grand mansion that was home to Lord Hughes. Part of it was a challenge. Could he break in? He'd suffered a terrible shock and

Lord Hughes deserved a return favor for the prank he pulled on him. Cat and mouse game? He would put an end to that.

Michael sneaked up the stairs and entered the private master suite. Lord Hughes slept on his stomach under the covers of a massive oak bed with intricate carvings. Michael got close to the bed and pressed sharp cold metal against the flesh of Lord Hughes's neck.

"Who are you and what do you want?" the man in bed whispered.

"I would like some answers, my lord." Michael removed and sheathed the knife and went to light some candles from the embers of the fireplace.

Lord Hughes arose and found his robe. "Sir Tidley. To what do I owe this unexpected pleasure?" The polite words were edged with steel.

"Miss Katrina Shepherd was shot tonight," Michael said baldly.

Lord Hughes blanched and fell into the chair close to him. "What happened?'

"I would like the answer myself, but she is not conscious to tell me. She obviously did not get my note of a change of location for our meeting and arrived at my home while it was again being pillaged by our enemy. It appears she fought skillfully, leaving three dead and one injured, but unable to tell us about who sent them."

"You said she was shot?"

"In the shoulder. She is at Lord Westcombe's being attended to by the lady of the house, and a doctor has been summoned. She has not awakened."

"How did you learn it was her? She was certain she would be able to pull this off with you none the wiser."

"She might have succeeded if I hadn't taken her to Westcombe. It was Phillip who recognized her. When I checked for a distinctive scar and birthmark, I was able to confirm his identification of our patient was correct." Michael stepped forward, and put his hands on the arms of the chair where Lord Hughes sat, getting into his face. "What were you thinking, to let her get involved in this mess? Lord Remington will have our heads," he hissed.

"Don't you think I realize that? She's a persuasive little lady, and I figured she would come to no harm and accomplish her task, as well as help you with yours."

"*Her* task?" Michael stood up and rocked back on his heels as he folded his arms in front of his chest.

"To clear her father's name. It's her mission."

"A noble cause, but couldn't you have assigned someone else do that?" Michael paced.

"We are at war. I have no spare people to work on restoring a deceased man's reputation."

"And if the daughter ends up dead, what's that to you?" Michael prodded dangerously.

Lord Hughes rose to his feet. "I held great admiration for Mr. Shepherd and long believed he was wrongly accused, but lacked evidence. Katrina thought she could find that proof, but she needed your help. Do you think you would have given it? Tidley, she is like a daughter to me. I failed her tonight. You said you changed location? When did you decide that? Why wasn't I informed?"

"I sent a message to you at Whitehall after six."

"I was there until eight."

"So what happened to the missive? If she received

that she wouldn't have walked into danger."

Lord Hughes strode over the window. "Perchance someone intercepted it?"

Michael strode to stand next to Lord Hughes and glanced at the older man's reflection. The man had aged ten years in one evening. The lines in his forehead and the grayish cast of his skin and sagging cheeks spoke of many worrisome days and nights. "You really do care about her?"

Lord Hughes met Michael's gaze reflected in the glass. "Yes."

Michael moved away from the glass. "How did she come to be a blonde rescuing me from the danger in that pub?"

"The girl has far more courage than is good for her."

"She killed three men tonight and wounded another. We could have used men like her on the battlefield. I almost wish I'd been able to watch her in action." Michael's voice took on a wistful tone.

Lord Hughes smiled. "She told me that everything she knows about fighting, shooting, and swordplay, she learned from you."

"Guilty as charged. What was I thinking to give in to the whims of a young girl determined to keep up with the big boys?"

"Perhaps you admired her pluck even back then."

"Maybe."

"Will you keep me informed as to her progress?"

"Who was she staying with and how do we communicate to that person about her? What do I tell the Westcombes? Phillip is asking uncomfortable questions and wants to inform Lord Remington. I've managed to convince him that we should wait."

Michael drained his glass and went to set it down.

"I'll take care of it in the morning." Lord Hughes walked over and extended his hand to Michael. "Sir Tidley, I am sorry to have deceived you. It was a lark to be able to trick you for once. But never in my wildest dreams would I have envisioned this."

Michael shook his hand. "Neither of us are omniscient. I hear only God knows the future."

"I wonder what He's up to then if that's the case." Lord Hughes's hand dropped back to his side.

"I need a favor while I'm here."

"Yes?"

"There is a prisoner and several dead bodies littering my house."

"I will send someone over to take care of that."

"Thank you." Michael yawned. "Good night. I'll be in contact."

"Thank you, Michael. And in case I haven't said it enough, I appreciate your work and couldn't ask for a better agent. Keep watch over our Mouse, will you?"

"I'll do the best I can, but that has to be the most impossible task you've ever given me." Michael gave a wry grin and winked at Lord Hughes before he slipped out of the room and made his way back to the Westcombe townhouse.

He sneaked into the house and found Phillip waiting for him in the library.

"How is she?" Michael asked.

"Beth and the doctor are with her. There have been no screams so I will hope that means she has remained unconscious for the surgery."

Michael nodded. He moved to a chair and sat down, slouched, and put his booted feet up on a table.

Phillip caught his friend's raised eyebrow.

"I cannot tell you how this all happened. I'm still not sure. I was not aware that Katrina would be there."

"I don't know that you ever really explained how you found her like this."

"You are correct. She got herself in a bad spot, fought, and was shot. But not without taking out a few men first. Our training her with knives and guns came in handy tonight."

Phillip sat across from him, setting his drink carefully on a side table. He leaned forward. "Are you into some kind of trouble, Michael?"

Michael tipped his head back and shook it. "Not the way you think."

"Is there anything I can do to help?"

"You already have, by caring for Katrina. We cannot tell Marcus about this yet."

"He'll be in town in a few short weeks. Surely he will be bound to learn something is up."

"Then it's good you don't know more than you do. Let any recriminations fall on my head, Phillip. If you can keep her safe and out of trouble, I would be grateful."

"I can keep her safe in the house. We are talking about Katrina. Unless she has changed significantly over the years, the 'out of trouble' part I do not think I can promise." Phillip smiled and shook his head. "I still remember some of the scrapes she got into. It was always you who rescued her even then."

Michael's eyes widened momentarily and shut. "I think you may be right, but I thought that was over years ago. We are no longer children and these are not lighthearted games with minimal risk."

There was a knock on the door. "Come in," Phillip called and stood as his wife entered the room.

Michael rose.

"How is she, Beth?" Phillip asked.

"She lost a lot of blood, but the wound looked clean. We will need to watch her for signs of infection. One of the maids is watching over her." Beth crossed the room to stand by Phillip's side, and he put his arm around her waist.

Michael walked over and took Beth's hand and raised it to his lips. "You are an angel of mercy. Thank you for taking care of Miss Shepherd." He straightened and turned to leave. "I'll be back later this morning to check on our patient."

Phillip drew his wife closer to his body and nodded to their departing guest. "Good night, Michael."

4

Katrina awoke to agony. She tried to move her left arm, but pain seared through her shoulder. She squeezed her eyes shut.

"You are finally waking up. That's a good sign," a soft voice said from the side of the bed.

Katrina discovered an attractive woman with reddish hair and green eyes that twinkled in the morning sunlight streaming in from the nearby window.

"You were shot, Miss Shepherd. Sir Tidley arrived here with you in his arms in the early morning hours. You stayed unconscious through the surgery, which was a blessing for us all. But now you are a guest of my husband, Lord Westcombe, and myself, and must do us the honor of recovering here. My name is Elizabeth."

"Phillip? I'm in Phillip's home?" Katrina grew dizzy trying to sort the memories of the previous night and the disconcerting sense of being off balance in the luxury of the beautifully appointed, blue-themed bedroom.

"You are acquainted with my husband?" The redhead's left eyebrow rose and there was a small smile on her face as if she were already aware of the answer.

"We were childhood playmates, my lady. Nothing more I assure you." Katrina's heart raced. Would

Phillip's bride believe her?

"You never pursued my handsome husband?" Beth queried.

"No. Never. T'was always Mi…I loved elsewhere."

"Perhaps Sir Tidley was the recipient of your affections?"

Katrina's face grew warm.

"Never fear, my dear Miss Shepherd. Phillip told me of your childhood connection through Lord Remington. I am not threatened by your presence here. It would appear, however, that Sir Michael has been blind to the precious gift that has been his for the taking."

"I don't understand." Katrina leaned her head back further on the pillow and closed her eyes.

"Sir Michael needed to be informed of your identity by Phillip. It came as quite a shock to the man. Now why could a man as observant and witty as Sir Tidley not recognize his childhood friend beneath that disguise? He is in denial of his affection for you."

"Please, do not tease me, my lady. I am in no mood for such this morning."

"Perhaps you are ready for tea, toast, and possibly some nutritious broth?" Elizabeth smiled broadly now. "You need to recover from your wound."

Katrina's stomach growled. "That would be lovely. Thank you."

After eating and having the doctor check her injury, Katrina was allowed out of bed. Her bruises ached all over, and there were a few surface scratches as well. Her face, thankfully, had not suffered too much from the battle. She sat by the window, wrapped in a borrowed dressing robe of silky royal purple, an imposter in this beautiful home. Her hair was even done by Elizabeth's maid into a soft and attractive style, although Elizabeth considered it a wasted effort to use curling tongs for an injured woman who would be confined to her sitting room for the day.

A mixture of anticipation and anger surged through her when she thought of Michael. Some of the anger was forced on herself. How'd she been exposed? If she hadn't been injured, she may have gotten away with it longer. She was not surprised that Phillip recognized her. He was an intelligent and observant man. He probably guessed long ago how much she loved Michael, but ever the gentleman, he never teased or chided her for her infatuation. He treated her with brotherly respect. Even when he came to visit this morning, he showed nothing more than the concern of an older brother.

He assured her that Michael cautioned him not to tell her cousin Marcus yet. How would she explain this without exposing her role in something bigger? How could she justify the risks she took to her virtuous cousin who held firm standards and would have done anything to make a life of comfort for her? He respected her decision to serve as a companion rather than face a season and the whispers that surrounded her about her father. Something about God having a plan that sometimes doesn't always follow what one expects. She never did understand his faith, but she respected it and admired his sweet wife, Josie.

She probably could have been comfortable in his home and had a good life. But she desired more than that. She wanted answers and to clear her father's name. She hadn't bothered to think about what life would be like when and if she accomplished her goal.

If? Where had that come from? Of course she would. She needed to. Doubts were not to be part of the equation. Now that Michael knew her identity, would Lord Hughes let her continue? Would Michael try to stop her?

She blushed as she remembered his kisses from a few nights ago, the feel of his arms around her, and her body against his. Even if he'd refused her help, it was worth the risks to have had those few moments of bliss in his arms. He'd never want her for a wife, but for a few minutes, she'd experienced what it was like to be desired as a woman. It wouldn't happen again. She would never love anyone the way she loved Michael.

She was even pleased that her moniker of Mouse failed to clue him in. People really only saw what they wanted to. Sadness overwhelmed her over how invisible she was to him. Wishes didn't always come true in real life. If there was a God, she was just as invisible to Him as she was to the man she adored.

She let out a deep sigh and settled against the chair. She winced as her shoulder brushed up against the fabric and adjusted her position so she still caught the view out the window and rested comfortably. Before she realized it, she'd drifted asleep.

~*~

Michael knocked before entering the room. He noticed someone by the window, and he smiled to think that Katrina awaited him. He glanced at her as she slept. Her hair washed free of whatever it was that she used to dull the color, now glimmered with honey highlights illuminated by the sunshine streaming in. It was a soft brown and quite straight normally but somehow today she possessed curls and they framed her features in an attractive way. The heart-shaped face always appeared so small to him. She was still petite, and her face matched her size giving her an appearance of fragility that was far from reality. She'd managed to fend off five men last night and come out the victor. Anger and admiration warred inside him.

What would he say to her? Apologize for not even recognizing her? Did he need to apologize for kissing her so thoroughly the other night? He'd enjoyed the moment nearly too much to regret it. But this was Katrina. Mouse. Childhood friend and playmate. She was not someone to think about romantically. He glanced down at her figure, fully covered but not hidden by the silky purple robe she wore. Her feet were tucked up underneath her. He remembered the feel of those curves. She was not a child anymore, but a woman full grown. Women cried. Women had expectations. He'd need to tread carefully. He possessed the means to support a wife, but his lifestyle wasn't conducive to marriage and he would never trap her in a loveless union.

He closed the door behind him and cleared his throat. A maid appeared from the other room and came to sit down in the corner to act as a chaperone. He was grateful he would be able to have at least a semi-private conversation. "Katrina?" He crossed the richly textured rug. Reaching her side, he found himself at a loss as to how to approach her.

Her chest rose and fell. Which shoulder did she injure? The bulkiness on the left indicated it was that one. He reached forward to touch her right shoulder and gently brushed his hand against her jaw. Her skin was soft. "Kat? Wake up, please. We need to talk."

The hazel eyes opened, and her gaze moved up from his waist to his face. "Michael. I was waiting for you." Her voice was husky, stirring memories of the alley.

"I thought you might be. How do you fare?" He brought another chair close to hers so they could converse quietly without the maid overhearing everything that needed to be said.

"Banged up. My shoulder throbs. I've experienced more enjoyable evenings." She blushed.

He wondered if she was remembering the night she'd rescued him.

"I'm sure you have. I am sorry for what happened. I sent a message through Lord Hughes to give you a different address for our meeting. Given a previous break-in, I thought it would be safer to be elsewhere." Michael's elbows were perched on his knees and his hands were clenched together in front of him as he leaned toward her.

"I didn't receive any letter."

"I realize that now. Lord Hughes was upset to learn of your injuries. He sends his regards."

"I failed, didn't I? He is disappointed in me and has forbidden me to continue on my mission."

"Your mission? I thought you were helping me with mine?"

"They dovetail."

"Care to explain?"

"I can't do that right now." She glanced past him to the maid who was doing mending in the corner.

"Fair enough."

They stared at one another.

"I'm sorry I didn't recognize you. Twice you tricked me and I'm kicking myself for being so dense."

"Three times." She said it so quietly he almost missed it.

"Three?"

"I was the one who passed you the note."

"At the ball? But I didn't…how?" Michael's eyes narrowed as he gazed at her. His voice stayed soft.

"You ran into me, spilling the drink I held."

"That was you? I'm not normally that clumsy."

"You weren't clumsy, Michael. I deliberately stepped into your path and spilled the wine on you. It was the easiest way to get the note into your pocket." She glanced away from him toward the window. She grew pale and there were dark shadows under her eyes.

"My valet may never forgive you for that. He said those pantaloons needed to be destroyed." Michael smiled.

"I can reimburse you out of my pin money if that will make him happy." Her tone was flat and she continued to give him her profile in shadow.

"There is no need. I can absorb the loss." He paused. "I could not tolerate losing you, however. How would I explain that to Lord Remington? Even now, at some point he will learn you were shot, that I'm somehow involved, and there will be hell to pay." His voice caught.

"Lord Hughes will keep you out of it. Bringing me here, having Phillip recognize me. That's where things went wrong. I apologize for jeopardizing your relationship with Marcus. I understand how important his friendship is to you." She leaned forward slightly to touch his arm with her right hand. She gave it a squeeze and sat back wincing.

"I don't think you do, Mouse." He shook his head

and lowered it. "I would do almost anything for that man."

~*~

"I understand." Katrina glanced out the window as an uncomfortable silence stretched between them. Outside the carriages drove by, the birds sang, and it was a beautiful day. Here in her sitting room, loneliness pulsed. He only cared about Marcus. She only caused discomfort for that. If she died, he wouldn't miss *her*. The pain of those thoughts hurt her heart worse than the physical ache in her shoulder. "I can still help you with the deciphering if you will let me," Katrina offered.

"That'll be up to Lord Hughes. If you possess a key, I can take it and give it a try. The code is unusual. I don't understand how you would have what is needed for this one." He held a hand up. "Don't explain. The less I know the better."

"We are running out of time. I insist you let me help you," Katrina implored softly.

Michael laughed. "You can't lift your arm. You need to heal. What is it you think you can do?"

Anger welled up Katrina. "Apparently, I can fool one of the best agents out there. I can save his life and fend off attackers and live to tell about it." *And I can hide the fact that I love you.*

Michael sat up straight, his eyes narrowed, and his fists clenched. His voice, when he spoke, was edged with steel even as he whispered to her. "You bested me. I admit it. I am grateful for your assistance, but I am well able to handle my own business. Without your interference. It was foolishness for you to be at that pub. You are a gently-bred woman. Your actions might have led to you being permanently compromised in the eyes of society if they ever discovered what happened," he growled. He stood and began pacing, arms now folded tightly in front of his body as if in an attempt to keep from strangling her. He got close and bent to her ear. "And what if you'd failed? What if those men had attacked? By myself, I might have managed to escape with my life, but having to defend a woman as well, could have meant death to us both and the lives of thousands of servicemen currently at war."

"Our mission."

"My mission. You seem to be misguided in thinking you are a part of this or that I even need you. I do not. I will accept the code. I will do the work. The risk is mine alone to take."

"What makes you so special that no one else can participate in the risks you assume?" Katrina grew weary and heartbroken, but she wasn't ready to surrender. Not yet.

"I have no family. No heritage to live up to. A few friends who will survive without me as they establish their families. I can afford the risk."

Katrina saw an emptiness in his eyes, a loneliness that called out to her soul and stirred compassion in the midst of her anger and fear of losing him. Losing him? He was already lost to her. *He was never mine to begin with.*

"I'm sorry, Michael. You are wrong. You minimize the grief your demise would cause simply to salve your conscience and give you freedom to take foolish risks. You are more loved and cared for than you realize."

"By whom, may I ask?" he hissed. "By my father who denied me his name or even the benefit of being born on the right side of the blanket? By my grandfather who cringed to look at me and is now gone to his noble reward? By my deceased mother who never recovered from the scandal of my birth and could barely look at me without shame for herself, who never really lived after I was born? Every person I touched in my life has suffered somehow."

"That's a lie. Your family situation is unfortunate. But you have friends who would fight for you and care deeply for you."

"Maybe so, but they would move on with their lives not having to be concerned for me. And I wouldn't need to watch them grow their families and regret that I possess nothing of value to offer a woman."

"You see your future as a short one?"

"I pray it would be. I have no desire to live to an old age."

"No desire to sample the best of what love would offer you?" Katrina whispered.

"Love? I am no great catch. I do not seek love. I have witnessed little of it."

"But what of Marcus and Josie, and Phillip and Beth?" She yawned and rose to stand, shaking out her robe to make sure her slippered feet were covered.

"What of them? They are unique. Blessed by God in ways I cannot understand. But I do not deceive myself that I am worthy of a woman's trust, adoration, or devotion. I would only destroy her in the long run."

She stood in the sunlit window, sorrow flowing off her in waves.

"I'm sorry to rant, Mouse. You need rest. I will

visit again soon." He reached forward and put his hand under her chin, lifting her face and bringing his close to hers.

Will he kiss me? She dared to hope as she closed her eyes in anticipation.

"Stay out of trouble, please?" he whispered against her lips. His hand dropped and he moved away abruptly.

She keenly rued the loss of his strength and the scent of horse and man. She sighed deeply as she opened her eyes. "I make no promises. I am not under your authority, Michael. You will do well to remember that. I have my own mission too, and you will not keep me from it, no matter how noble your motives are."

With that, Katrina rose and walked to the door to the bedroom, and addressed the maid with a voice that went above the whisper in which they had been speaking, "Penny, I'm going to rest. I am suddenly quite weary."

The maid rose to follow Katrina out of the room, shutting the door firmly behind her.

5

He'd been dismissed.

Michael sighed and left Phillip's home. Why did he feel he'd just lost something?

Back in his rooms at the Savoy, he sat down at the desk, picked up his quill, and drew out some paper. He doodled while his mind worked through the problems ahead of him. How could he crack the code? Who knew he even possessed the document? In all his years he'd never been discovered. There'd been some close calls, but his secret identity had been secure. That was no longer the case. Would this be his last opportunity to serve his country as a spy?

Life would have been easier had he stayed in the Horse Guards. He might not even be alive at this point, but that wasn't much of a concern to him. His only purpose was fulfilling the next mission. Life held no pleasures for him anymore. Once Theo found a wife he would be the odd man out at any event with his friends. He didn't want to be around for that. He didn't begrudge them their happiness, but it would only highlight his lack of those same joys.

The clouds moved in front of the sun casting the room into dark shadows that reflected his mood. His sketches illustrated the faces of one woman in various guises. Katrina. How had he overlooked her? Was he getting too old for this business? What else might he be missing? Was his enemy someone closer than he realized?

He lifted the paper and glanced at the images in front of him. The mousy servant who spilled wine down his pants to get a message to him. He admitted it was clever and he'd wondered about that event until Mouse had told him about it today. The brazen blonde who kissed with such fiery passion. *Katrina?* This was the image hardest for him to reconcile with the mousy yet spirited little girl who tagged after a gang of boys out at Rose Hill when they came home on holidays. His heart beat wildly when he took in the image and remembered the warmth of her in his arms.

Katrina? He should never feel that way about her. She was like a sister. Marcus would behead him if he ever found out—after marching his tortured corpse down the aisle with a Special License. Michael shook his head sadly. It had happened to Phillip, although that marriage seemed to be working out well for all involved.

The final image of a young boy, hat pulled low, dirty face with a determined chin. How could he have thought those eyelashes were anything but feminine? And those lips. Again his mind strayed to heated kisses shared in the alley. *Enough of this!* He crumpled up the paper and rose to throw it in the fireplace, but before doing so he paused, un-crumpled the paper to view the fourth image. Katrina today, with curls framing her heart-shaped face and those large hazel eyes turned a stormy gray in her anger and stubbornness. Curves that somehow emerged in the years that had lain between their time apart. A woman now. Not a child. Cheekbones and not so rounded face. Perky nose and mischievous smile.

A tinge of alarm skittered up his back. She would

not be deterred from whatever her mission was. Could he accomplish what he needed to do and keep her safe as well? She wouldn't obey orders. He took a deep breath, ripped the paper to shreds and let them fall into the flames and burn. He didn't need the drawings to remember this woman. They were written on his heart—what little of it he still possessed.

He walked back to the desk and sat down to go through the invitations and letters that Tristan left for him. His faithful servant was supervising setting the townhouse to rights with a small army of servants hired for the work. If the danger passed, he'd return home soon. The Savoy was a high-end hotel and the furnishings were luxuriously appointed, but it wasn't home. But then, was anyplace?

He owned few personal belongings that he really cared about. His trunk of memories was stored at Rose Hill for the nonce, and he wondered if he would ever reclaim it. What purpose would it serve when he was gone? He shrugged. It didn't matter. He slapped the invitations down and opened the right-hand drawer. Inside was a book Marcus gave him a few years ago. He pulled it out and randomly opened it up to Romans chapter three to read.

For what if some did not believe? Shall their unbelief make the faith of God without effect? God forbid: yea, let God be true, but every man a liar; as it is written, That thou mightest be justified in thy sayings, and mightest overcome when thou art judged. But if our unrighteousness commend the righteousness of God, what shall we say? Is God unrighteous who taketh vengeance? (I speak as a man) God forbid: for then how shall God judge the world? For if the truth of God hath more abounded through my lie unto his glory; why yet am I also judged as a sinner? And not rather, (as we be slanderously reported, and as some affirm that we say,) Let us do evil, that good may come? whose damnation is just. What then? are we better than they? No, in no wise: for we have before proved both Jews and Gentiles, that they are all under sin; As it is written, There is none righteous, no, not one…

Michael leaned back. He never assumed he was righteous, but he always considered the cause he served was. But by whose standard? He believed in God, but not like Marcus and Phillip. Marcus never tried to coerce him to faith like some who were passionate about Jesus.

He was a sinner, of that there was no doubt. He engaged in lies and deceit as part of his stock in trade. When had he grown so maudlin? What happened to the happy-go-lucky man whom the *ton* adored? Lately…lately a weight bore down on his soul and the stakes had been raised higher than ever before.

While he didn't sense imminent danger, Michael suspected this was a final mission. His end was coming and it would not be pretty. Did kissing a beautiful woman in the dark lead him to such melancholy thoughts? Tempted by what he couldn't commit to, had he swung to ambiguity toward his own death? Maybe Katrina was right. Maybe he recklessly took risks that were propelling him to that end. Why would she care? And what was so important about her mission that she couldn't share it with him? He was saddened at the thought that he was only a means to an end. Could not even Katrina have a little affection for him?

He shook his head. He didn't need her or anyone's love or approval. He was self-sufficient. He flipped the Bible in front of him to the Old Testament and fell upon verses in Proverbs 7:

He goeth after her straightway, as an ox goeth to the slaughter, or as a fool to the correction of the stocks; Till a dart strike through his liver; as a bird hasteth to the snare, and knoweth not that it is for his life. (Pro 7:22-23)

Michael laughed out loud. Well, if God had a sense of humor He definitely spoke through this. Seeking affection from a woman was a sure way to death in this business. There was no room in his life for the distraction of Katrina or anyone else. He closed his eyes and the sensation of holding her in his arms in the alley assaulted him. He blinked and shook his head. Closing the book, he put it back in the drawer and rose. He might have work to do but first, he longed for some fresh air. He summoned a servant to ready his black stallion, Pepper, for a ride. He needed to clear his head of all his thoughts of sin, death, slaughter, and a young woman whose kisses haunted him.

~*~

Traffic impeded his way through town to Hyde Park. It took all Michael's skill to restrain his horse. Once they reached a more distant area of the park, he let Pepper have his head and they tore off over the turf as one. When the stallion had satisfied his need to run, Michael drew to a canter and made his way back through town to the hotel.

After Michael rewarded his horse, he returned to his suite. Tristan remained absent. Instinct warned caution. Someone had been here. A maid perhaps? Michael did a thorough survey of the room and finally came back to the main sitting area. Someone had gone through the papers on his desk. While he made it no secret he was staying at this establishment, security was tight. How did anyone gain entrance? He was on the third floor. The windows were locked. Unlike previous attempts to find the papers, this search had been far more discreet. Was it the same person, or were others after the document?

An hour later, Tristan entered the suite.

"Sir Michael. I heard you had gone for a ride?"

"I did, and returned an hour hence."

"Everything appears to be in order at the townhouse. All is cleaned up and the dead bodies are gone." Tristan stood at attention.

"At ease. We are no longer in the military. How long were you over there?"

The man relaxed. "The past two hours or more. Why?"

"Curious. I probably owe you extra pay for that job."

"Tis no matter, sir. How is the young lady?"

Michael's attention had wandered, but at this question he became alert. "Young lady?"

"Yes, the one who was shot? Was she part of the group searching for the document?"

"No, she was my contact last night. The message never got to her."

"That little girl was your contact?"

Michael nodded. *Far from a girl.* "Did I ever tell you about how a young woman tagged along after my friends and me during our summer vacations at Rose Hill?"

Tristan's head bobbed up and down, his eyes beseeched Michael to continue.

"She is one and the same as the woman who was shot last night."

"If you trained her, that would explain her skill with a knife and gun."

"If I were honest, Tris, she is superior to me in all areas. She is also an amazing archer, something I was never very skilled at. So if I ever ask you to put an apple on your head, run as far away as you can."

Tristan grinned but didn't move.

"Why are you standing there, Tris? It's not like you to not be busy doing, well, something. Anything."

"Pardon me. I'll tend to my work after I deliver your letters to your desk." Tristan moved forward to cross the room. Michael stood and intercepted him.

"Hand them here, I'll peruse them now. I'm famished. Could you go to the kitchen and scare up some kind of food? I cannot recall when I last ate." Michael sat in a leather chair near the fireplace and began to sort through the letters and invitations received.

"I shall return with a meal." Tristan departed the suite, closing the door quietly behind him.

~*~

Michael wandered around the suite, searching for clues as he casually flipped through invitation after invitation, making a pile for further consideration and those that he would send regrets to. A few bills that needed to be paid. He would take care of those later. Someone had been here, though, but if it hadn't been Tristan, then who? Tristan had no clue where the papers were hidden. He learned long ago that even with the best of partners, it was better to be cautious because the enemy might terrorize people closest to him. The less they knew, the safer they were. It bugged Tristan that he refused to share such information with him, but it was for his own good. If Michael were to die, the document would remain safely hidden, although that would also mean that it would also remain undecoded. He had already taken care of that eventuality as well, and only one other person possessed the information. Again, a closely guarded secret.

Michael slumped into a chair, throwing the rest of the cards on the table next to him. Weariness seeped into his bones. All the secrets, the lies, the loneliness. They grew heavy. He'd seen many friends sacrifice their lives over the years. The grief he could never express or release due to the urgency of the work at hand. The grisly deaths he had seen and participated in, all for the sake of a cause, left scars on his soul that never fully healed. Every new death, every valiant life wasted, every son whose blood was shed because he had not done his job well, rested as boulders on his soul.

Michael rubbed his hand over his face from forehead to chin and left it to rest there. Finish the mission. Get it over with. Resign. But then what? Retire to the country? Find some nice little estate and become a farmer? Grow old in London, dancing with beautiful women who enjoyed his company but would never take his name? Life was wearisome.

He remembered Marcus telling him something about King Solomon at one time, and how he wrote about the vanity of life, how futile it was. His own experience echoed that. Michael shook his head. That ride through the park obviously didn't do enough to clear his head. He leaned back against the chair and closed his eyes briefly.

She walked into the room and he glanced over to

her. A diaphanous robe emphasized her figure and hinted at wonders yet to be revealed. His mouth watered. She smiled at him. That sensuous smile spoke of secret delights. A smile that was for him and him alone. Her gown was a virginal white and her hair was down, a satiny brown curtain flowing with glimmers from fading light coming in through the windows. He couldn't move, so he waited for her to approach.

"Michael," that soft musical voice spoke his name with reverence and he experienced a sense of awe that she would be here. He licked his lips but words failed him. His mouth grew dry. Her hips swayed as she walked closer and he caught a glimpse of her feet peeking from beneath the gown. There was no hesitation in her steps but she took forever to get to him. He watched and waited, his breath stolen from him. Had he ever seen someone so beautiful? A delightful blush rose up in her cheeks and he grinned in appreciation. She reached for him with her right hand.

The door to the outside hallway opened with a click, followed by a clatter as Tristan came in with a tray containing his evening meal.

Michael startled. His eyes flashed from the door to the room around him. There was no woman present. He sat up and leaned forward, burying his face in his hands as he slowed his heartbeat. She wasn't real. But he wanted her to be. What was happening? Why couldn't he move forward without thinking of Katrina? It was her he'd envisioned.

"Sir?" Tristan asked cautiously as he brought the food to place on the table nearby.

"Thank you, Tris. I'm just tired."

"Will there be anything else? This was my night

off."

"No, thank you, Tristan. I can manage from here. Enjoy your evening. I will see you in the morning."

"Yes, sir." With that, Tristan departed, leaving Michael to deal with a meal he was no longer hungry for and struggling with desires out of place with the work at hand.

After he ate, he paced the sitting room like a caged tiger. The document needed to be deciphered. Time was of the essence. He gained nothing by attending the spate of balls and recitals that were open to him for this evening. Theo might be at the club, but he was too anxious for that. Fidget followed in his wake clicking at him.

"I realize that. I need to get this done, Fidget. So you think I should allow Mouse to help me?"

Fidget jumped from the floor to the chair and in a swift leap was on Michael's shoulder giving him kisses.

"I don't want to deal with Phillip. How am I to accomplish this if she is under such guard? Will she even agree to help me anymore?"

The ferret's eye was close to his own. The animal jumped down and attacked the meat on the plate that Michael hadn't finished.

Michael shook his head. He needed to see her, but how to do that in Phillip's house without anyone being aware? Well, he wasn't in this business for anything, but there would be hell to pay if he got caught. For some reason, that hell wasn't looking so bad anymore.

6

Katrina rested and her appetite had returned. Her hostess spent some time visiting but with a young child to care for, was occupied elsewhere and exhausted. Katrina made it clear that she did not need Elizabeth hovering over her. She had a book from Phillip's library and Phillip had managed to bring a box of her belongings from Lady Orion's home, who was informed that she was taking a much-needed holiday at Phillip's request, keeping any injury out of the discussion.

Lady Orion graciously acquiesced, knowing of the long-term relationship and assuming that Katrina was there to assist in caring for the baby.

Carriages could be heard through the slightly opened window. She strained to catch a view past the gas streetlights to any stars, but a fog shrouded the city, even this early in the spring. The smell of rain was once again in the air, and a full moon rose faintly, casting eerie light through the clouds. The night had a surreal quality to it and she shivered, not so much due to the cool air coming in, but due to her fanciful imagination thinking something was about to happen. She wrapped her robe around her, taking care not to lift her arm. The throbbing in her shoulder and resulting weakness persisted. She reached for the glass sitting on the table by her side and lifted it to her lips. The brandy burned its way down her throat and warmed her from the inside out. Phillip would be shocked to see her drinking this, but she learned a long time ago that there were times when even a lady needed a good stiff drink. It was either that or the laudanum which she abhorred.

Her slippered feet on the floor touched something warm and soft before it made a small noise. She fought to not scream. Did Phillip have a cat she was unaware of? She slowly set her glass down and raised her feet. Two beady eyes peered up at her and a little nose wiggled as the creature made a clicking noise. This wasn't a cat. She wasn't quite sure what it was, but she swallowed the sounds that she wanted to emit. *Be brave.*

The little creature bared his sharply edged teeth in a perverse little smile. Her heartbeat quickened and adrenaline surged through her. Before she could kick the animal to the side, it skittered away toward the window and perched itself on the sill in front of her. Finally, it stretched out with his eyes focused on the view outside of the glass. Little ears perked up and twitched.

Katrina rose to her feet. The black, white, and brown animal gazed back at her as if daring her to leave. She went to her bag. With one eye on the animal, she reached her right hand in and withdrew the small pistol. She checked to make sure it was loaded and primed when a voice behind her made her jump.

"I hope you were not planning to use that on me."

Katrina turned quickly with the gun pointed but dropped her arm to her side when she recognized Michael. She closed her eyes briefly before opening them again. "How dare you scare me like that."

"I'm sorry. I expected you to be asleep at half past

ten." He exhaled.

"For most of the city, the fun has just begun. You don't expect a bullet wound to keep me from enjoying my season in London." Her chin came up a fraction.

"Season? Most debutantes don't spend their seasons dressed in gray, taking on a life of service and twice tempting death with their foolhardy actions." Michael folded his arms.

The animal from the window managed to jump up from the bed onto his shoulders and wrap himself around the back of Michael's neck. Clicking and kissing Michael, it stared at her with beady eyes and a grin.

"What, or who, is that?" She pointed to the animal with the gun still in her hand.

Michael reached out and removed the pistol. "I don't think you'll be needing this tonight." He placed it back in the bag while still holding her right hand with his other one. He brought the hand up to his mouth and left a kiss on her skin.

Scandalous rogue!

Heat sizzled up her arm at his touch.

Michael continued to hold her gaze with his coffee-colored eyes. "This, my dear, is my associate, Fidget. He is a ferret and has at times been useful in my work. He insisted on joining me tonight." Michael brought her hand up to Fidget's nose and the ferret sniffed her fingers before licking her. Michael dropped her hand between them but didn't release her.

"The pleasure is all mine, Fidget. So nice to meet another agent who has the challenge of working with Sir Michael."

"Drop the Sir, please, Katrina? We've known each other too long to stand on ceremony and the title—

well, it's an anomaly and not my identity."

"You earned that title through honest and courageous actions. Why despise it?" Katrina tugged her hand free and walked back to her seat by the window. She closed the glass and pulled the drapes shut before seating herself in the chair and picking up her glass again.

"Maybe so, but I'm still Michael. A simple man, caught between the worlds of respectable aristocracy and social outcast. The title gives me a bit more cachet than I deserve." He walked over toward the window. Pulling up a chair in front of her, he sat.

"Why are you here, Michael, in the middle of the night and with a ferret? I'm assuming you did not make your entrance by the front door and your presence here is unknown to my hosts?"

"You definitely were never one to let things slip by you, were you?" He winked and that little smirk made her want to slap him.

"You refuse to answer the question?"

"Question? You were asking a question?" Michael raised his left finger to tap his nose several times as he squinted his eyes. "Oh, yes. Why am I here? Or how did I get in here? Which one concerns you the most?" He gave her his most winning smile.

She fought a grin. Something about those dark eyes twinkling in the candle-lit room, caused her heart to flip. She lifted her glass to her lips. She closed her eyes as she savored the warmth and calming of the brandy. "Never mind. It doesn't matter," she said as she leaned back on her right shoulder while cradling the glass.

He reached out, took the glass and took a sip. He held the glass out and looked at it. "French? Where would Phillip procure French brandy?"

"Probably from his father." She took the glass back and set it on the table.

"Most likely."

Katrina drank in the sight of him. Dark hair pulled back into a que at his neck. She remembered the softness of those locks as her fingers ran through them. Was that only two nights ago? She took in the thick arched brows above dark eyes. The stubble on his face. He was dressed all in black and his boots were well worn and scuffed with a softer sole. No wonder she hadn't heard him come in. He was not nicknamed "Cat" without good reason.

"Do I pass inspection?" With one eyebrow raised, amusement tinged Michael's words.

"You'll do, I suppose." She gave him a smirk.

"How do you fare?" Concern was now evident and written in the lines between his brows and the frown on his face.

"As well as can be expected for someone who has been shot. I couldn't sleep anymore. I did that almost all day." She blushed as she glanced past him to the bed behind him with the covers pulled back as if in invitation. The impropriety of the situation struck her. "You really shouldn't be here."

"I had to come."

"You did? Why?"

"Because you possess something I need."

Her breath caught. She whispered the words, "I do?"

"The code," Michael whispered.

"Did you bring the document?"

"I brought a part of it."

"Fair enough." She rose and started to make her

way to her bag. "You want to begin work on that now?"

Michael nodded. "We don't have time to lose."

"Right." Katrina dug into the bag, pulled out her father's old journal. With a golden embossed cover and tattered pages, it appeared older than it really was. Even though it was about to fall apart, it was the most precious possession she owned. She hugged the book close to her for a moment and fought back the memories of her father. Tears often accompanied touching this book that bared her father's heart to her. With a heavy sigh, she turned.

He stood and followed her to the low table by the fireplace. She set the book down reverently and slowly slid to her knees, bracing herself with her right arm. Michael fished out the sample scrap of code and came to kneel beside her, placing paper on the table for her to view.

She gave him a small smile as her finger touched the paper and glanced at what he had written down. Opening the journal, she flipped to a spot towards the end with similar drawings, and she started to whisper the secrets of the document he had struggled with for so long.

"You broke the code."

She remained silent, closed the journal, and handed him back the scrap. He took the paper and ripped it up and tossed it into the fireplace.

"Why did you do that?" she asked.

"It is a mere copy and only one fragment of a much larger document. I brought that little bit to make sure what you claimed was true." He reached out to clasp her right hand and give it a reassuring squeeze.

She glanced down at their joined hands, reveling

in the warmth of his touch and the sensations it aroused in her. His dark eyes reflected the light of the fire.

"Does that mean you believe me now? That we can be partners?"

"I despise bringing you into this. Your life is at risk if it is discovered you were involved."

"But if I don't help you, how will you ever do this?" She removed her hand and instantly grew chilled.

Michael frowned at her withdrawal. "Give me the journal and I shall do it alone."

"I cannot part with this." She picked up the book with her one good hand and held it to her chest.

"Why? It's just an old book."

"No. It's more than that. This holds the key to absolving my father of the lies that were compiled against him as he lay dead and unable to defend himself."

"If I use the book to crack the code, you still get what you want and your life would not be at risk." Michael's voice held a gentle plea.

"You don't understand, Michael. This is all I have left of him. It's more than the codes. His hopes, dreams, plans. His love for me and for God are all written in these pages. I would never willingly part from this."

"Not even for King and country?"

Katrina's lips pursed together and anger flared inside. She struggled to rise and he gently helped her up, but kept his hand on her right elbow.

He cleared his throat. "Katrina," he whispered.

She glanced up into his face.

Their eyes held and a connection from years before

seemed to flash to fresh life.

He leaned forward and his lips met hers in a tender tribute. She whimpered in response and he deepened the kiss, drawing her body closer to his.

She finally pulled her head back, dizzy with pleasure and confusion over the emotions at war within her. "We shouldn't. I think you need to leave." She took a step back out of his embrace.

"Katrina, I—"

"—am sorry and it won't happen again." She walked over to the bed to put her journal back in the bag, only to discover something or someone, warm and fuzzy in there. She gave a stifled squeal as she pulled her hand out, book clutched tightly. A small furry head popped up and grinned. Katrina tried to slow her heartbeat. "Michael, I think your pet needs to depart with you."

Michael came up behind her and glanced over her shoulder. "Fidget. Come here." Michael reached out his hand. The ferret scampered up and weaseled his way into an interior pocket in Michael's coat.

Fascinating. She put the journal in the bag. Turning, she faced Michael and giggled at the squirming lump on the left side of his chest.

Michael grinned. "Fidget, shhhh!" The ferret stopped moving completely but the lump remained. Michael glanced up at Katrina, his eyes dancing.

"Please let me help."

His smile faded. "I don't want you hurt."

"It's a bit late for that, don't you think?" She touched her injured shoulder with her good hand.

"I'm sorry. It should never have happened. I still don't understand why you didn't receive that note. Lord Hughes never got it either." His eyebrows almost met as he squinted in concentration.

Katrina's hand came up and she smoothed the lines between his eyes with her thumb before she even realized she was doing it.

Michael grasped her wrist and held it gently.

They stared at each other. Michael's gaze went to her lips again and he licked his own as if preparing for a feast. Katrina longed for more of those kisses, but her resistance to him was weak. She took back her hand and stepped away. "You need to leave."

Michael grinned. "You are correct. What is it about you, Mouse? You infuriate and attract me all at the same time."

Katrina smiled. "I can relate. We sometimes want most what we can't have." Her voice was soft and tender. "Good night, Michael. Sleep well, and stay safe."

Michael leaned in to give her a peck on the cheek. As he turned to leave the room a clicking sound came from his coat. "Shhhhh, Fidget. This is not the time for that."

The door closed and weariness overtook her in his absence. Banking the fire and blowing out the candles, she climbed into bed, her thoughts dwelling on kisses that awakened dead dreams she knew she'd never achieve. She cried herself to sleep.

Michael, I love you. If only you understood that.

~*~

The next day, Michael found himself once again summoned to Lord Hughes's office at Whitehall. This time, he was ushered in immediately.

"Good morning, Michael. Please sit." Lord Hughes

motioned to a chair as he resumed his seat behind the large mahogany desk practically covered with piles of papers everywhere.

Michael sat, folded his arms in front of his chest, and waited.

"So how is she?"

"She?"

"Mouse, you idiot. Let's not play games, Michael. I have no time for that."

"It's only been a day. She's in pain, and as full of sass as she ever was. Still being stubborn, insisting on helping me break this code."

"Can she do it?"

Michael nodded and frowned.

"Why can't we let her?"

"I'm going to have a hard-enough time explaining to Lord Remington about his cousin being shot. If any more harm comes to her, how do I justify that? I don't want her involved, it's too dangerous." His voice was terse and words came out clipped through clenched teeth.

Lord Hughes leaned back in his chair. "You care about her."

"As a human being, yes. She is nothing more to me and never could be."

"She'd be perfect for you."

"I don't need anyone."

"I beg to differ. In this case, you need Miss Katrina Shepherd and I plan to give you an order that you will obey. Let her help you. Get this done and do everything in your power to ensure she stays safe."

Michael's chin went up. He swallowed his anger as he glared at Lord Hughes. That man, older and wiser, stared back.

"It will be as you wish, Lord Hughes. But heaven help you if any harm does befall her. By helping me she may be walking into greater danger than you realize and I will not be held responsible for the consequences."

"She is your responsibility. I expect you to protect her as fervently as any man would his wife."

"Katrina is *not* my wife."

"No, but she could be."

"You don't know what you are asking of me."

"I think I do. Get it done, Michael. And quickly. Men are dying while we play our little games here. Let's put a halt to some of that needless carnage."

"Yes, my lord." Michael strode toward the door. His back was straight and shoulders squared. He turned as he reached the knob. "This is my last case. When this is completed, I intend to resign my position with the War Office." Michael opened the door and closed it behind him with a slam.

~*~

Katrina struggled to rest. She read through her father's journal again and found comfort in his words, even when they were the simple tasks of a day being recorded. How investments progressed or neighborhood news. It reminded her of happier days.

Michael failed to visit the past few days and she found herself pacing at night, hoping he would show up to work on the document. She needed to prove her father had not been a traitor. While she understood that Lord Hughes and Lord Remington did not believe those rumors, she wanted more comprehensive proof so that word could spread through the *ton* exonerating his name posthumously.

That was her purpose. It disturbed her when her thoughts dwelt on the image and desire for a certain spy. Dark eyes glinting a challenge to her. His soft hair. Those lips. *Stop!* There was no time or place for that kind of childish mooning over a man who didn't want her. Well, that might not be completely true. He desired her as a woman. But he didn't desire Katrina Maria Shepherd. He didn't need her in his life and he did not want her in on this case. She brushed away tears.

Michael didn't realize it, but someone was out to kill him. She strained to remember the comments of the men she fought that night at his house. She caught them by surprise. They'd been bragging about the money they would gain if they achieved access to the document, but also managed to kill Sir Michael. She longed to get that information to Lord Hughes, but she couldn't even leave her room.

Anticipating Michael's nocturnal visits every night, Katrina took to sleeping during the day. It kept questions at bay from her hosts, but it also left her pacing and lonely in the dark—alone with her thoughts and her father's words.

She took heart as she read his journal. He had quoted from the book of Joshua. They were God's words to her about being strong and having courage. Reading them infused her with power to overcome whatever might be ahead. It wasn't a promise. She wasn't sure what she believed about Marcus's God, but her father seemed to also possess his own brand of quiet faith that emerged more and more as she read. She wondered what she'd missed when he was alive.

She'd been too caught up in managing the

household and nursing him in his last months, to ever think of a time when he wouldn't be around and she would not be able to ask him about these things. She really believed he would survive. Now she wondered. Had he been hunted as Michael was now? Could she have prevented his death? She wasn't sure how.

Who would be after Michael? She didn't know many amongst the *beau monde* but somehow, she thought it was not someone directly connected to Michael. But who? She wished she understood more about his life and past missions. Had he made enemies? How could she ever find out? He would never tell her. Katrina sighed.

If only he would come!

He presented such a mass of conflicting emotions within her. Temptation as a woman. She was not above being lured by his handsome appearance. She had loved him since she wore her hair up. He didn't reciprocate that. He infuriated her with his prideful I-don't-need-anyone mentality. He needed her and refused to accept that. How could she possibly change his mind?

Seduce him. She smiled to herself. Her wound was healing, but her shoulder still ached terribly. How was she to tempt this handsome, virile, and self-contained man who only saw her as a little girl out to annoy him? She spent hours thinking about this and trying to imagine different scenarios in which she could arouse his interest and gain his cooperation. But the question always nagged at her. How far was she willing to go?

She wanted to vindicate her father. Was it worth it to give up her virtue for that? Was the cost too high? She struggled inside. She'd already gone beyond the pale and compromised herself by her actions to date. If anyone found out, her ruination was certain even though she was still as pure as the day she was born. Or was she? If she were honest with herself, she had dreams that were far more inappropriate than any maid had a right to.

She admitted she was jealous too. Phillip and his bride seemed so deliriously happy that she grieved her lonely state. She was happy for Phillip and amazed at the transformation that his bride brought to his life. He was more relaxed than he ever was. He was still in some ways as serious, and liked things done "his way" around the house. But then he would hold his son and laugh while being drooled on. The normally fastidious young man had grown in depth. Love had transformed him. He also embraced this Jesus that Marcus had been so passionate about.

But what kind of God would allow her to become motherless at such a young age? What kind of God permitted her beloved father to die and then have that man's name dragged through the mud? She respected God and even feared Him. She attended church and tried to listen and live according to the vicar's words. She never measured up. When her father died, God stole love from her and she resented Him for that. *Be strong and courageous* were God's words to Joshua. She sucked in a deep breath and held it for a moment, closing her eyes and then letting it all out in one exhale, all the fear, worries, longings.

Empty.

During the day she slept with her father's journal under her pillow. She did not doubt that if Michael wanted to, he could take it from her and do the work alone. But she would never let it out of her hands. She just couldn't. It was all she had left in the world of her beloved father. His book. His words of love to her. She dared not risk it being lost to her forever.

7

That dratted woman. She haunted him everywhere.

He shook his head to concentrate, trying to remember the limited bits of code in Katrina's journal. But there were too many gaps. He couldn't make out the message. He would need to humble himself and visit her again. Several times at the Savoy and even now, back in his own townhouse, there had been other subtler attempts to gain access to the document in his possession. He would have laughed at the futility of what the individual attempted, but lately, he hadn't been feeling well.

Weaker somehow.

"Tristan, who is the new cook we have?" Michael inquired that morning.

"Maggie, sir. Has there been a problem with your meals?" Tristan asked with stoic politeness.

"The food has been unexceptionable. My preferences are simple. But the taste of certain things has been 'off'. Like the pudding last night. Something didn't taste right about it, but I'm not sure why." Michael sipped his coffee and grimaced, setting the cup down. "And if you could teach her how to make a halfway decent cup of coffee I would appreciate it." Michael yawned and rose from the table in his room. "I'll wear the buff pantaloons today and the cranberry waistcoat and blue coat."

"Very well." Tristan left the room to gather the

items from the wardrobe and returned to shave Michael.

"I prefer to do this myself," Michael said as the process began.

"I am trying to earn my wages, Sir Michael. Please allow me to do so." Tristan did not meet Michael's eyes in the mirror, staying focused on the task at hand.

Unusual. Normally Tristan was far more talkative and shared in the humor of things. Michael fought to sit still. Humor? That vanished the night Katrina had been shot. Perhaps, once this case was solved, he would find it again.

His mind flashed to younger days, laughing and carefree under the shade of a huge oak at Rose Hill. Marcus and Phillip went fishing and Theo sat in the house reading a book. Michael kept Katrina company. She did not like handling worms and touching fish. She couldn't even eat fish if they were served with the head still attached and the eyes gazing out at her. Michael fought to not smile as the razor moved along his neck and face.

"Michael, what do you want to be when you grow up?" Kat once asked in that curious way of hers.

"I don't know. I'm too irreverent to become a vicar, don't you think, Mouse?" He nudged her as they sat there side by side, watching the young men further down the hill by the stream.

Katrina laughed in that musical way of hers, unfettered by the worries of life. She sat there with her sun-kissed face and her straight hair pulled back but falling down all the way to her waist. "No, definitely not a vicar, Michael. I've heard the tales of the mischief Remy and the rest were forced to rescue you from. What about a steward?"

"Numbers and I have an acrimonious relationship. Definitely not a good option for *moi*."

"Ohhhh, you've been mastering your French? Maybe you can travel on the Continent."

"While that might be entertaining, it doesn't pay very well." Michael chuckled at her innocence.

"There is no dream that you hold dear?"

He was slow in answering as he took in the estate around him. "I have no one. No purpose or dream. I live for today and let tomorrow take care of itself." He shrugged and glanced over at her.

Katrina looked as if he had taken away a prized toy. Tears pooled. She didn't argue with him. She reached out a hand to lay it on his arm. "That has to be the saddest thing I've ever heard, Michael. I predict you will go on to do wonderful things. There is greatness in you."

Michael shook his head. "You'd be the only one to believe that, Mouse. If I live long enough to be an adult, I doubt any good will come of it. What about you? What dreams do you have?"

"The dreams most young girls have. To go to London for a season of balls and dancing and somehow find a man who would fall madly in love with a small insignificant woman of little fortune. To live with him and raise a family. Happily-ever-after."

Michael didn't laugh at her. "I hope you get that, Katrina."

"It's a dream, but it may not match reality. Maybe I need to live like you in the meantime." She looked up into the branches above. "Right now, I would like to climb this tree. I've always wondered what the view would be like from the top."

Michael studied the strong sturdy branches. "It's a

pretty tall tree. It might be dangerous to climb up it. I don't think it would be wise."

Katrina stood and shook out her skirts. "Oh? You doubt I can do it?"

"I didn't say that. I don't think it would be smart. You might get hurt. You're a girl." Michael recognized the minute he said those words, that they were the wrong ones.

Her eyes narrowed and her clenched hands went to her waist. Without another word, she stared at the trunk of the tree. Hiking her skirt, she grabbed a lower hanging branch, managed to swing herself up, and began to climb. Michael watched, hoping she would not fall. Occasionally, he glanced down to the riverbank. Marcus and Phillip remained oblivious to Katrina's daring adventure.

Katrina climbed as high as she could. "Michael! It's amazing up here!" she shouted down to him. "You should come up!"

"Thank you for the invitation, but I'll stay here on *terra firma*."

"Coward." Her laughter filtered down through the leaves like droplets of sunlight that broke through from the sky above, dappling everything around him with joy.

Michael waited. He could no longer see her. He heard rustling at points and sounds of discomfort. "Are you coming down, Mouse?"

"Trying. It's. Much. Harder."

"Take it slow, you'll be fine." Michael tried to catch sight of her.

"Oooomph! Owwww!"

"Are you all right?"

"No," came the reply. It sounded as though she

might be crying.

"Can you climb down?" Alarm tinged his words.

"No. Please. Help." The plaintive cry did something to Michael's heart. The joy evaporated into fear and anxiety. Michael kicked off his boots, swung himself up and started his own climb.

Katrina came into view. Her leg was at an odd angle and her face had a grayish pallor. She gamely tried not to cry.

"Hey, Mouse. What's wrong?"

"My leg."

Michael inched closer on the branch, leveraging himself and holding on with one arm, he touched the leg. "Do you think you broke it?"

Katrina's teeth clenched. She nodded.

"I'm afraid we need to go down the way we came up."

Katrina's eyes filled with tears. "You'll help me?"

"Sure, Mouse, I'll help you as best I can, but I'm not sure how I can avoid hurting you."

"Hold my hand at least."

Somehow, they slowly made their way down the rest of the tree. Michael dropped to the ground to catch her. She was reluctant to let go of that last branch and when she did, it cut deeply into the side of her palm and up her pinky. Katrina wept then, clinging tightly to Michael.

Even now his heart clenched at the memory.

"It'll be all right, Mouse. I'll carry you to the house." He leaned her against the trunk and removed his cravat to bind her hand before lifting her into his arms. She'd been so slight then. He thought back to a few nights past when he carried that same girl, with a new injury, in his arms. The curves and that desire to protect her, to take away her pain, was only heightened by the memory of the last time he'd done that. How many more trees would he need to rescue her from before this was over?

Shaving completed, Michael finished dressing and recalled other memories of summers with Katrina. The one attempt she tried at fishing failed, her shrieks and giggles keeping the fish away. How eager she was to learn to shoot and how she could put an arrow through a target with greater efficiency than he could. She would crow about that.

Michael grinned. The only true laughter and joy he ever experienced in life had been with that girl. The same young woman who sat healing from a bullet wound and eager to help him down a tree he couldn't manage on his own. Maybe he owed her the opportunity to help. There were no other options.

Michael worried he was losing his edge. He'd been dead serious when he'd told Lord Hughes he was quitting. At times, he couldn't concentrate. He forgot simple things as if he walked in a fog, unsure of his direction. He understood his mission. But an invisible wall kept him from reaching his goal.

He laughed at his own inability to describe his mental state. But that was the issue. He feared he was losing his mind. He hoped he could hold on to it long enough to solve the riddle of this document and keep Katrina safe. After that, he could slide into insanity and live there quite happily. He shook his head. Everything appeared the same, but fuzziness haunted the edges of his vision. He feared this time he might fail.

Fail the mission.

Fail his country.

Fail Mouse.

~*~

The dark corner of the pub obscured the identity of the two men meeting there, to all appearances sharing a table and enjoying the brew available.

Cap pulled low, the brawny tall man spoke in a whisper. "Where is it? We are running out of time. You realize that if you don't get your hands on that document before he figures it out, that you will soon find yourself…" The man motioned with his finger moving across his own neck.

The smaller man paled and his hands trembled slightly as they gripped the mug in front of him and raised it to his lips to drink. He rubbed his sleeve across his mouth to wipe away the foam left behind. "Don't tell me things I don't already know. I've searched everywhere. I've even taken some other measures to try to get him to confide in me. At least the girl is out of the picture. I was a bit worried about her interfering."

"The Black Diamond will not be thwarted. The stakes are high and there are forces at work that you don't want to encounter."

The pale man's eyes shifted quickly to the face of the one threatening him. "Forces? What forces?"

"Evil. Unexplainably diabolical. He will achieve his ends with or without your help." The man's voice dropped to a sinister sounding whisper, "You will be richly rewarded when you succeed."

"If I succeed."

"When. There is no if. Deliver the document." The bigger man drained his mug. Slamming it down on the table he rose to leave. "Do not disappoint me. You will not live to regret it." He slipped through the tables to the back corridor and was gone.

The man remaining frowned. He pushed away the rest of his ale and rose as well, nerves shaken. Time was running out and he despised himself for the bargain he'd made. He had a job to do and he could not afford to fail.

~*~

Katrina learned from Phillip that Michael had returned to his home. She debated endlessly that day about waiting for him to come to her or go to him. Her arm hurt and the doctor warned her about any physical exertion. But surely slipping in a back door of the townhouse wouldn't be too onerous. It wasn't last time either. What if she met with other resistance? She wandered in her sitting room as she debated. The clock struck eleven and the household had settled in for the night. Did she dare?

She sat down by the fire and picked up the glass of port. Phillip laughed when she'd asked for some after dinner, but it had become a drink she learned to love while sitting at the end of meals with her father, discussing the events of the day. She sipped the wine, enjoying the darker tones and full body of the drink as warmth slowly spread throughout her chest. She leaned back in the chair, relishing her freedom from the insane stays that were so often dictated by society. She stretched her legs out in front of her, exposing her feet and ankles to the cool night air and the warmth radiating from the fire. She crossed her feet at the ankles and closed her eyes. So much for the proper companion. She smiled. There was freedom in her isolation that she didn't mind.

She rested there for a moment while she thought back on the past two years. Nursing her father and running of the estate. Writing up letters and reading the Bible to him as he lay in bed, weak and struggling mentally to comprehend all that was going on around him.

~*~

She awoke with a start and opened her eyes to find Michael sitting across from her.

"You snore in the most delightful way, Mouse." His eyes twinkled as he sipped from her glass of port.

"I do not." She tried to sit up and arrange her nightgown and robe to cover up her ankles and feet.

"You most certainly do, but it was charming."

"Why are you here?" she hissed at him, and reached over to grab her glass back. She was about to take a sip, but thought better of it and set it on the table.

"I need your help." Michael's smile faded and his eyes pleaded. "Please?"

"I've been waiting to hear those words." She smiled. "Did you bring the whole thing?"

Michael shook his head. "Only part of it. Based on what we did the other night, I figured it would take more than one sitting for us to decipher this. I can deliver whatever we finish to Lord Hughes tomorrow. And follow-up with the remainder the next day.

"Are you still being watched and threatened?" She leaned forward and placed a hand on his arm. Warmth radiated through her simply by that touch.

Michael flinched and shook his head. "Someone is

still searching my rooms, but it is far subtler. Less violent. I am always on the alert, but between my valet and I, it is rare for someone not to be around. How they are doing this I haven't figured out."

"How are you safeguarding the document?"

"The original is with Lord Hughes. I only carry a copy, it never leaves me. I guard it with my life."

She nodded. "So, you are willing now to let me help you?"

He smiled sheepishly. "I am, if you are still willing to throw your lot in with the likes of me. You've already proven yourself to be an intrepid partner. I could do with worse."

Katrina's eyebrows rose and her eyes widened as her chin went up. "Really? I'm not sure if I should be flattered, insulted, or both. Probably both. But fine, let's see what we can accomplish. We won't have much time before Lady Westcombe peeks in on me."

"She peeks in?"

"She sees light and is aware I am often up at night. When she goes to take care of the baby, she comes to check in on me too."

"How much time do we have?"

"Less than an hour."

Michael pulled out the document and went to the table by the fire and Katrina followed with her father's journal. It was a low table on a soft lush carpet so both fell to their knees just like the last time.

Michael got up again and went to a nearby desk to bring the quill and ink. They worked feverishly, both focused only on the task at hand.

After three-quarters of an hour, Katrina reached up to rub her neck and yawned. "I think we need to stop."

Michael nodded and began to fold up the sanded pages and shove them in his coat. "We've accomplished a lot. I will get these notes to Lord Hughes in the morning. May I return tomorrow night?"

Katrina shook her head as she closed the journal. "Tomorrow will find me returning to Lady Orion's. She thinks I fell and hurt my shoulder. She came to visit today and that's the word she's spreading around town. Phillip and Elizabeth are not happy about the lie, but won't contradict it. Hopefully, by the time Marcus gets here that is all he will be told. I took a tumble and hurt myself. Just like trying to climb down a tree." She winked at him as he helped her rise to her feet. A surge of heat followed that touch.

"You realize you might be as sought after as I am. Katrina, are you prepared for that?"

"I doubt I'm in danger. It's you I worry about. You don't seem quite yourself tonight." She withdrew her hand from his grasp.

"Truth be told, I'm not. What I am, I don't know." He sighed. "Let's accomplish this quickly so that we can both be free. Where can I find you tomorrow night at Lady Orion's? Where is your room?"

"Fourth floor, last room on the left as you come up the servants' stairs."

"Any other entrance?"

"No vines or tree on that side of the house. No." She moved away and set the journal down on the desk before turning to face him again.

Michael reached up to touch her cheek, sending tingles all the way to her toes. He bent his head to hers and gave her a kiss.

"Mmmm. Michael." She pulled back before

leaning her forehead against his chest. Her pulse was rapid. His hand came down to the small of her back and rested there.

He kissed the top of her head and took a tiny step back. "I should apologize, Mouse. I have no right to take such liberties."

Her head rose. "Then why?"

"I wish I knew. Something about you…it's my fault. Please, forgive me." He stepped back and before she could respond, he was gone.

Katrina put her fingers up to touch her lips. She fell asleep hugging the memory of that kiss and others close to her heart. Perhaps Michael held her in affection after all.

~*~

Michael managed to get back to his rooms without Tristan being any the wiser that he'd even left. He sat in front of the fireplace and drained a bottle of wine. Why did he keep kissing the girl? *Idiot!* He took another drink and berated himself further. *If you are going to lose your mind and your head, don't take her with you. She deserves better.* As he slipped into a restless sleep, all he could think of was a young woman with hazel eyes, brown hair, and a heart shaped face. What would he do with her?

~*~

The next morning, Michael awoke to the rhythm of a horse galloping across his skull. He groaned and rolled over. Tristan had obviously been in the room. His clothing was set out and a vile drink was on a tray by his bed.

Tristan walked in with Michael's freshly polished Hennisons. "Good morning, sir. I took the liberty of making you a special concoction, deducing from the bottle on the floor that you might be in need." Tristan was loud and way too chipper for Michael's sensitivities.

"You can leave me to dress myself. I am in no mood for your chatter this morning, and I need to be off soon."

Tristan put one hand to his chest and bowed. "I apologize if I have offended you, sir. Please, allow me to assist you. I earn little enough of the wages you pay me."

"You are here more for my consequence and appearances than out of any genuine urgency I have for a valet, and you fully well know it. Go enjoy your day. I will apprise you later if I have need of you."

"May I inquire as to where you will be?"

"You may, but I right now refuse to answer that question because I don't know fully myself. I will go where the wind takes me. Right now, it is calling me to the withdrawing room."

Michael made it in time to relieve himself of the effects of his night's drinking binge.

8

The noise in Michael's head was reduced to a dull roar by the time he presented himself at the Ministry of Defense at Whitehall, outside of Lord Hughes's office.

His wait was short and he was ushered in before the older man.

"Michael. You bring me good news I hope?" Lord Hughes put his quill back in the ink pot. Quickly standing and folding the paper before him, he finally gave Michael his full attention.

Michael handed him the document that had been deciphered. "This is not the complete work, but it's a start." He sat down and waited while Lord Hughes perused the contents.

"This is excellent. Important news indeed. How soon can you complete the rest?"

"My hope is that by tomorrow morning we will have it for you. Miss Shepherd is moving back to Lady Orion's today. I will seek her out this evening."

"Where will you meet? She hasn't fully recovered yet, has she?"

"No, The story of the injured shoulder was brilliant, though. It will buy us time."

"Injured shoulder?"

"That's the word that Lady Orion is spreading about Miss Shepherd. I thought it began with you."

Lord Hughes shook his head. "That woman is a force to be reckoned with. But don't let that worry you.

It serves our purposes very well. Even Lord Remington will not fault either of us in this instance."

"Lord and Lady Westcombe are aware of the truth, however, but will not be inclined to counter the *ton*'s rumor mill."

"Where will you meet tonight?"

"At Lady Orion's. With her shoulder, I cannot expect her to risk any more injury by meeting elsewhere."

"If you get caught there you realize you will be forced to marry her."

"I won't get caught."

Lord Hughes's eyes narrowed. "Let's make this clear. *If* you are caught, you will do the honorable thing."

Michael glared back. "Like I said. I *won't* get caught."

Lord Hughes was silent for a moment and frowned. "You don't look good, Michael."

"I don't feel well."

"Anything you care to share?"

"No. If that is all, may I be excused? I need to pay my respects at Lady Orion's." Michael stood but wavered on his feet a bit before gripping the edge of the desk to steady himself.

Lord Hughes's eyes narrowed further. "You are sick. You should go home and rest. I can send a doctor to you."

"How kind of you, I'm sure. I'll be fine." Michael made his way to the door but gripped the knob hard before opening it as a wave of dizziness flowed over him. Taking a deep breath, he opened the door and headed out into the busy streets of London.

Somehow, he managed to make it to Lady Orion's

home. He didn't remember the journey and fear began to take root deeper in this soul than ever before. *Tonight. I only need to make it through tonight to break the code and be done with this case. Then they can lock me up in Bedlam and throw away the key.* He smiled and bent to place a kiss an inch above Lady Orion's gloved hand.

The older lady took him in with a considering eye. "Sir Tidley. To what do we owe this unexpected pleasure? You haven't been at any to the balls of late to flirt shamelessly with all the young debutantes and make sure all the wallflowers get at least one dance. I must say, are you well? Have a seat." Lady Orion took back her hand and leaned forward to pour a cup of tea for her visitor.

Michael was seated next to her, relieved when the room stopped spinning. He accepted the tea. It removed the metallic taste in his mouth.

"Sir Tidley, I believe you have met but not been introduced to my companion, Miss Katrina Shepherd." Lady Orion motioned to the young lady sitting across from them in a chair. He eyed Katrina closely. The woman before him was so entirely not the same young woman he kissed last night. Her hair was now pulled back into a tight bun and under a cap. Her gown was gray and she was wearing…spectacles! No wonder he hadn't recognized her before. Katrina always wore spectacles. She couldn't see very well. He was observing another side of this woman and she baffled him even more.

He lifted his teacup toward her and bowed his head, maintaining eye contact with her. "Miss Shepherd, what a pleasure to finally meet you."

She nodded to him and her eyes flashed briefly. She wore a sling around her arm and shoulder.

"It appears you have been injured?"

"Miss Shepherd fell and hurt her shoulder. She may be unable to accompany me in society for some time. I've been considering sending her to her cousin in the country to recuperate. She won't be doing me any good here in town except to be eating my food. Lady Remington would not mind having her for company."

Sir Michael glanced over at Katrina with a raised eyebrow.

"As you say, my lady." She bent her head down glancing at her fingers and avoiding Michael's gaze.

"I thought Lord and Lady Remington were due in town soon? Surely a trip to Rose Hill would be more taxing on Miss Shepherd than resting in your care."

"Do you think so, Sir Tidley? Every time I see her I shiver in horror at the pain she must endure, and I admit I am selfish and do not like that. But I cannot keep her confined to her room either." Lady Orion said this in a most confidential air as she leaned towards him.

"I fully understand your sensibilities, ma'am, but even your kindheartedness would not sacrifice her healing for your comfort. All of the *beau monde* is aware of your generous nature." Michael gave her his most winning smile.

Lady Orion sat up a little taller under this flattery. "Well, of course you must be correct. Yet a vacation to the country could easily be arranged and she would return refreshed when Lord Remington arrives in a few weeks." She glanced at Katrina who kept her eyes downcast. "What do you have to say for yourself, Miss Shepherd?"

Michael caught the flash of anger before it dimmed and her eyes appeared glassy as she answered

Lady Orion. "I will do whatever you desire, my lady. I would not like to discomfit you after all your kindness to me."

"There, you see, Sir Tidley? She is willing to accede to my wishes in this matter. Well, that settles it. You will be on your way within the hour. You do not have much to pack and I expect one of the maids shall assist you. The carriage will be at the door. You may arrive relatively late, but you should not need to make an overnight stop if you hurry off." Turning to Sir Michael she spoke in a lower voice, "See, I am most considerate of her needs with this."

Sir Michael nodded and stood as Miss Shepherd rose to her feet.

"Sir Tidley. Lady Orion." She gave small courtesies to them both before departing the room without a sound.

Sir Michael bent to set his cup and saucer down on the table in front of him. "I must be off too, Lady Orion. It has been a pleasure to have been able to visit you again."

"Sir Tidley, heed my words. You do not appear well. It might behoove you to make a country cure as well. 'Tis too early in the season for you to be as careworn as you are."

"I will consider your advice, my lady." Sir Michael bowed and turned to leave.

Back at his home, he threw some items into an overnight bag to place on Pepper. If ridden well, the stallion could make the journey. Otherwise, he would be required to switch horses at least once. He made sure his purse was sufficient. As he finished packing up, Tristan entered with a tray of food.

"Sir. You are leaving?" Tristan quickly placed the

food on the table with a clang. He wrung his hands together. "Without me?"

"I need to make a journey to Rose Hill for a day or so." Michael walked over and picked up some cold ham and cheese and placed them on a piece of bread. He managed to eat the food in a few quick bites and swallow a glass of lemonade. He shivered as he set the glass down. "Those were some bitter tasting lemons, my good man. Tell the housekeeper that I like a little more sugar in my lemonade."

"Yes, sir. You are not taking me with you on your journey?" The man's foot was now tapping.

"I need you here in case someone else tries to break in. You can let Lord Hughes know if something happens. I'll be back in a few days." Michael threw his bag over his shoulder. "Don't worry, Tristan. This will soon be over and we can be comfortable again. I'm thinking of retiring when this case is done."

Tristan paled. "Retiring? Sir?"

"I'm done with this kind of work. If my life will be too bland for you, I will gladly write you a good reference to find another position. I won't be offended. You have served me faithfully and well over the years." Michael turned to survey the room. "Fidget? Where are you?" Without warning the long, furry ferret was swathed around his neck. "Ready to go?"

Michael was greeted with kisses and smiled. "Ah, at least someone loves me." Tipping his hat to Tristan he headed for the door. "In a few days, Tristan, that's all. Stay out of trouble."

"Sir." Tristan stood upright with his shoulders back and eyes wide. He stammered to say more.

"Relax, my good man. I am joking. Take care, the enemy might be getting desperate and I would hate for anything to happen to you."

"Yes, sir."

~*~

Katrina rested against the squabs of the shabby coach she was given for the ride to Rose Hill. It was better than riding on the stage. She hadn't warranted a maid to travel with. Keeping her injured shoulder from being banged against the carriage was her main challenge. As she stared out at the passing scenery, she wondered if Sir Tidley would head to Rose Hill as well. At least she hadn't needed to worry about him arriving in her room tonight and finding her gone. They would get this document done and redeem her father's reputation.

She thought back to her father's last few weeks and how weak and dizzy he'd become. His manservant at the time insisted on making sure that all the food and drink was prepared especially for him. She had hated having to let the young Irishman go after his faithful service. His accent had been fun and his eye twinkled with mischief as he teased her.

She frowned. Even now with her reputation, career choice, lack of fortune and age, a valet would be considered a respectable match. Her heart sank.

When she finally restored her father's good name, then what? Did she continue as a companion to a dragon of the *ton* like Lady Orion and hope that someday a man might notice her? Tears sprang to her eyes. They were so close to realizing her dream. After that, the future stretched out as a black void of unknown. Her heart filled with grief for all she'd lost and how now, with her choices, she stood to lose even more. Sir Michael's love she'd never possessed and grieved that she never would.

Her father was gone and restoring his reputation would not bring him back. Her youth had been stolen by caring for him in his illness. Her position as a young, marriageable lady of the upper-ten-thousand was set aside the minute she chose to serve Lady Orion.

Maybe she could still work through the war office as a spy at *ton* events? Even that had lost its allure. She would be a servant at someone else's beck and call, with her life and spirit diminishing with each passing year, curtsey, and 'Yes, ma'am.' Her hair would turn gray and she would enjoy no more kisses with a certain coffee-eyed man whose humor and strength had been the lifeblood of her younger years, and the figment of dreams that sustained her thus far as an adult.

Foolish heart!

She let the tears flow freely now. Tonight, she was certain that Michael would come to her for the last time. They'd finish the work that would free them both from any further entanglements. She leaned back on her right shoulder and tried to rest her head. Loneliness overwhelmed her. The sound of dirt and stone under the wheels and the steady clomp-clomp-clomp of the carriage horses all mocked her.

Even the weather seemed to be in accordance with her gloomy mood. A cold rain began to fall in earnest as the day progressed. Mentally, she tallied the amount of money she possessed and whether it would be enough to get a room at an inn on the way. When the early spring rain turned to snow, the carriage started to slip on the road and the way became harder to see. Her fate was sealed and the expense would be unavoidable. They pulled into a small town and she prepared herself mentally for the humiliation of trying to find a room. A single, unattached female was in a less than enviable position when coming to a country inn—alone.

When she reached The Crown in the little town, she found the door opened by none other than Sir Michael Tidley. "My dearest love, how I worried about you on these roads. Come, I have already arranged for a private dining room and a suite for us for the evening." Sir Tidley helped her down from the carriage and linked her right arm through his left. With his back straight and his head high he led her into the inn. She was surprised to find the innkeeper bowing and scraping before her as if she were royalty.

"My dear wife, please allow Mrs. Finch to escort you to your room to refresh yourself. I look forward to your company in our private dining room for a repast that is already being set out for us." Michael winked at her.

"Thank you, my dear." She gave him a solemn nod and headed off after the rather rotund body of Mrs. Finch.

"What a horrible thing spring weather can be, Mrs. Tidley. But we are right glad that you have deigned to spend the night with us. We hope to make you most comfortable. I can send a maid up to assist you with changing your gown if you desire?" The landlady was eager to please with her bright eyes, rosy cheeks, and rapid speech.

"Thank you, Mrs. Finch." Katrina took in the humble room with the large four poster bed, fireplace, and screen for dressing. "My husband spoke of a suite of rooms?"

"Due to the storm, we only had this available. Although for newlyweds that shouldn't be too much of a problem?" Mrs. Finch gave a giggle and a wink. "Will there be anything else, ye be needin'?"

"No. Thank you, Mrs. Finch." Katrina walked the lady to the door and shot the bolt home as she leaned against it and closed her eyes.

Michael had spared her the humiliation she expected. And the room was much nicer than she anticipated. She pushed herself away from the door, untied her cloak, and hung it on the coat rack. Untying her bonnet, she shook off the snow, and hung that as well. She untied her half boots and dug in her bag for a pair of slippers to wear instead. Her toes felt so cold she hoped Michael wouldn't mind her warming them by the fire downstairs. She laughed at how improper she had become. Taking care of her needs and freshening up her hair as best she could with one hand, she grabbed a shawl and her father's book, and headed down the stairs to the private room where her false bridegroom awaited her.

Oh, how she wished they were not pretending.

~*~

Michael watched Katrina go upstairs with the landlady. He'd ridden Pepper hard. Lady Orion's coachman followed through on Michael's instructions, although the weather definitely made the decision to stop seem less suspicious. Michael had stopped twice on the journey to cast up his accounts by the side of the road. He shivered even in his greatcoat and headed to the private parlor to stand by the fireplace, placing his hand on the mantle to steady himself.

They needed to finish working on the document. Tonight. There was no more time. He was growing sicker and weaker. He would not be able to get this done later. Sweat beaded up on his forehead even as he shivered in front of the fire. The wind howled outside and a flash of fear jolted him. He closed his eyes tight, fighting the sense of losing control. A wave of dizziness crashed into him as he fought against the darkness that threatened. *I'm dying*.

Fidget ran in circles making a clicking sound.

That was the last thing Michael remembered.

~*~

Katrina entered the private parlor expecting Michael to be waiting for her with a sly grin on his face. She was fully prepared to deliver a good set down and make sure he understood that business would be all that would be done this night. All thoughts of their task fled when she entered the empty room. She closed the door behind her and reached for her knife hidden in a side pocket of her gown. The room was wreathed in shadows and the curtains were drawn against the stormy night. The smell of cider, soup, and fresh baked bread assailed her and her stomach rumbled in response. She licked her lips and her gaze darted from wall to wall taking in the furnishings.

The hair stood up on the back of her neck. She slowly made her way around the table, checking underneath the heavy rustic wood. Coming around to the fireplace her heart dropped to her solar plexus as she saw Michael lying there, so still. Fidget was guarding him and bared his teeth at her.

No! Not Michael! Please Lord, not him! She rushed to his side, put away her knife, knelt alongside his body and leaned over to check his breathing by placing a hand lightly on his chest. The ferret sniffed her fingers and backed off. Michael's heart beat steady beneath the layers of his clothing. She sat back on her heels and gave a sigh of relief. She moved to untie his cravat and unbuttoned his vest and shirt. She grew warm spying the dark hair peeking through. Had that always been there? She placed her hand against the warm hot flesh. His head moved and a moan escaped. A hand came to clamp her wrist tightly, startling her.

"Oh!" She tried to pull her arm back but it remained still. She glanced at Michael's face as his eyes flickered open in an unfocused way. "Michael?"

~*~

Michael should let her go, but he couldn't. Her distinctive scent tickled his senses. Vanilla. He tried to make out her face but she seemed blurry to him. "Please. Don't leave me," was all he could gasp out before he released her and closed his eyes again. She moved away from him and he wanted to cry. He despised his own weakness. His breathing quickened as he feared being left here, but then her presence was beside him again. A small hand moved behind his neck, lifting his head slightly.

"Drink."

The mug was to his lips and he tried to comply. Water dribbled down his cheeks. He forced his eyes open and focused on the face in front of him. The concern in her eyes, the pink lips pursed together in worry. *For him?* When had anyone really cared about what happened to him?

"Good job." She set the mug down and using both hands, lowered his head, bending over to kiss his forehead.

"More?" He grinned. "A little lower?"

"Michael? What happened?"

He shook his head and instantly regretted it. "No time. You need to finish the document. Now. I must return to Lord Hughes, before…"

"Before someone manages to finally kill you?" she whispered.

"Something like that." He tried to grin.

"Don't do that."

"Do what?"

"Go dying on me. I won't allow it." She touched the side of his head tenderly and her face came into focus.

"Can you help me get up, Mouse?" He tried to rise. She leveraged him to a sitting position and then she stood and leaned over to help him up. It was a clumsy process as she avoided using her injured arm, but finally, he sat in a chair by the table, was able to put his elbows there and lean his head on his hands.

"What happened?" She pulled up a chair beside him.

He shook his head weakly. "Not feeling well. Need to finish this job. Get you to Marcus so you'll be safe."

"I can worry about myself. How long have you been unwell?"

Could that be anxiety in her soft voice? It washed over him like a lover's caress and he focused on her lips. "A week or so, I don't remember. Never been this bad. Getting worse."

"Can you eat something?"

"I'll try."

Katrina rose and moved to fill a bowl with soup,

dipped some bread into it, brought it to his mouth. He ate eagerly and when the bread was gone he licked her fingers.

Her eyes widened.

"I'm sorry, Mouse. I'm a rogue and you were wise to never fall for the likes of me."

Katrina's pale hazel-gray eyes grew moist.

"Don't cry, Mouse. I'm not worth your tears."

"Don't tell me not to care, Michael."

Katrina moved to get the mug from the floor, filled it with some ale, and again brought it to his lips. He managed to take it from her. She withdrew from his touch when he had hold of the mug. He leaned back against the chair and let the ale slide down his throat, warming him.

"More soup?"

"Certainly." She rose to refill his bowl and set it down in front of him. She filled a bowl for herself. She picked up her spoon to eat.

Who was this woman? How did she get to be so beautiful? Why did he need her so much? Beyond this job, how was he to walk away from her and slide into oblivion, never to hear her laughter, or feel her touch, and savor her kisses? He no longer remembered kissing her that night and thinking of her as that tiny blonde spitfire. No, she was his hazel-eyed, brown haired beauty. She deserved better than him.

Katrina ate and said nothing.

He picked up his spoon and tried to put away the bowl of soup before him. He got halfway through and set the spoon down. "I'm sorry I waylaid you, Katrina. I need that document done. Too much is at stake. They are closing in and I don't know how much time we have left."

Katrina nodded and moved away from the food to the end of the table. She went to a corner desk and brought back the ink pot, feather pen, and paper. She drew the journal out of the bag she had with her but before she was seated, she locked the door and checked the windows.

Michael produced the remainder of the document to be deciphered and smoothed it out on the table.

Silently, they sat down to work.

9

Two hours passed. Katrina allowed the landlord to clear the table and bring in some pudding and a bottle of port.

Michael folded up the finished document and leaned back in his chair.

Katrina put the writing elements away and tucked her journal in her bag. She wandered to the window and pushed the drapes back to watch the falling snow. "He will wash you whiter than snow. I never completely understood that."

"What are you talking about?"

"Jesus. He's supposed to wash away our sin, with His blood, until we are whiter than snow."

"Makes no sense." Michael leaned back in his chair.

"I know. But do you think it's possible?"

"What's possible?"

"That God could wash away our sin by His innocent blood?"

"I don't know."

"Neither do I."

"Mouse?" She turned and looked at him, allowing the curtain to fall shut.

"What is it, Michael?"

"I need you."

She gave a half-grin with one dimple showing up

on her right cheek. "You needed me, but we are done. You have the proof that my father is innocent. I have that comfort and can now prove it to Lord Hughes. Thank you. You have what you need."

"I…"

"Michael, I understand you only ever spent time with me because you needed that journal. It's done. It's over. You need never see me again."

Michael struggled to rise. "No. I don't think you do, Mouse. At first, that may have been true, but now…"

"Now?"

"Now I can't imagine living life without you." There. He said it.

Katrina was silent.

Michael stood, holding tightly to his chair with both hands.

"Michael, you are not well. Please, sit, before you collapse. How will you ever make it back to London by yourself?"

"Maybe you should go with me?" Michael obediently sat, but stretched out a hand to her.

Katrina walked over to him. She yawned, but moved into his embrace and held his head to her chest. "I would go to the ends of the earth for you, Michael," she murmured.

Michael's face came up. "What did you say? I couldn't hear you." He drew her down to sit on his knee.

Katrina put her uninjured arm around his neck.

Their eyes met and slowly her head lowered closer to his as he angled up for a kiss. Their lips met in sweet communion.

A knock on the door brought Katrina to her feet

and a blush to her cheeks.

"Who is it?" Michael barked.

"Tristan."

Katrina started and her eyes were wide. "Tristan?" she whispered.

"My valet. He served with me in the war as a batman. You can let him in. I'm not sure why he followed me here."

Katrina bent down before Michael. "What does he look like?"

The knock was louder this time. "Just a minute!" Michael called out.

"Irish heritage, reddish brown hair, blue eyes and medium build."

Katrina paled.

"Why? Katrina, what's wrong?"

"How long has he been serving you?"

"We met about four years ago in France, but parted when I left the Horse Guards. I only hired him on a few months ago."

The knock was more insistent.

Michael raised his eyebrows.

Katrina shook her head and wandered over to the fireplace.

"Mouse?"

"He sounds like the valet who cared for my father in the last years of his life. Nice man, sure, but disappeared the minute my father was dead. Now you are sick like he was…"

"What are you saying?"

"I often wondered if my father had been poisoned. I could never prove it."

"Open the door, Katrina." Michael rose to his feet.

Katrina shot him a venomous look but did as he

bid, walking over to the door and pulling back the bolt. The door shot open and was slammed shut by the newest occupant of the room.

Katrina took several steps away, and her hand came to cover her mouth.

Tristan stood staring at her. "You! What are you doing here, Miss Shepherd?"

"You know each other?" Michael said casually.

Katrina nodded.

Tristan collected himself and walked towards Sir Tidley. "Sir, I could not stay home and wonder as to your well-being. Forgive my impudence in following you."

"How noble of you, Tris. You have difficulty obeying direct orders, however."

Tristan lowered his head a fraction. When he raised it again his chin went higher and he moved to pull a gun out of his inner coat pocket, pointing it at Michael. "I obey orders, just happens that I am taking them from someone other than you."

Michael remained outwardly calm. Katrina reached slowly into her pocket. He hoped she had her knife. Michael tensed for a fight.

"What do you want, Tristan?"

"The document."

"So you were the one?"

Tristan nodded.

"Why? I thought you loved England. I thought you were on our side."

"So did Mr. Shepherd, much good it did him."

Michael walked over to the fireplace and stirred the coals so the fire blazed fully again.

"Did you kill Mr. Shepherd?"

"Slowly poisoned him. He was a stubborn old

coot. Far too noble in defending his cause."

"So when you couldn't get what you wanted from him, you killed him?"

"Of course, he was expendable."

Katrina leaned against the wall, trying to not draw notice to herself. *Leave. Just leave!* He longed to yell to her.

"Why?" she asked.

Tristan turned to her while keeping the gun trained on Sir Michael.

"He was an enemy to Napoleon. A spy passing on information. I couldn't discover his secrets so I was ordered to eliminate him and collect his papers."

"It was you who poisoned him? You were the one who decimated all his records?"

Tristan nodded. "But somehow the one book I needed eluded me. He was gone so it was of no importance."

"What book was that?" Michael asked, drawing Tristan's attention back to himself.

"His journal. He kept his codes in there. I only ever saw it once but could never find it."

Michael frowned. "So why are you here now?"

"I told you, I want the document."

"It was you who was searching my things?"

Tristan nodded.

"And you who has been poisoning me?"

The red head once again went up and down. "I have no more time to play games. Hand over the papers."

Michael reached into his pocket and pulled out papers. "You mean these?"

Tristan nodded and his eyes grew wide. "Yes. I am assuming you finished them. I was hoping you wouldn't be successful because now you know too much."

Michael crumpled up the papers and threw them into the fireplace where the flames eagerly licked them to ashes.

"Tis no matter, Sir Michael. I only needed to make sure they didn't get into the wrong hands. But if you managed to decipher them it means that this lovely woman here has had her father's code all along."

Tristan advanced on Michael but stood out of arm's reach and cocked the hammer on the pistol. "Miss Shepherd. If you value this man's life, you may want to consider handing over that code to me now."

Katrina walked over to the table and the bag where the journal was stored.

"You don't need to give it to him, Mouse." Michael stood straight, with the gun aimed at his chest. His eyes spoke to her of finality and love. He motioned with his eyes for her to leave, to save herself.

"It was you, Tristan, who spread the rumors about my father, wasn't it?"

Tristan nodded. "I had to make sure that if the code book surfaced no one at Whitehall would seriously consider it a valuable tool."

Katrina gave a rueful laugh. "You misjudged me, didn't you?"

"Apparently so. A mistake I do not intend to make twice. The book?"

Katrina took the journal out of the bag and opened it to the pages of code they had used. She tried to rip them out, but the paper wouldn't cooperate and tear.

"What are you doing?" Tristan asked.

"Trying to help you out," Katrina said with a lightness in her voice. Her hands shook, betraying her fear.

"Give me the journal."

"And what? What do you promise me in exchange for this?"

"I'll let your lover live."

"My lover?"

Tristan waved his gun towards Michael's face. "Him."

Katrina looked to Michael and their eyes met. She walked around the table as far from Tristan as she could and came to the fireplace next to Sir Tidley.

"I don't believe you, Tristan. You poisoned and killed my father. You have been poisoning Sir Michael. You are an enemy to the King."

"The King who is as mad as this man here, or worse? How does one swear allegiance to such as him?"

Katrina hugged the journal to herself for a moment and then glanced at Michael.

Michael shook his head and whispered, "Don't do it, Mouse."

Katrina turned and dropped the journal into the fire. The flames roared up around it to devour its pages.

"No!" Tristan rushed forward to try to find a way to remove it from the fireplace, but was defeated when Katrina rushed forward to throw the contents of a glass of brandy into the mix. The blaze roared, singeing Tristan's eyebrows, and the odor of burning hair filled the room.

Katrina and Michael both stepped back. The flames destroyed the last memory of her father and tears welled up in her eyes. "I'm sorry, Father."

Michael moved toward her and put his arm

around her. "You didn't need to do that, sweetheart." He held her close and watched Tristan. The book was black and the contents irretrievable.

The man before them swelled with rage. The gun was again raised and Michael shoved Katrina behind him.

"I will kill you." Tristan's teeth were clenched and his face was fierce.

"I saved your life on the battlefield more than once, Tris. And you saved mine as well. Before you end my pathetic existence, would you at least give me a reason as to why? Why you would betray me and your country?"

"My country?" Tristan gave a cold bark of laughter. "What have I here that is mine? I own no land, no title, no wealth."

"I thought we were friends."

Tristan's voice cracked. "Maybe at one time. I'm sorry for that Michael, but it's either your life or mine."

"Who is forcing you?"

Tristan looked uncertain for a minute and shrugged. "I can tell you. Calls himself 'Black Diamond.' I've never met him, but he has power. And the reward is great if I bring him what he wants." Tristan's eyes took on a bleak look. "But you denied me my victory and prize, so only certain death awaits me now. However, I will not meet my end alone." The gun shook a bit before raising a fraction higher.

Katrina backed away from Michael.

Tristan watched and uncertainty filled his gaze.

"You don't want her anyway, Tris. It's me you really mean to destroy, isn't it?" Michael drew his attention back to himself.

Tristan shook his head. "I need you both dead. I

cannot risk that you somehow tricked me."

In a flash, a black and white bundle of fur climbed Tristan's back and began nipping at his neck. Tristan frantically moved around, wildly waving the gun in an attempt to fend off the ferret's attack.

Katrina withdrew her knife and aimed. She tossed it. The knife sliced through the air and found its home in Tristan's neck. Blood spurted. The gun went off, knocking a picture off the wall and the man fell to the ground.

"You've been practicing, haven't you? That had to be the most brilliant throw I've ever watched you make." Michael moved over to the body of his valet, scooped up Fidget and lifted him to his shoulder. He felt for the pulse of the man laying at his feet.

A knock came at the door, followed by the landlord's voice. "Do I need to call the magistrate?"

"No. We are fine," Michael yelled.

"Did I…" Katrina asked.

Michael nodded and rose to his feet. Bringing Fidget off his neck, he set the ferret at the table to forage. He walked over to Katrina and enfolded her in his arms, making sure she could not see the dead man across the room. He loosened the pins from her hair and softly petted the silky strands as she sobbed in his arms. A wave of protectiveness flowed through him. He could not imagine living life without this woman by his side. He didn't know if he could continue in this line of work with her. A formidable partner, she would be an asset, but he couldn't handle any more instances where her life would possibly be in danger.

When the tears subsided, he pushed her away. He placed a kiss gently on her forehead as he wiped away a stray tear with his thumb.

"The ugly cry. I still think you are beautiful even now, Katrina. Why don't you take Fidget up to our room and I'll clean up here. There is no need for us to be up any longer."

Katrina nodded, grabbed the unfinished bottle of port with her free hand and gave Michael a weak smile. The ferret leaped to her shoulders for a ride upstairs.

"Lock the door in case there are others with him. I doubt it, but let's be safe. You remember my secret knock?"

Katrina nodded.

"Don't open to anyone except me."

She walked to the door, unlatched the bolt, and left him to dispose of the body.

~*~

Michael arrived up at the room and knocked. He heard the shuffling sounds within. The bolt moved and the door opened. Fidget skittered around his ankles as he came in and sat in a chair by the fire. A glass of wine waited for him there and he grabbed it and sipped.

Katrina bolted the door and padded across the small room to sit. She was dressed in her night rail and robe and her pink toes peeked out at him from under the folds of cotton. So young and innocent. Her eyes, however, told a different story.

"I'm sorry about your journal, Katrina. I understand how much that meant to you."

"I'm sorry you had to destroy all our hard work."

"I didn't."

"Excuse me?" Her tired eyes widened and

eyebrows rose.

"I pulled out a piece that had some nonsense written on it. I didn't sacrifice the document. Tristan didn't suspect anything and had no chance to look at it. We can still get the completed translation to Lord Hughes when the roads clear. Will you come with me? We can still exonerate your father, even without the journal."

Katrina leaned back, closed her eyes, and a soft smile emerged. "Thank you, Michael."

"Would you help me get these boots off, Katrina? I find that I'm in need of the services of a valet and am short staffed at the moment."

"Please don't make light of his death, Michael."

"He killed your father and planned to murder both of us as well. If he hadn't been so sure of himself, he might have succeeded. Don't feel bad about doing what you did. Fidget was pretty close to finding a strategic spot to bite as well, he was doomed regardless."

"I didn't know ferrets could kill people."

"Pretty rare, but he and Tris never got along."

Katrina moved to pull off Michael's boots and set them to the side. He relaxed in the chair. "I'm exhausted, Mouse. How are you faring?"

"Tired, sad. Confused." She sat down with her feet curled up underneath her. Her voice got soft. "Michael, you told the landlord we were married. We are alone in a room together." She blushed, glancing towards the bed in the far corner.

"I'm sorry for the lies. I'll grab a blanket and sleep here on the floor with Fidget. I've had far worse accommodations. Your virtue is safe with me."

"But is yours safe with me?" Katrina whispered.

She glanced back at him and held his gaze.

"The snow has stopped and we have a job to do. Tomorrow we will go back to London. Can you still ride astride like you used to?"

"If I dress as a man. I have the clothes with me, but not a warm enough cloak."

"Your shoulder?"

"I think I can manage if we don't push too hard."

"Good. Why don't we both get some sleep? We need to leave early in the morning."

Katrina clenched her fingers in her lap. She released them slowly, pulled her feet out from under her, and rose. She padded across the room, removed a pillow and a blanket from the bed, returned to the hearth and made up a pallet. She came to him.

"Michael."

"Kat?" He reached out and held one of her hands.

"I'm glad you will live, that the poisoning is over. I was terrified."

"I know, Mouse. All is well." He raised her hand to kiss it and let it go. "Off to bed with you, sweetheart."

Michael tried not to watch as Katrina blew out candles near the bed leaving only the light from the fire to illuminate the room. He kept his eyes focused away but her movements reflected in the standing mirror in the corner. A gentleman would avert his gaze, but tonight, Michael did not feel like a gentleman. Far from it. As Katrina slipped under the covers and snuggled into the pillow, he swallowed what was left of the wine and rose to climb under the covers of the pallet placed in front of the fire. He rested with his back to the dwindling flames and watched the shadows dance on the wall and ceiling. He wondered if hell was made of unfulfilled longings.

10

Michael woke early and dressed quickly. He went below stairs to get some coffee and toast before returning to awaken Katrina. When he came back, however, he found the bed empty and sounds coming from behind the screen. With little illumination, there were no shadows but that didn't stop his imagination. He cleared his throat as he closed the door and moved into the room towards the fire, setting the food down on the table.

Katrina emerged from behind the screen and once again appeared as the young man whom Michael had found half-dead on his bedroom floor. Her hair was tucked up under a cap. Her pants and coat fit her well. She wore riding boots. There was no hint of the woman who drove him mad with longing. She'd abandoned her sling.

Katrina came forward and grabbed a piece of toast. "Thank you for thinking to bring up some food."

"You're welcome. I hope you don't mind coffee. I needed that over tea this morning. I wasn't sure what your preference was."

"It used to be hot cocoa but I appreciate a coffee now and then." She reached down to pour a cup and add in some sugar. She stirred it and took a sip. "Hot." She put it down and nibbled on her toast as she found the chair.

Michael poured a cup, grabbed a piece of buttered

toast, and sat down across from her. "Did you sleep well?"

"I was fine in that comfortable bed—but how about you?"

"I was fine."

"How you are going to explain our absence and return here?"

"You're belongings will be taken to Rose Hill. Maybe we'll even be married by then." He grinned as he lifted his cup to his lips.

Katrina stared at him. She stopped chewing and set her cup down on the side table. She stood and started pacing.

"Mouse?"

Katrina waved him away but didn't answer. She had one hand over her nose and mouth and her eyes would periodically squeeze shut as she shook her head.

As she came back through her route he stopped her with a wall of solid muscle and arms enfolding her.

"I'm sorry if I upset you."

She looked up into his face, so close to her own. His brown eyes were warm and searching as he gazed into her hazel ones.

~*~

It was so good to be snuggled into Michael's arms as she wept. She wished he would not joke about marriage. All she'd ever wanted was to be his wife. She had no clue where they'd even live. Her only consolation in that dream of living and loving together was that she would finally be able to enjoy his touch and kisses without feeling as if it was wrong. She shuddered, sniffled, lifted her lips to his and kissed him softly.

He pulled back. "Mouse, we can't. You don't understand what you do to me."

Katrina nodded and stepped away. "I'm sorry." She walked to her cup of coffee and drank it down. She grabbed her hat and put it on top of her head. "Maybe we should depart?"

Michael followed suit, finishing his drink and grabbing his greatcoat and hat. "I found a coat for you. I borrowed it from Lady Orion's servant. I hope you don't mind that it doesn't smell very fresh."

He brought it to her.

She put it on and slid on her leather gloves.

"I'll be fine. The more nondescript I look, the better. Shall we go?"

Michael nodded and checked the hallway before letting her out the door. They ended up on the first floor landing and took a side door to the back toward the stables. Once there, Michael led a fresh Pepper out into the snow that fell.

The blast of cold air sucked the breath out of her for a moment and cooled off any remaining ardor. Katrina spoke softly to the gelding he'd procured for her. She swung up into the saddle and put the horse through some paces to make sure he knew who was boss.

Michael swung up onto his own black stallion and without a word the two were off, heading into the rising sun, toward London.

Katrina was shortly cursing her bravado the night before. After a few hours in the saddle, her leg muscles cramped and she was sore all over, especially her wounded shoulder. Her head throbbed. They stopped for a short break and when she swung down from the horse, she fell into the snow and lay there, allowing the cold to seep in through her many layers.

Michael's shadow came over her and he reached his hand out.

"Leave me here. I can't go on." Katrina closed her eyes.

"Underestimated how hard this would be?" Michael asked.

Silence.

"I suppose, if you really can't go on, I can't either. The mission will be lost and we can have the comfort of knowing we were together at the end." He plopped into the snow next to her and lay down. "Ah, Mouse, you might have something here. A bed of ice is infinitely preferable to a fluffy pillow and feather bed warmed by a brick."

Katrina started to giggle. She rolled onto her right arm to face Michael, placing her hand on his chest. She leaned forward to kiss him. Before he could react, she jumped to her feet, gathered up some snow and lobbed it at him. Michael howled as the snow spattered all over his face. He jumped to his feet, packing snow to return the favor. Soon they were hiding behind trees laughing and throwing snow and getting cold and wet. Finally, Katrina stopped and leaned against a tree. Michael came up to her. Both were breathing heavily. The laughter was gone.

Michael put one hand on Katrina's head and leaned in. "I know you're exhausted, Mouse. Do you think you can go on? We only have another hour to travel."

Katrina nodded. "I'll make it. We have to." She sighed deeply.

"I wish…" he whispered.

"What?" She held his gaze. He said no more words but communicated his longing through his eyes before pushing away from the tree and escorting her to her horse. She climbed up, wincing, She would be rubbed raw from this day's riding.

They arrived later in the afternoon and made sure the horses were cared for and well fed. Michael escorted her into his townhouse and up the stairs to a room adjoining his. Katrina sank into a chair in front of a fire he started for her. He came to pull off her boots and left. She dozed off, still fully dressed. When Michael awoke her a short time later, it was to find a tub in the room filled with hot water.

"I don't have a closet of dresses for you, but I found some clothes that might fit if you can stand being a man for a few more hours."

"Thank you, Michael," she said with weariness. She untied her cravat and took off the greatcoat and lay it over the back of a chair to dry.

"I'll leave you now. You can find me in the study downstairs when you are ready to go with me to visit Lord Hughes." Michael turned to leave.

"Isn't it too late? Won't Whitehall be closed?"

"We will find Lord Hughes tonight. Never fear. We will finish this so you can have your life back." With that, he strode from the room closing the door firmly behind him.

Katrina stripped, gingerly stepped into the hot tub, relaxed into the heat and the smell of…vanilla. She smiled. He'd noticed.

Michael also left a salve for her sore spots. When she felt presentable she made her way to the study on the first floor. Michael sat there with a tray of food, meat, cheese and some fruit.

He rose when she entered, walked over, placed a kiss on her cheek, and inhaled deeply. He stepped back and smiled. "Better?"

She nodded.

Michael placed a glass of brandy in her hand. "Here, drink this, it will help warm you up. A carriage will be ready in half an hour and we can set out to find Lord Hughes."

~*~

Michael almost helped her into the carriage and Katrina bit back a grin.

They headed first to the Ministry of Defense at Whitehall, but Lord Hughes was not there. They went to his home, but again, Lord Hughes eluded them.

Michael sank against the squabs, his teeth clenched, his mouth a thin line.

Katrina grew alarmed. "What? What's wrong, Michael?"

"I think we may have to track Lord Hughes down at his club. But I wonder if I can get you in without your reputation being ruined."

"I can play the role of a man. You needn't worry for me, Michael. I take responsibility for my own choices and their consequences."

"As a man, I take responsibility for caring for you. Remember, we don't know who the 'Black Diamond' is. He might be a member of this club. We need to be careful."

"You have the document?"

"A copy. The original is hiding elsewhere."

"So, if something happens to you, how am I to find

it?"

"Nothing will happen to me."

"You don't know that, Michael."

"Trust me, Kat. It will all turn out fine. Lord Hughes knows where to look for it."

"Are we bringing Fidget in with us?" Katrina motioned to the ferret that hid in a basket on the floor near the heated brick.

"Try to keep him out."

Katrina's eyebrow raised but she said no more.

The carriage pulled up to the curb at Brooks. Michael alit from the carriage and stood to wait for Katrina.

At the door, Michael was recognized and he introduced Katrina as Mr. Shepherd. They gained entrance and learned that Lord Hughes was present but currently dining in a private parlor. Michael sent a note to him and then he and Katrina found a place to sit. He ordered a bottle of wine.

Michael admired Katrina's adaptation to the role of a man. Gone was the feminine sway of the hips for a loose-limbed manly strut without the swagger. She held herself straight and was unafraid to look others in the eyes as he introduced Mr. Shepherd to those curious as to who this unknown young sprig was with him.

Mr. Shepherd declined invitations to play cards and soon the two were sitting comfortably at a table with a bottle of wine between them, watching the other occupants of the room as they awaited Lord Hughes.

"I hope Lord Hughes won't be long, Michael. I won't be able to prop my eyelids up for much longer."

"Would you like to go back to the house? I can handle things here. You can rest and I can report to you in the morning."

"No, thank you. We have come this far together. I would like to see this to its conclusion."

"That's a good man, Mouse."

Katrina shot him a look of disdain.

"What?"

~*~

The Black Diamond sat at a table with several others, observing Sir Tidley and his companion. "Who is that with Sir Tidley? And how did Tidley come to be so hale and hearty? His servant said he would be on his deathbed by now." His piercing eyes dared the men around him to give him an answer and warned of reprisals if the answer did not meet his approval.

"My lord, Tristan left town and has yet to return. Word was that Sir Tidley departed."

"Tristan has yet to report?"

"Correct, my lord," said a nervous young blond man to the right.

The Black Diamond frowned. Those around him waited with bated breath. Finally, he motioned them in and they all leaned forward to hear his whispered instructions.

~*~

Katrina tried to contain her curiosity as they sat by the wall. Michael seemed so at ease here, leaning back, drinking his wine, his legs stretched out in front of him, boots crossed at the ankle. As Mr. Shepherd, she felt horribly underdressed, but that didn't seem to bother Michael at all. She hoped that Lord Hughes would be available soon so they could get some sleep.

Shadows appeared and Katrina looked up and gasped in dismay.

"Sir Tidley, what a surprise to see you here with, um…" Lord Phillip Westcombe left the sentence unfinished as he gazed at Katrina. Emotion crossed his features. Surprise, and then anger as he turned back to Michael. "You had better have a good explanation for this."

"I do, but I will not defend myself right now. You need to trust me."

Phillip took a deep inhale as he stared at his friend. Exhaling, he finally spoke. "Fine. But he needs to go." Turning to Katrina, "Elizabeth would love to see you again. I will escort you to my carriage."

Katrina set her glass down and glanced at Michael, who gave her a resigned nod. Frowning, she rose and followed Phillip out of the club. Once they exited, she yawned.

"You look exhausted, Katrina. He hasn't compromised you, has he?" Phillip's tone was soft and low.

Katrina shook her head. "Phillip, I do not want a forced marriage."

"You've loved him for years, it would not be a bad match for either of you."

Katrina sighed. "You don't understand."

"You don't think so? Ask Elizabeth how we came to be married. A 'have to' can end up being a beautiful thing." The carriage pulled up and Phillip opened the door.

Katrina stepped up but glanced around to Phillip. His face was hidden in shadow and the light from the nearby gas street lamp illuminated his blond head like a halo. "You have always lived a charmed life, Phillip. But realize that God doesn't have that same kind of favor for everyone." She climbed into the carriage and reached to shut the door before Phillip could answer. She thought she heard him say, "Ask Beth."

Phillip waved the carriage off and headed back into the club.

~*~

Katrina rested against the comfortable cushioned seats of Phillip's carriage. The rich, royal blue looked black in the moonlight and she gazed out the window as the city passed by. She felt lulled to sleep by the clippity-clop of the horses's matched gait as they traveled through the nighttime streets of London. Her eyes grew heavy and she fought to keep them open. It was a battle she lost.

~*~

Michael took advantage of Phillip's exit to steal away. Some men eyed him suspiciously and the hair stood up on the back of his neck. A sure warning sign that something was about to go wrong. He slipped further into the club and awaited Lord Hughes.

~*~

Michael awoke to the sounds of water in the near distance. His stomach protested the stench of the river as well as other raunchy smells he wasn't sure he wanted to identify, from the cloth covering his mouth. He fought to keep the nausea at bay. His hands were tied behind him and his feet were secured. His boots were missing and his toes were numb from the cold. The dirt floor beneath him was rough and he struggled to move to avoid the few stones that poked up through the floor to torment him. He heard a moan behind him.

He tilted toward the sound, moved his fingers slightly, and touched someone else's cold fingers. Petite hands. He closed his eyes and for the first time in years, he prayed.

11

Katrina's throbbing shoulder got her attention first. Her toes and fingers were numb. Her neck was twisted at an odd angle and the muscles cramped as she tried to move. She moaned. She was afraid to open her eyes. Water lapped against something outside. She almost screamed when fingers touch hers. *Michael*? Her heart sank further. How did they manage to catch both of them? She fought the tears that threatened. Did they come this far only to fail now?

Her thoughts were scattered like the rats in a warehouse as a light appeared in the periphery of her vision. Dark shadows moved toward her and she could make out human shapes. She suspected the souls inside were anything but.

"Build the fire, men," the tall central figure said.

The bodies did not come any nearer. A blaze started. The cold of the floor seeped deeper into her. Pain in her head and shoulder kept her from moving to try to touch Michael again. It was enough to know he was near. What was their fate? She hoped she would not have to watch him die. Oh, if only she had never become involved. Had Lord Hughes received the document? Would the men they sought to save benefit from the work they did and the suffering they had undergone?

Papa, I failed you, the tears came freely now. *I will never get to prove that you didn't betray the land you loved or redeem your good and honorable name. I failed you and I failed my king.* Despair washed over her like the waves over the stones on the side of the Thames.

Footsteps drew closer. Katrina was yanked to her unbound feet by her arms tied behind her back. Her legs lacked the strength to stand.

"Don't make me carry you." The tough voice was accompanied by a foul-smelling breath. His appearance was hidden in the dark. She shivered more from fear than from the cold as he forcefully yanked her forward, grabbing her left arm. The pain from the abuse and her injured shoulder made her cry out involuntarily.

Show no weakness. Have courage. Don't let them see your fear.

It almost sounded as though Michael were whispering to her soul those words of encouragement. She tried to glance towards Michael, but found a hand forcefully meeting her cheek in response to her attempt.

~*~

They dragged Mouse away and Michael's heart sank. The man slapped her and anger welled up within him. He moved his wrists feverishly to try to get his hands loose but it was futile and only netted him raw bloody skin. He struggled to see what was transpiring. With the fire beyond them, all was wreathed in dark shadows and he could not make out the features of the people who were there. He groaned and tried to relax his muscles in spite of the twisted position he found himself in.

~*~

Katrina was brought close to the blaze and shoved face down across some boards elevated a few feet off the floor. Her body was fastened to the wood at the knees and waist with a rope. She found the wood and the position to be painful. The boards were supported at various points by something solid but she couldn't tell what. Her head was torqued to the left and the muscles in her shoulders scream in pain. They pulled the gag out of her mouth. She gasped for air and tried to get the taste of the foul-smelling fabric off her tongue but was unsuccessful. A knife cut into her coat and shirt, exposing her right shoulder and arm.

A voice came from behind her. Sinister and dark. "You should have stayed out of this, Miss Shepherd. Your father meddled where he wasn't wanted and you regrettably followed in his footsteps. You wasted precious time in my planning. But before I kill you, I want your partner to understand a pain he has never experienced before. He will watch you suffer for his failure to accomplish his task. He'll hear your screams of pain. But don't worry about being disfigured. You won't be left alive in your pain for long. Your body, however, will be found as a warning to those who might seek to follow your path and undermine our efforts to support Napoleon in this war. You might even be 'branded' as a traitor yourself." A sinister laugh followed this.

Fear exploded deep in the pit of Katrina's stomach. She swallowed and willed herself not to throw up.

~*~

The smell of burning wood and smoke combined with pain, cold, and odors of the wharf made Michael dizzy. He fought to retain consciousness. Vibrations alerted him to someone moving towards him and he struggled to open his eyes. The dark figure was a menacing shadow made larger by the angle of the light behind him.

"Sir Michael Tidley. Finally, we meet but you seem to be at a disadvantage at the moment. Tristan didn't do a very good job at finishing you off, but the fact that my men overcame you at least proves his attempt. The old *Cat* would have never been caught. Believe me, I've been trying for years." The dark figure moved in closer and while Michael could not see him he could detect the scent of wine and tobacco on his warm moist breath. "Or maybe, just maybe, the poisoning isn't what weakened you." The man looked pointedly over to where Katrina was bound.

Her eyes blazed into his even in the darkness and he drew strength from her with that gaze.

The deep voice continued. "Maybe it is a woman that has proven to be the undoing of the incomparable Sir Michael Tidley."

Michael couldn't answer but defeat emanated from Katrina. He shook his head and with the pain that ensued had to fight down the urge again to vomit. He perversely thought of how gratifying it would be to do so on the polished shoes in front of him. *Was this the Black Diamond*?

The body moved away and stood next to Katrina. "You have caused me more trouble than any woman is worth. Therefore, you shall suffer for it. You may have been, in another world and time, a suitable match for my son. But I find you a tiresome inconvenience."

Katrina gasped out, "I haven't had the honor of meeting your son."

The dark man laughed, his robust sound was menacing and loud, reverberating off the walls of the empty warehouse. He smiled and she could make out the brightness of his white teeth illuminated by the fire while the rest of his features remained in shadow. She shivered.

"You've been half in love with him most of your life. I was aware of that even if he wasn't." The Black Diamond laughed again and walked away while casually telling the men by the fire, "Get this over with."

Michael watched in horror as one of the men stuck a long metal stick in the fire with something on the end. The man held it there for a while before drawing it out, steam emanating from the metal as it hit the cold air.

"Be quick about it. I have a ball to attend." The Black Diamond was somewhere nearby but out of sight.

The man with the branding iron came toward Katrina and holding the metal bar vertical to her shoulder he pressed it down into her exposed flesh.

The scream of pain was one that Michael would never forget. He tried to keep his eyes on her, to give her courage to communicate his love, but hers were closed even as the brand was withdrawn and shoved in a bucket of water to cool it down. She convulsed with pain, struggling against the ties that bound her tight until finally, she stopped.

The heavy tread of footsteps drew near again, this time from behind him. "She is mine now, son. You will never have her. Could there ever be a more fitting punishment for your interference? I withheld my name and now I take from you the woman you love. Even if for some reason you would survive this night, which I highly doubt, you will always remember it. A torture to your soul that the one person who so unwisely gave you her heart, you were unable to save." The man loosened the cloth that bound his mouth. "I'll give you the benefit of conversation as you die. But don't be hopeful. If you are not dead by morning, I will personally see to the deed myself. Too bad you chose the wrong side of the war, son. You would have been a worthy ally."

The heavy tread moved further away and whispered conversations could be heard by the other men. The bucket of water was tossed onto the fire and the hiss and steam rose up high as the flames were doused. They all departed from view and a door slammed.

~*~

Lord Phillip seethed. Michael disappeared while Phillip escorted Katrina outside. He sat down and awaited Lord Harrow who was due to meet him. It wasn't long however before not only Lord Harrow, but also Lord Remington strode into the club looking ready for a fight.

"Where is she, Phillip?" Marcus, Viscount Remington asked. "I got a letter from Lady Orion and I couldn't make heads or tails of what was up with Miss Shepherd. I got held up by the snow but am here now. Where is she and what has Michael been up to?"

Phillip set his glass down and sighed. "I sent Katrina home in my own carriage. We can go there and talk far more privately."

"Then let's leave," Lord Harrow said, and the three men departed, with a small furry creature following them.

~*~

Reaching the house, Phillip escorted the men to the study and rang for a servant to give word to his wife to have Miss Shepherd brought down when she was presentable.

Lady Elizabeth Westcombe came into the study a few moments later. "Phillip, you returned much sooner than expected. What is this request for Miss Shepherd about? I thought Lady Orion sent her to Rose Hill?"

Phillip put his arm around his wife's shoulders. "I am not sure why she was here in town, but she was and I sent her to you not an hour past. Is she resting?"

"My lord, she never arrived here."

Lord Harrow spoke up. "I'll head out to your livery to inquire as to your coach."

"Thanks, Theo. Something is seriously wrong."

"While we wait for Theodore to return, would someone mind explaining to me what is going on? I confess to being confused. The letter I received spoke of an injured shoulder and that Michael was making mooncalf eyes at Katrina."

Beth bristled. "Michael is your friend. Why would you mind if he liked Miss Shepherd? I found her unexceptionally delightful and suspect that she has had a tendre for Sir Tidley for some time."

"Beth, I have no objection to a match between the two, but something seems havey-cavey about the whole business."

"Michael was very closemouthed about how Katrina was injured, and believe me, I tried to get the information out of him, Marcus. You know how Michael can be, winsome and yet, over the years it felt like there was so much he didn't say about his life and how he occupied his time."

"How was he knighted, Phillip? I don't believe I ever heard the tale," Beth inquired.

"Probably because Michael has failed to regale us with the reason for that honor. Not that we haven't asked, my love, but he has artfully dodged the questions whenever possible." Phillip released his wife and went to the sideboard to pour a glass of brandy. He offered it to Marcus who took it with a nod of thanks.

Marcus began to pace. "Something is definitely afoot. Do you think Michael is in trouble?"

The door opened and Theodore entered, clearing his throat. Accompanying him was a young man wearing the Westcombe livery but with rips in the clothing, a bloodied face, and swollen eye. "Phillip, it seems that you have a sorely abused servant and a missing carriage and horses. He had a long walk home and just arrived."

"Where is Miss Shepherd, young man?" Marcus came forward toward the servant.

The servant recoiled in fear. "I don't know nutin' 'bout no lady. The young gent were kidnapped a few blocks from the club. I t'weren't expecting 'em. Sorry, m' lord." The man's downcast face indicated he expected to be discharged from his position.

"Can you describe the men who assailed you?" Theodore asked with a softer voice.

The interrogation continued for some time with

Marcus in the lead until Beth called the men off. "The poor man cannot tell you much more than he already has. He needs to get those cuts tended to." She escorted the man out of the room.

"So all we know is that Katrina is dressed as a man and has been kidnapped. And Michael is missing." Theodore was now pouring himself a brandy from the sideboard.

"But what do we do about it? How do we find them?"

"Might I suggest we start with prayer?" came the voice from the hallway as Elizabeth once again entered the room.

The men stared at her for a moment, nonplussed.

Finally, Marcus nodded and briefly making eye contact with the other two men, he bowed his head and prayed.

When he finished they all opened their eyes.

"Phillip? What is that furry thing by your feet?" asked his wife.

Everyone stared at Phillip's boots.

"I believe, my dear, that would be an elongated rat, otherwise known as a ferret. Didn't I tell you that Michael owned one?" Phillip reached down to scoop up the animal.

The ferret gazed at him with dark beady eyes and clicked his tongue rapidly before jumping down and running for the door. He stopped to glance over his shoulder to make sure he was being followed.

"Gentleman, I believe we may have found the answer to our prayer." Marcus smiled.

"Do you really believe God would use a ferret to lead us to Michael and Katrina?" Theo looked skeptical.

"If God can use a donkey to speak to a man, I believe He could use a ferret to lead us to our friends." Marcus grabbed his greatcoat from the back of a chair as he headed toward the door.

"A crow led me to Beth when she had been injured." Phillip came to his wife and gave her a kiss. The other men looked away. Phillip grabbed his coat as well and soon the three men and a ferret were out the door to find their missing friends.

~*~

Silence enshrouded the dark of the old warehouse. It was too cold for them to last for long and Katrina had burned and exposed skin as well. Michael listened closely to detect if anyone was still present but his senses told him they were alone.

"Michael?"

He could hear the fear in her voice.

"I'm still here, sweetheart."

"It hurts," she whimpered.

Michael fought back the tears in his own eyes as he tried to figure out what to do. The distance between them seemed so far but he slowly and painfully began to wiggle his body forward, wincing at the rocks that would bite into his chest and legs, and the pull of his arms as they remained firmly tied against his back. Finally reaching the bench, he lay on the ground and looked up at her. His eyes could see little in the dark as moonlight streamed in some high windows.

"I'm here." He gazed into her eyes to tell her without words just how sorry he was.

"It's not your fault. I willingly chose this path." She closed her eyes tight, wrinkling up her face as she fought the pain.

Michael tried to leverage himself to a kneeling position beside her. The largest of the knots was on the side by her middle back. He began to use his teeth to try to worry the knot.

"Michael, let me die. You need to get the papers to Lord Hughes. The mission has to come first." She groaned as fresh pain lanced through her when the bonds pulled at her arm.

Michael stopped for a few moments and leaned his head against her side. "Katrina, I love you and would rather die than leave you here. Lord Hughes has the document."

"How?"

"I'm the *Cat*, aren't I? But I'll admit I had a little help from Fidget."

"Where is Fidget?"

"I don't know. But don't worry about him, he'll be fine. He can hunt. He's a survivor and he has served me well regardless."

"Do you have a way to call him?"

"Yeah."

"Then do it."

"Why? He's not here."

"You don't know that. I didn't realize he had made it into the club either."

"True, he is pretty sneaky."

"Call him."

Michael gave a low series of whistles. "There. Done. Now let me try to get this loose."

Michael continued to worry the bonds and his teeth ached from the effort.

"Michael, he called you son. Who is the Black Diamond? Is it possible he really is your father?"

The bonds around her arms broke free. Katrina let her hands dangle to the ground, unable to move them.

Michael collapsed on the ground to his side, exhausted.

"Does it matter if he's my father or if he's just toying with me? I would rather he weren't but would kill him either way if the chance presented itself."

Katrina tried to reach with her hands to loosen the bonds that held her waist tight to the board. She wept in frustration and pain as Michael lay there and watched, the knot being in a position he couldn't maneuver himself to. Finally, that was loose. Katrina tried to raise her head and then lay it back down, but facing away from him.

"Mouse?"

"Give me a few minutes, please. Everything hurts."

Silence hung between them in the dark like a chasm. Michael was falling into that pit—deep, and irretrievable. He closed his eyes and let the grief wash over him. He failed Katrina, the only woman who ever loved and believed in him. Even his mother struggled to look at him. His darker features were more from his father than from the Tidley lineage. He inherited her small stature. Could that large, dark man really be his father? Michael shuddered at the thought and tried to focus on how Mouse fared.

"Michael?"

"Hmmm?" he grunted wearily, cold seeping deeper into his bones and sapping any strength.

"Can you get closer to my left hand with your wrists?"

"I'll try."

Michael shifted to his other side and then inched

his way toward Katrina's hand that was loosely dangling from the bench to the floor. He grunted with the effort, every move bringing pain to his shoulders, neck, back, and wrists. Finally, he was there. He tried to grasp at her hand with his stiff and cold fingers.

"I think that's about as good as I can get," Michael whispered and closed his eyes against the dark and pain as Katrina painstakingly tried, one-handed, to loosen his bonds.

~*~

Katrina mumbled and whimpered. Her fingers were so cold, but she needed to free Michael. The branding she received was probably already festering with dirt and her other wound had reopened. Her energy dwindled. If she could at least get Michael free she would feel better about dying. She'd seen the agony in his eyes after she was branded. She despised her weakness in crying but she was so tired, and she longed for the suffering to end. All of it.

It didn't matter to her anymore if her father's reputation was restored. It didn't matter that hers was tattered beyond belief should her activities come to light. She didn't want to face Marcus with the reality of what happened and the shame of what she had wished she had done.

She fumbled away, slowly the bonds loosened, and she removed the cloth from the wrists rubbed raw and bleeding till Michael's hands were free. She let her hand drop and closed her eyes. The rest was up to him.

~*~

Michael gritted his teeth as Katrina worked. The tugging and pulling against his wrists was agonizing and he hoped she would be successful. He longed to see her. He wished he had the words to encourage her but he despised giving false hope. When his hands came free he slowly moved his arms and rolled onto his back. He lay there for what seemed like forever before he could move against the soreness everywhere to undo the bonds at his ankles.

He went to the fire and threw the rags in. After hunting for another flint, he managed to get a meager flame to burn. He came to stand over Katrina, whose eyes were closed. He took off his coat and lay it on her back to try to warm her up. She moaned as it hit her shoulder and he shuddered in empathy for her pain.

"Hold on, Mouse. We'll get out of this yet," he whispered. He knelt down and with the light of the fire to guide him he began to work on the bonds at her feet. The going was slow, but he finally got her freed from the bench. He slowly worked to sit her up but she kept leaning forward against him. Finally, he brought her to the floor.

They were both free. Michael rubbed Katrina's stocking feet and put them near the fire next to his own. He held up her hands and rubbed them and held them out to the fire as well. She moaned as her arms moved, increasing the pain in her shoulder, but she failed to awaken. The cold was taking her away from him and he experienced fear like never before.

Michael struggled to rise and bring circulation to his legs. He gingerly lifted Katrina in his arms and made his way to the door of the warehouse, into the bleak coldness and damp air. He set her down by the wall and listened carefully at the door. Were guards posted there?

"Michael, wait." Katrina pulled him down beside her as she leaned wearily against the wall of the warehouse, tears involuntarily coming due to the pain.

Michael was on one knee before her and gently placed one hand alongside her face. "What is it, Mouse?" His thumb wiped away a tear. His other hand came up and pushed hair out of her eyes. Her pins had come out during her capture and the rough treatment she had endured. Michael swallowed the big lump in his throat as he searched her face.

She peered up at him. "You need to leave me. I can provide a distraction and you can escape. Get help. I can't go any further."

Michael frowned. "I would sooner die than leave you here to be tortured by those pagans."

"If you take me with you, you may get your wish, but I don't know that I could live with being the cause even if I survived."

"You care about me that much?" Michael asked softly.

"I've always loved you, Michael. For as long as I remember, it was always and only you." Her eyes drooped and he watched the eyelashes fanning across her dirty cheeks.

"Sweetheart, I don't know when I began to love you, but maybe I always have. I never felt worthy of your admiration but I craved it. You were the one I wished I could share the truth of my double life with. But I couldn't, so I stayed away. But now…"

"Now you can move into a future free of my childhood infatuation."

"I'd rather move into the future with you always by my side."

"Be realistic, Michael." Her gaze was once again focused on his face and the grim set of his mouth.

"Marry me. Let me prove to you just how real I am."

"I will consider that when this is over after we have recovered. If we make it out of here alive."

She lied. He could tell by the way her eyes shifted around as she said the words. She inhaled deeply and with one hand reached up to touch his face. "Just one more kiss…"

He acquiesced to her request.

12

Noise from outside tore them apart. A shuffle of feet and the sound of punches thrown. Yells of pain and shouts of victory. Michael spun around and stood with Katrina still on the floor behind him slumped against the wall. The key turned the lock and the door opened.

~*~

Katrina couldn't bear to look. She retreated deep inside herself, away from the pain, from everything. Fear and shame seared her deep within. Unworthy of love and adoration, even from the one man she'd always longed for. She fought to not sniff back her running nose and she swiped it instead with her sleeve. So cold, even with Michael's coat. She tipped her head down and let her hair cover her face so she would melt into the wall around her. She'd always been the master of being invisible. She hoped she could do the same now, although she was equally determined to assist Michael in any way possible, even if it meant risking her life. She kept an eye on the door which she could see just past Michael's thigh.

~*~

A small thin furry creature entered. Spying

Michael, Fidget ran to him, climbed up to his shoulder, and clicked noisily at him.

"Shhhhh," Michael said as he waited, holding his breath. He scooped up Fidget and dropped him into Katrina's lap. "Guard her, Fidget." The ferret gave Katrina a kiss on the cheek and set to work warming up her fingers with his body.

Slowly, one after another, three men entered the room, their once pristine appearances now disheveled and torn.

"Michael?" a voice cautiously called out. "Katrina?"

"Marcus?" Michael asked.

The three men turned to see Michael behind them near the door.

Marcus stepped forward. "Are we alone in here?"

Michael nodded.

"Katrina?"

"Behind me. She's been tortured, she's weak and tired. I hope you brought the coach," Michael said as he stepped aside so the men could see the dark figure slumped on the floor with a ferret in her lap.

Katrina looked up. "Hi, cousin. Fancy meeting you here."

Marcus frowned and came forward.

Michael stepped in his way. "I'll carry her."

Marcus stood several inches taller than Michael. "Don't be a fool. You've suffered enough. I will take care of Miss Shepherd now. She is my concern, after all."

"I would make her mine," Michael said boldly with his chin lifting a fraction and not letting his eye contact fall.

"So, is that the way the land lies? Good. Often

believed she was the one for you. Yet, I insist as head of the household, that you let me care for my family member as I deem appropriate." With that, Marcus pushed Michael aside.

Michael stepped toward Phillip. "The Black Diamond branded her."

Phillip's face turned gray in the moonlight. He shifted his gaze to the girl and watched as Marcus bent down to lift her up. Phillip's eyes sought Michael's. "He did this in front of you?"

Michael nodded, unsmiling, as he fought back tears.

Phillip put an arm around Michael. "He's getting closer and bolder. We will all work to help protect her and you now."

Michael lay his head against his friend's shoulder. "Thank you, Phillip. I definitely need it."

"Keeping track of Mouse? It always took all three of us to keep her out of trouble. But once you marry her, you will be on your own," Phillip said.

Michael grinned and nodded. "I think that once we are married I will handle those responsibilities just fine, and without your assistance."

Phillip grinned back as they all made their way out of the warehouse into Marcus's waiting carriage.

It was a tight squeeze.

Lord Harrow decided to ride on top with the coachman with a gun primed and ready.

~*~

Michael couldn't take his eyes off Katrina. Anger surged from Marcus and he knew his accounting was coming. He'd led Katrina into danger. He would pay a price for that. In spite of his own pain, he ached at what she had endured because of him.

Since Josie remained at Rose Hill, it was decided to descend once again on Phillip's home.

Beth was up, waiting at the door when the carriage pulled up.

Marcus came up the stairs with the limp woman in his arms, with Michael on his heels. She quickly called out orders to her staff for a doctor to be fetched, a bath to be drawn, and clothing to be gathered. She led them up the stairs to a room adjacent to the one Katrina previously occupied. This room was done all in creams with accents of mint green and Rosewood furniture.

Marcus carried Katrina to a couch and lay her gently down. "She's been injured, Beth. Branded on her right shoulder."

Beth paled at these words.

Michael swallowed hard as he was dragged from the room. He didn't protest. He wished God were real and could somehow swoop down to repair the damage he'd done to the one woman who mattered most.

~*~

Katrina struggled to cooperate with Beth and the maid as they eased her into the bathtub. The hot soapy water felt good until it hit her burn and she cried out in pain. A glass of brandy was handed to her along with a low-voiced apology as the women set about getting Katrina bathed and dressed for the doctor. In lieu of a night rail, a chemise was chosen so that her wounds were more easily accessed. After she had been treated and fed some toast, Katrina fell into a deep, dreamless sleep.

~*~

Michael was not treated with as much kindness. He was allowed to bathe and change in the room that had typically been his on his visits. A servant had been dispatched to his own townhouse to fetch clean clothing for him since Tristan was no longer in service, the explanation he gave to his friends.

When he finally entered Phillip's study, his three friends sat by the fireplace with their own hair damp from their attempts to clean up from the events of the evening.

Michael reluctantly entered and wearily sat in the one remaining chair.

"Brandy?" Phillip offered.

Michael shook his head and put a flat hand up to refuse the offered drink. "Begin the interrogation, unless you would be gracious enough to let me rest and you can tear me apart in the morning."

"One question first," Marcus spoke softly.

Michael nodded. "I'm at your disposal."

"How serious are you about marrying Katrina?"

"Deadly serious. If she will have me."

"After what I perceive as her shenanigans, Michael, she will be more than eager to take you for her groom."

"Don't count on it, Marcus. That girl has a mind of her own and is not easily swayed."

"Except for when it comes to you. Don't downplay your charms with the fairer sex," Theo stated.

Michael glared at him. "Can I seek my bed now?" Michael asked.

Phillip rose. "You may. We're just glad you are

both alive."

"Thank you for coming for us. I wouldn't have blamed you if you'd left me there. It's what I deserve." Michael rose and departed before they could respond.

He slowly climbed the stairs to his room, the suite that had been occupied by Mouse during her previous stay. She was in the adjoining room and after having his boots removed by a servant, he excused the man, locked his door, and padded across the room to the door separating his room from hers. He slowly opened it and crossed the rug to the side of the bed where she slept.

With both shoulders freshly bandaged, she looked uncomfortable no matter what position she would be in. She rested on her stomach with her arm embracing her pillow. Fidget was curled up next to her and raised his head to let him know he had not abandoned his post.

"Good job, Fidget," Michael whispered as he smiled at his pet. The ferret lay his head back down and closed his eyes.

Michael knelt by the bed, folded his hands, and bent his head to the mattress. *Lord, thank You for bringing us out alive. I did nothing to deserve You rescuing us from the Black Diamond. I'm ready. I'm ready to set aside my sinful ways and follow You. I'm ready to live life Your way, because mine doesn't seem to be working out too well. Please heal Katrina and incline her to accept me as a husband. I love her and it broke my heart to watch her suffer tonight because of my foolishness. I'll quit my work with the War Office and do whatever it is You would have me do. Even if Katrina refuses to be a part of that, I will follow, but it would break my heart to not have her in my life after coming to realize how much she means to me.*

Michael brushed away an errant tear. In frustration at his weakness, he rose and gazed down for a time at the young woman lying asleep. Her profile highlighted her perky nose, the dark lashes fanning her cheeks, and the brown hair braided down her back that made him itch to loosen the strands so he could touch it again. He sighed, turned to leave, locked the door, and shoved the key under it. Would she even realize he'd been there?

~*~

The next morning Michael sneaked out of the house and made his way to the War Office to meet with Lord Hughes. He was ushered in immediately.

"You look like hell, Tidley."

"After I got the document to you last night, the Black Diamond came after me and Miss Shepherd." Michael stood before the heavy wood desk with his arms at his sides, clenching and unclenching, his bandaged wrists hidden.

"Did you get his identity?"

Michael shook his head and frowned. "Only that he was tall, dark, and had a deep voice. The others referred to him as 'my lord' and..." Michael blinked hard and sucked in a breath.

"And?"

"He claims to be my father."

Thick silence filled the room as Lord Hughes leaned back in his chair.

"Well, that was unexpected. The progeny of the Black Diamond happens to be one of my best agents?"

"I resign my commission as of this moment."

"I don't think so. I need you to finish this job."

"I decoded and delivered the papers. I kept Miss Shepherd alive although she was," he gulped, "branded by the Black Diamond's cohorts."

"Branded?"

"Metal in a fire, applied to the skin. Branded."

Lord Hughes closed his eyes and swore under his breath. "We're in deep trouble now."

"Viscount Remington, Lord Westcombe, and Lord Harrow rescued us last night. Somehow Fidget was able to lead them to us."

Lord Hughes's head rolled back and he stared at the ceiling. Gold trimmed the perimeter of the molding with intricate detail that went largely unappreciated at this precise moment. "You will deliver this document to Captain Allendale in France. You leave from Bristol on the evening tide."

"No."

"You will comply or you will be locked in the tower."

"You can't do that."

"I can and I will. You leave immediately. There is passage booked for two. Tristan can accompany you."

"Tristan is dead. He was a traitor and had been poisoning me."

"How certain are you that he is dead?"

"Katrina stabbed him and I left him buried in the snow."

"Any more surprises you would like to regale me with this morning?"

"Only a question."

"And that would be…?"

"Remington, Westcombe, and Harrow want to know what happened. They are involved now just as they have been with the last few cases we dealt with.

Only now they suspect my secret. They want an accounting for Miss Shepherd's involvement. What shall I tell them?"

"Nothing. You tell them nothing. You leave for Bristol immediately."

"I will go, but not to Bristol. I will find my own way across the channel. Make your arrangements. I am not going to tell you my plans. I will complete your mission and if I come back alive, I am done. Lock me up if you will. But my goal now is to marry Miss Shepherd. I could not bear to see her suffer again as she did last night."

"They made you watch?"

Michael swallowed hard, gritted his teeth, trying to avoid the tears at the memory of Katrina's scream of pain, the hiss of the branding, and the stench of burning skin. He nodded.

"I'm sorry, Michael. You've seen a lot in your years with us, but it is different when it is someone you care deeply for."

"Love. I love her."

Lord Hughes frowned. "Doubly painful then." The older man looked out towards the window. "There is a cemetery out there, with my beloved wife in it." He turned back to Michael with unshed tears in his eyes. "I wish I could have made a better choice. Did she need to be sacrificed so I could serve my king? I failed her."

"Katrina's alive. Remember it was her choice to participate in this. She could have gone on to Rose Hill several days ago and been safe. I dragged her with me so she could be here before you to exonerate her father's name. She says she is not concerned for that anymore, but will you…? For her?"

Lord Hughes smiled. "I most certainly can do that. I will start with the Sefton's ball tonight. I know just the right ears to tickle."

Michael sighed. "I will be off."

Lord Hughes handed him the paperwork. "Realize this is going via a variety of methods to Wellesley. You are but one, but you are an important one."

Michael turned to leave.

"Sir Tidley?"

Michael stepped back, considering Lord Hughes. "Yes, my lord?"

"Well done. I couldn't ask for better. I'm proud to have worked with you."

Michael nodded gravely. "Thank you." And with that, he was gone.

~*~

Michael entered his home discreetly and packed his bag for the journey to France. He walked into his office, drafted a few letters, and disappeared from London.

~*~

Lord Westcombe and Lord Harrow met at the Remington townhouse at two in the afternoon to meet with Michael as prearranged. They were led into the study where Marcus sat at his desk, frowning.

"Marcus, you look as though someone divested you of all your stocks," said Lord Harrow cheerfully.

"Worse, Theodore. Michael has disappeared."

Phillip came toward the desk. "Explain."

"He's gone and this was delivered a short time ago

via some street urchin." Marcus handed the simple stationary to Phillip. "Read it out loud so we are all informed. And maybe I will believe its contents."

Phillip nodded and cleared his throat, and read:

Dear Lord Remington, Lord Westcombe, and Lord Harrow,

I regret that I am unable to give you the accounting you desire and deserve. I need to leave for a time but, Lord willing, I will return safely and be ready to assume the reins of Miss Shepherd in marriage.

I am not escaping your censure for what happened to Mouse. I deserve all that and am unworthy of her hand in marriage for more reasons than I could count. Forgive me for my departure. You will have answers but they will come from someone other than myself.

You have been my dearest friends for longer than I can remember and no truer men would I desire to entrust so great a chore as to guard Katrina and keep her safe for me. Thank you for your able rescue last night. Post the banns as I hope to wed her upon my return.

Sincerely,

M.T.

The three men looked at each other grimly.

"I've never known Michael to go back on his word before." Marcus started as he rose and motioned the other men to the chairs at the center of the room.

As they were seated, Theo spoke, "He didn't precisely break his word, did he? He could have disappeared without a note. It sounds as though he wanted to honor his promise to us to share what happened. Perhaps he was forced to disappear."

Phillip leaned forward, supporting his chin with his hand, the elbow resting on his knee. "Over the years, it seems that since Michael left the Horse

Guards, we've had little knowledge of his activities, of how he spends his time when he is not with us, or attending parties amongst the *ton*. There is no talk of romantic conquests. No gossip of business he is involved in. He will regale us with tales of others' exploits and news of the world, but doesn't really ever share anything relating to himself."

"You are correct. Why have we not noticed this before? We've been friends since school. Do you suppose his birth makes him feel as if he is not one of us? He's always been kind of set apart from us even when we used to hang out at Rose Hill." Marcus was speaking now, leaning back and taking up most of a loveseat.

"I thought that was because he was babysitting Mouse for us. She clung to him, desired his attentions, and he seemed willing to provide that so we could do things he wasn't as interested in, like fishing."

Marcus nodded and smiled. "Yeah, and instead he got caught having to rescue her out of that huge tree. He felt terrible when she broke her leg."

"Remember how humbled he was when he taught her archery and she was able to out-shoot him every time?" Phillip grinned.

"I always questioned the wisdom of him teaching her how to throw knives and shoot a gun, but she was undeterred and he couldn't say no to her," Marcus added.

"He lost his heart to her years ago, didn't he? I mean, I always knew that Katrina adored him, but he only seemed to tolerate her," Theo mused.

Marcus smiled. "I think they will have a great marriage. Michael hinted that Katrina was not amenable to that, however, and I wonder why. What happened between them to change her mind?"

"You had better hope nothing 'happened,' Marcus. If word got out of her activities, she would be ruined amongst the *beau monde,* but if she were truly compromised…" Phillip frowned.

"Michael is a gentleman, surely he wouldn't…" Marcus queried, his forehead furrowed in worry.

"Marcus, not all of us are the paragons of virtue that you are. He is a man and can be tempted. I gather they have been alone together several times. It is possible." Theo frowned.

"But, we're talking about Mouse here, not some sumptuous beauty," Marcus said.

"You of all people should know that it's not the outward appearance that attracts a man in the long run, but the heart of the woman," Phillip added.

"That's nonsense." Marcus's tone darkened as he challenged his friend. "I fell in love with Josie the first time I saw her."

"An unconscious woman bloodied in a carriage accident?" Phillip's eyebrows rose in disbelief.

Marcus nodded. "And what about you, Phillip? You can't tell me that Beth didn't attract you from the start either."

Phillip grinned broadly at that remembrance. "I won't deny it, Marcus. She was so hauntingly beautiful. But I was not the man of integrity that you are when it comes to women. However, by the time I met Elizabeth I was trying to walk a more gentlemanly path."

"You have no evidence that Michael has ever played fast and loose with women or even sought them in the brothels. No word of any of that has ever circulated amongst the *ton* and he has certainly never mentioned his exploits to us," Theo said.

Marcus laughed. "I doubt that would be the kind of thing he would ever share with me, so I'll take your word for it."

Theo sobered up. "So when and from whom will we discover what's been going on? Michael's been playing least in sight the past few months and I confess, after his close call last night and what Katrina went through, I have a horrible feeling about what might be next."

The other men nodded. A knock came and a servant entered with an urgent missive for Lord Remington. Marcus excused the servant and requested he wait in the kitchen.

"Men, we may have received our answer." Marcus rose to go to his desk and break the seal on the envelope. "It's from Lord Hughes, at the Ministry of Defense. He requests that we join him there at four of the clock, today." Marcus glanced at the clock. "That gives us little over an hour." He returned to his seat. "I guess that would confirm our suspicion that Michael's life has been far more secretive than we realized."

"Why would he keep us in the dark? After all we went through with both your wives, and the impact the Black Diamond has already had in our lives, why would he keep this a secret?" Theo asked to no one in particular.

"It's the nature of the game, and in tune with who Michael is naturally. I feel bad that I didn't pick up on how lonely he must be with no family but us in his life. Since Phillip and I married we've been less involved with him and with you, Theo. I'm sorry I have neglected you both."

Theo shrugged. "It goes both ways, Marcus. I'm

aware I am always welcome in either of your homes as part of your extended family. Do I feel a bit *persona non grata* when wives and babies are around? Perhaps to a certain extent. But maybe my day will come as well when I get those joys, so I do not begrudge either of you your happiness. But for Michael? I cannot speak for him. I admit that I was surprised at his reference to faith in his letter."

"Faith? Marcus, let me see that letter again." Phillip took it and read. "*Lord willing,* he wrote. You are right, Theo, that is out of character for him. Has he perhaps had a spiritual epiphany through all of this?" He handed the letter back to Marcus, who silently read it again himself.

"Either way, we should be praying for his safety. The man who tortured Katrina and left them both to freeze to death in that warehouse is still at large. That means both of them could be in grave danger. Michael clearly asks us to protect Katrina which indicates that he's not thinking of her own willful and impulsive nature, but that there might be some outside threat to her safety. He was more traumatized by what happened to her last night than he let on. I suspect that if he left her side at this time, it was not by choice."

"Shall we prepare to go to the Ministry of Defense? It seems that we have an appointment with the man who might supply our answers."

"Who'll watch over Katrina until we return?" Marcus asked.

"I've a few footmen who are ex-military, and I'm sure Beth is more than capable of keeping watch over her as well."

The men all rose and agreed to meet at the war office at the appointed time.

13

Deep agony plagued Katrina. She wanted to stretch but her bandages kept her movement limited and any shifting of position caused more pain. She was sore from the long ride as well and she could feel the bruises on her face and other parts of her body from the rough treatment of the brutes from the night before. She opened her eyes and closed them against the shards of glass that shot through her with the bright sunlight streaming in the window.

"Are you finally awake? I was getting worried about you, Miss Shepherd." Beth sat there in a pink gown that emphasized her figure in all the right ways. Little adornment but cool and composed, she rose to move to the window. "Shall I draw the drapes? Is that sunlight too much?"

"Yes. Thank you." Katrina's tongue stuck like cotton in her mouth. "And something to drink would be nice."

"Gladly." Lady Westcombe closed the curtain and pulled the bell to summon a servant. She returned to the side of the bed. "Can I assist you up?"

Katrina nodded and accepted Beth's help out of bed. She was surprised at how weak she was. After taking care of some personal needs she was settled by the fire with a warm robe and a blanket across her legs. Food was spread out on the table next to her. Her stomach growled.

Her hostess laughed. "You'd better eat, you must be ravenous. You didn't eat when you arrived and Michael indicated that you'd not had much to eat yesterday with your travels and adventures. What was he thinking to not take better care of you?" She shook her head and smiled. "Always a charmer, but that man will need some lessons on how to provide for a wife. You are just the one to teach him."

Katrina almost spit out her tea. "Wife? I haven't agreed to marry him."

"Protests accompanied by your maidenly blushes give your heart away, Katrina. You love him. When you are finished, a letter has arrived for you and I'm sure you will want to read it in private." In a *de soto* voice she added, "I think it might be a love letter." She winked at Katrina as she smiled.

Katrina frowned. "A love letter? I doubt it. Let me see that now, please." She set down her cup and saucer and reached her hand for the document.

"Very well, but I will stay to see if I am correct." The envelope exchanged hands.

Katrina inspected the handwriting. "It's from Michael." She broke the seal and pulled out the stationary.

Dearest Mouse,

I regret that I have been called into service to complete my mission. I hope I will not be gone from your side for long. I am praying for your protection. Please be careful, my dear, for I could not bear it if any more harm befell you. You are all that is most good and precious to me. Lord willing, I will return to your side to remain your ever-devoted servant, dedicating my life to reminding you how beautiful you are to me.

All my love, now and forever, is yours,

Michael

P.S. I needed to leave Fidget behind. Please take good care of him. He seems to have taken a liking to you.

Katrina let her hand with the letter drop to her lap. "He's gone? He left without even saying good-bye." For once the ache in her heart hurt more than the pains in her body. She fought back the tears.

Beth was by her side instantly. "Gone? Trust me that man would not leave if he didn't need to. He adores you."

Katrina shook her head. "He is being noble and reacting to the circumstances. We had an adventure together, but it is no more than that and it is foolish for my heart to think otherwise." She inhaled with a shudder wracking her whole body. She blinked back the tears. "I'll be fine. It is as it should be. He has work to do and my part is done. I need to move on."

Beth pursed her lips and squeezed Katrina's hand. "What does moving on look like?"

"I need to go to Rose Hill to rest and recover. I have always felt at peace there."

"I will talk to Phillip. You realize that Lord Remington is in town and was one of your rescuers last night?"

"Marcus was there? I don't remember much except arguing with Michael. I longed to go to sleep and never wake up. The pain in my body and my heart was too much to bear."

"But you would wake up eventually. Katrina, where would that put you?"

"You mean, would I have been in heaven or hell?"

Beth nodded.

"I suppose that would put me in hell if I were to believe all that Marcus ever shared with me through the years and what I read in the Bible."

"Is that where you want your forever home to be?"

"Forever home?"

"This life is short on earth, but once we leave, we go somewhere and that place becomes a permanent dwelling for us. Hell is not described as being a very inviting home to spend eternity in. But heaven, to be with Jesus face-to-face and to experience no more fear or pain and to know perfect love? Those are our choices."

"I didn't realize that by not choosing one I was selecting the other."

"But that is what you are doing. Just as if you refuse to accept Michael's love, you by default decide to live a lifetime here on earth without him."

Katrina yawned. "I'll consider your words. I'm worn out. May I return to bed? I want to sleep."

"Certainly. You've been through a terrible ordeal. Here, let me help you." Beth rose to her feet and assisted Katrina to hers. Katrina held on to Michael's letter even as she divested herself of the robe and crawled under the covers.

"Rest well, Katrina. Heal. I will pray for you. A maid will come to sit with you in case you need anything." With that, the elegant Lady Westcombe sailed from the room, shutting the door behind her silently.

Katrina fell asleep with Michael's note under her pillow.

~*~

Michael reluctantly left London and found a group

of smugglers near Folkestone willing to get him into France for a small fee. Once he made land near Boulogne, he skirted through the countryside like the cat he was known to be, staying hidden, quiet, out of sight of anyone who might be seeking him. He acquired a horse when he could, but found himself making much of the long journey on foot. Fortunately, Jared wasn't in the South of France for this assignation. He managed to connect up with Captain Jared Allenton outside of Reims to hand off the information.

"Sir Tidley. Well met." Captain Allendale greeted him warmly as he invited him into a lean-to he had set up.

"You appear well. I have not seen you since Marcus and Josie's wedding."

Jared nodded and frowned. "And now I'm an uncle and have yet to meet my niece. Tell me, is Marcus well and happy?"

Michael smiled. "Very much so."

"Good. It's nice to know that someone is having a normal life and that my feeble efforts here are providing some peace and security for them."

Michael nodded. "I possess papers for you to deliver to Sir Wellesley."

Captain Allendale perused the document and frowned. "This will be valuable to him. I will depart at nightfall to head south to deliver this. Thank you."

Michael nodded and rose as if to leave.

"Please, Michael, stay and sit. Inform me of what's happening back home. I receive so little news out here. How did you get this?"

Michael regaled Jared with the tale of how he and Mouse deciphered the code and the appearance of the Black Diamond.

"The Black Diamond. He was behind that initial threat to Henrietta and Josie I believe. Sir Bastion kept murmuring something about that man but we never could determine who he was."

"Phillip's bride had a run in with one of his minions too. A diamond was cut into her right shoulder."

"And now you say Mouse was branded? He's becoming either more cruel or more desperate. Poor Mouse. She always was a pesky little thing. Has she grown up any?"

"She is still petite, but yes, Jared, she has matured into a lovely young woman."

"A young woman you perchance have an interest in?"

"I hope to marry her when I return to England."

"About time, ol' man. I'm happy for you, and for her. I think she always did have a decided preference for you, even after you let her break her leg."

"Let her? Did you ever try to stop her from doing what she wanted?"

"No, as the younger brother, I was more interested in making life difficult for Marcus than for my cousin. After all, she was a girl and my sister was often at boarding school or a friend's home. At that time, I had no interest in the fairer sex."

Michael laughed. "Neither did I, but she was stuck to me like a burr almost every summer and holiday from university."

"I remember. I pray you make it back safely. My family cannot know we met."

"I understand that too well. I will be glad to leave my secret life behind when I return."

"Good luck with that, and stay safe, Michael. If the

Black Diamond is out there, none of us can rest. He is tenacious."

Michael nodded. Together they shared a simple meal and Michael regaled him with the latest news of the *ton* before slipping into the evening heading north, while Jared headed south.

As he walked Michael prayed. He longed for his Bible but it had been too much to have it with him on this mission. He kept a small book of psalms and prayers in his breast pocket and he found comfort in reading that during times of rest. Often, he thought of his Mouse and things he wished he could share with her. He smiled, thinking about how life would change for him. Maybe they could purchase a small cottage somewhere to start a family. He could work as a steward, or maybe they could purchase some land he could farm. Or breed horses. He had always loved horses. He would need to talk to her about what she wanted and dreamed of. He smiled. The future was theirs. But first, he must make it home—alive.

~*~

"Katrina, I think it's time we had a little chat." Lady Westcome interrupted an unprofitable reverie. Katrina had been plagued by melancholy in the wake of Michael's defection. Lady Westcombe came to sit beside her on the couch in front of the fireplace in her sitting room.

"We do?" Katrina asked. Nothing moved her. It was as if her heart were frozen.

"We do. I'm not sure where to begin." Lady Elizabeth Westcombe leaned back and sighed. "I was saddened after they rescued you and I saw the mark on your shoulder. To be perfectly honest, I thought I was going to faint." Lady Westcombe sat up and reached for Beth's hand. "I have a similar mark on my right shoulder as well, only mine was carved with a knife. Thankfully, I was unconscious at the time, unlike the terror you experienced." Tears came to her eyes. "I wondered if Phillip could bear to look at me after that. I felt tainted." Beth now smiled. "I learned, however, that my husband had greater love for me than my outward appearance. In fact, I think he loved me more because of my wound. I came into the marriage believing I was unlovable due to my past. I was haunted."

"Why are you telling me this?" Katrina asked.

"Because you mope about in your rooms, refusing to visit your childhood friends, and denying yourself the comfort they would offer. You cling to a letter and wonder, 'Will he come back to me? Will he still want me?'"

"I'm tired."

"You're always tired. And part of that is the healing your body and your heart need to do. But what about your soul, Katrina? Have you considered that you carry some deep wounds there that God longs to heal?"

"I don't know what you are talking about, Lady Westcombe."

"Come now, I'm Elizabeth, Lizzy, or Beth. Whichever suits you to call me. We are part of the same 'family' so we might as well be comfortable with one another."

"Thank you, Beth. I think that one suits you best."

Lady Westcombe smiled. "I'm glad you think so. For years, I was called Lizzy and it didn't always hold good memories. When Phillip began to call me Beth instead, I was given new life, a fresh beginning. I ended up taking a new last name when I married him, but I got a new first name as well. In the Old Testament God did that often with people he called to himself. Abram became Abraham and Sarai became Sarah, Jacob became Israel, and in the new testament, Saul became Paul."

"That's nice, what has that to do with me?"

Beth smiled warmly. "Why do these men all call you Mouse?"

Katrina shrugged. "I have always been so small." She grinned suddenly. "I did seem to like to take their cheese and other things from them when they weren't looking. And they said I squeaked when I was excited."

"Boys. That might have been fine for a little girl, but you are a woman grown. You need to fulfill the destiny of your name, Katrina. Did you know it's Greek and means 'pure'?"

"Katrina was my Russian grandmother's name. I have been Mouse for so long I don't really even see myself as a Katrina, much less pure."

"Why?"

"No one ever noticed me. I am a little gray mouse. I can fade into the crowd and no one can see me. Even Michael overlooked me when I left off my spectacles. I'm quiet and can be sneaky. I am Mouse."

"But what if God wanted to change your name to Katrina."

Katrina laughed. "God wouldn't want anything to do with me."

"Why? He died for you. I dare say that if Michael had been given the opportunity, he would have endured that brand for you. Jesus died to take the weight and pain of our sin, on his pure and blameless shoulders. He was branded for your sin with whips and nails."

Katrina shuddered.

"You are tired and have been through a lot. You need to realize that you are not stuck being who you were. That mark on your back does not prevent you from accepting the love and joy that awaits you in the future if you accept it."

"The only thing waiting for me, Beth, is possibly a position as a companion to Lady Orion or some other woman. To read books to her, sew, live what is left of my days in obscurity."

Beth's smile faded. "Is that what you want? In your heart, is that the future you desire?"

"We don't always get what we long for. My father didn't. My mother died when I was young. He was devastated. What about Michael? He's accepted for some unknown act of valor that resulted in him being knighted, but no young lady of the *ton* will marry a man born on the wrong side of the blanket."

"Except you."

"I'm not marrying him."

"You would if you could."

"I told him no."

"Why?"

Katrina sighed. "I don't want a man to marry me out of a sense of obligation. I long to be wanted. He doesn't love me. He didn't all these years that I waited and wished…"

"Men are not always aware of what they need or what they are missing. I think Michael had his own issues obscuring him from seeing you. He needed the glasses of your adventure together to realize what he missed and what he really needed."

"If that were so, why did he leave? He didn't even say good-bye."

"He sent you a letter."

"It's not the same as a, a…oh, never mind." Katrina blushed.

"It's not the same as a kiss perhaps?"

Katrina pursed her lips.

Beth smiled. "Don't worry, if you miss his kisses that much, I expect he is missing them even more." With that, she got up and left her guest alone to think about many things.

~*~

A few days later, Katrina found herself in a carriage once again heading west of London to Lord Remington's Rose Hill estate. Her father's name had been exonerated. She silently thanked Lord Hughes for that.

As she watched the scenery pass by, she recalled her moments with Michael and the tenderness and care he'd repeatedly showed her. Even as they'd worked on the code, he'd never belittled her ability to assist in spite of his initial reluctance for her to be involved. His premonition about the dangers was more real than she'd anticipated. She was now permanently marked by the experience and the very thought of that wound being with her always sent shivers of fear up her spine. She'd been so naïve.

Now she felt old. Cast aside and unneeded by anyone. Even Lady Orion didn't really need her. Lord Hughes initially resisted her quest to help. Michael was gone and she was being shipped off to Rose Hill to heal in obscurity and endure the weight of how alone she really was in the world.

Josie would welcome her warmly, but being there and seeing their child, her second cousin, would only remind her of all she'd never have. A family. A home of her own. But what made her so special that she deserved that? Did many of the servants even have that? Did an accident of birth give her rights others didn't have?

Her shoulder throbbed and she closed her eyes to rest.

~*~

A letter came two weeks later and found her at Rose Hill. She went to her favorite spot in the garden to be alone to read it.

Dearest Mouse,

Have you recovered from our adventures? I pray you have but worry that you would think that I view you as less beautiful for your injuries. I want to assure you that is not the case. I long to be with you. To see the sparkle in your eyes when you smile at me. I long to touch you and assure myself that you really are whole and well. My task is almost accomplished. I pray I can be home by your side soon. I think about you often and pray for you. I am as well as can be expected.

All my love, now and forever,

Michael

Would he really love her as she wanted? Or when reality hit and they met again would it be like before? With him acting as a big brother and treating her like a little girl instead of a woman? Maybe if she wore the blonde wig when she saw him again? She giggled at the thought and shook her head as she remembered things a maiden shouldn't even know, much less have experienced. She missed him even more.

~*~

Pure. What would it be like to be pure? Katrina looked out on the beautiful landscape of Rose Hill. Flowers blooming, the sun shining, and the light reflecting off the pond, where Marcus and his friends used to fish. She was sitting beneath that same tree she had broken her leg in. She stared up into the branches to see the dappled sunlight peeking through the new leaves. She listened to the songs of the birds and watched as Fidget wrapped himself in and around her feet over and over again. Memories of her childhood made her cringe. She had followed Michael around pathetically, seeking any crumb of attention he would dole out to her. She liked Marcus, Phillip, and Theo just fine, but for some reason, it was always Michael who occupied her thoughts and who played the hero in her dreams.

In the end, even he couldn't spare her from the consequences of her choices. Not from her willfulness in climbing this tree or from coming along to his club that night. She shivered at the thought of what might have happened had he gone alone. She might have been spared, but would he have lived? Was the Black Diamond somehow proud of his illegitimate son in some way to have not killed him outright? Had he wanted Michael to escape?

Katrina pulled at the grass and let the pieces fall over her lap. She was healing well. Josie had been gracious about not going back to London until Katrina was ready. Would she ever be ready? She removed her spectacles and rubbed them on her shawl to clean some dirt off of them.

Pure. What would it be like to be emptied of all the darkness? Would Jesus really be a friend to her? Josie encouraged her to read the book of John. Jesus was Light. A good Shepherd. Jesus was so many things. She was lonely. She wanted to die in that warehouse, but hell didn't seem like a place she would fit into. She didn't qualify for heaven either.

Kind of like her real life. She didn't fit in anywhere. Not really here at Rose Hill and not in London amongst the *ton.* She didn't even fit in with the servants when she'd served as a companion. She was alone in the world. She only ever felt "home" when she was with Michael—and he had abandoned her.

She was not without some support, but inside, she was alone. Jesus was a compelling person. He had compassion on lonely, broken people. Josie and Beth called her Katrina instead of Mouse and she was getting used to the sound. Was God changing her name? If He changed her name could He change her heart too? Would He welcome her into His home? Even now, would He walk with her through her loneliness and the uncertainty of her future? She leaned her head back and closed her eyes. Prayer. That's what people called talking to God. So, she would pray, and ask Him all her questions.

14

Michael traveled primarily at night. His feet hurt from blisters and his boots were worn. It was late spring and warmer than it had been a few weeks past in England. His only comforts through the treacherous journey were the words he daily read in the small book, and his conversations with God as he traveled and prayed. He found comfort in thinking about the woman waiting for him.

Home. The closest thing he could think of was Rose Hill. His townhouse was a building and he stored few personal belongings there, but it wasn't home. He never had the opportunity to stay in one place very long over the past few years. This kept his expenses low, however, and his investments had prospered. He wasn't as wealthy as his friends, but he possessed a comfortable income to live on, sufficient to support a wife and family in comfort. He grinned at the thought of Mouse as his wife. Of waking with her by his side. He imagined her holding a child of theirs in her arms. He'd never thought of becoming a father. But now, he longed to do that—with her. She would keep life lively and far from dull and he would be deeply content moving into the future with her by his side.

He noted the change in the air as he neared the coast and the vessel he hoped would transport him back to his homeland. He never longed to be back on English soil as much as he did now. He ventured toward a farmhouse where he'd sought shelter in years past. He found the old farmer still there but with little to offer due to the deprivations of war. What little food he had to share he more than made up with in his conversation.

"Cat is hunted," the grizzled man said. His clothes were dirty and torn and his fingernails broken with dirt underneath as he cut up some bread and cheese to share with his guest.

The farmer's wife came forward with a bowl of soup. No meat due to the lean times but the broth was still enough to make Michael's mouth water and stomach growl in appreciation.

"Ah, you like?" she asked with a smile that showed missing teeth. Her hair was gray, pulled back in a bun, and covered with a cap.

Michael nodded as he sipped some of the salty warm broth, wiping his chin with his sleeve.

"A trap, huh? Someone's out hunting cat?" Michael asked softly. "Interesting. One trapper or more?"

"Only one. A foxy one."

Michael's eyebrows rose as he continued to sip his soup and yet made eye contact with the farmer. *Tristan?* Had Tristan somehow survived and followed him to France? Michael chafed at how this might delay him, but he would rather get home late and alive than in a wooden box. Just when he thought he could retire…

"Thank you, Marcel. Your hospitality is always appreciated." Michael swiped the last of the broth from his mouth and swallowed the mug of water. He came to the kitchen and found a small metal container for coriander, popped it open, and dropped some French coin in there. More than enough to help this couple get through the next month or more if necessary.

He slipped into the basement into a tunnel but didn't exit. He remained below for several hours in the dark, resting. Later, he sneaked back into a sleeping house and out the side door to slink behind the trees. What kind of trap had his former servant set for him? He debated back-tracking and finding another route to the coast or facing the enemy and ending this once and for all. He leaned against a tall tree in the woods, melting into the darkness as he prayed for wisdom. He had read that the Bible was a light to his path, but would God really show the way for him to take? He smiled. The God he'd been reading about was perfectly capable of doing that.

Michael waited in the dark for well over an hour. No light appeared, but soon he heard the rustling of leaves. Tristan never mastered stealth which was one reason Michael often preferred to leave him behind at a base camp during missions. It also meant that as much as the Fox knew about the Cat, he didn't know everything. Michael grabbed the pistol out of his coat, it was primed and ready. He held a knife in his other hand. While not as skilled as Mouse, he was good with a short sword in close battle. He didn't doubt his ability to best his foe.

Silently thanking God for showing him his path, and relieved that soon, one way or another this challenge would be over, he moved around to come up behind the Fox.

"We didn't leave you dead enough the first time. A mistake I don't intend to repeat," Cat spoke with a purr.

Fox hissed, "I heal fast. You and Mouse escaped

me and the Black Diamond, but it ends here. Tonight."

"I agree. It ends now. But who will be the victor—you who serve the evil demon Black Diamond, or me who serves Jesus Christ and the King of England?"

"King? That mad-man? Or his ludicrous excuse for a son? And Jesus? Since when have you ever needed God?" Tristan sneered.

"I've always needed Him, but only recently bent my knee to Him as my Sovereign. I fight you in the name of Jesus, and King George."

"Noble words, but your long and illustrious career is destined to end tonight." Tristan raised his right arm with a pistol primed and pointed across the expanse, aiming for Michael.

"Don't you want to do this like civilized gentleman and fight hand to hand?"

"Too much time has been lost. You. Die. Now." With a flash in the dark night the gun exploded and the bullet found a home in Michael's chest. His own gun simultaneously fired. Both men fell to the ground and there was silence.

~*~

The sounds of the forest resumed. An owl hooted a call to her mate and an eager response was given. Michael flickered open his eyes, not sure whether to expect to see God before him, or to still be in the black of the woods. Pain throbbed in his chest and he moved his hand to the spot. There was no blood. He reached inside his coat and vest to make doubly sure. Again no blood. The clouds cleared and moonlight spilled down through the tree branches. Michael pulled out his small book. The bullet had lodged there but had gone no further. Michael pried the bullet out and returned the book to his pocket, slipping into the blackness and making his way around to where Fox lay still on the ground. He held his gun as he went, slowly watching the body. He came up to the head and saw no movement. Kneeling by Tristan's side he felt for the pulse. There was none. He checked for the wound and his aim had been true. Blood seeped into the ground.

Michael took Tristan's hat and placed it over the man's face. "May God have mercy on you, Tristan." With that, the Cat slinked away into the darkness, resuming his journey home.

~*~

Michael had never been fond of water. A dip in a pond was fine, but boating across the channel in a smuggler's skiff was something else entirely. The night was dark and overcast, perfect for stealth but difficult for navigating choppy waters. Michael's stomach did flip flops. It had been a few years since he cast up his accounts due to *mal de mar* but tonight he was coming close to revisiting that again. He lay low in the bottom of the boat, covered himself up with a tarp, and tried to pray away his sickness. The need to lean overboard passed.

He remembered the story of Jesus sleeping in such a boat through a storm and how scared the disciples had been. Jesus rebuked them for their lack of faith. As lightning illuminated the sky and thunder reverberated around them, Michael found a strange sense of peace.

He wondered if Mouse even realized he had requested that Marcus post the banns in church for his marriage to her. That could throw off the enemy. He didn't want to wait to claim her as his wife, and she deserved to be married in the church. With his newfound faith, he was more than ready to commit himself to this woman before God. He needed to make landfall first.

A huge wave threw the boat high into the air and it came crashing down. The men inside screamed in fright as they were plunged into the icy waters along with shattered planks of wood. Bootleg brandy sank to the bottom.

Michael was a strong swimmer, but he wasn't sure right now which direction was the shore. He managed to hold onto a plank. He somehow removed his boots and his outer coat which restricted too much movement. He hung on through the waves that crashed over him. He fought to stay afloat. Some of the other men had not been so fortunate. Michael prayed and waited with his eyes wide open. Another flash of lightning lit up the landscape and whether it was England or France at this point, Michael didn't care. He began to kick with all his might to get there.

Michael was wet, cold, and exhausted when he finally crawled up on rocks on the shoreline. His hands and feet were numb and he wanted to curl up into a ball and sleep. The storm continued to rage and a loud clap of thunder shook the ground as light flashed at the same time. Michael discovered a small fishing shanty, pulled himself upright, and stumbled to the shelter.

The place was deserted but there was kindling for a fire and a flint. Michael struggled to get the fire started with his shivering and numb fingers. Finally, a blaze roared in the hearth and Michael warmed himself, stripping off layers of clothing and wrapping himself in a rough homespun wool. He wandered around the tiny shack. He found hard tack, a bag of nuts, and some coffee. He got a kettle of water over the fire. Walking to the table he discovered a London newspaper from several weeks ago. Michael grinned. England had not given a gracious welcome, but he was here.

Michael sipped the bitter coffee, and warmth seeped deep inside of him. He grabbed a few more rough-hewn blankets, put more wood on the fire, and settled down to sleep.

~*~

The wind rattled the fisherman's hut and the room was cold even as dawn crept in the dingy windows. Michael's clothes remained damp from his swim, but he didn't have much choice, he needed to wear them. He stoked the fire and chewed on another piece of salty tack while warming up some water for a cup of coffee. He glanced at his bare feet, blistered and raw, and now with no shoes, his journey home would be even more painful. When he was finished with his drink and sufficiently warmed, he left the shack and headed north.

He walked only a few miles when he came upon a small cottage. He went to the door and knocked.

A young woman answered, neatly dressed in homespun cloth. She had two little ones at her skirt, peeking up at him with wide eyes.

"Ma'am. I apologize for bothering you. The boat I was aboard last night was destroyed in a squall. I managed to make it to shore and found shelter, but am in desperate need of some dry clothes and a pair of boots. I am willing to pay for them."

"Are you a smuggler or French?"

"Neither, my name is Sir Michael Tidley. I returned from France but it was in service to our King that I even ventured there." He held out some coin to the woman.

"You could use a shave and haircut too." Turning back into the cottage she yelled, "Harry, we have company!" She opened the door wider and motioned for Michael to enter.

"Come to the kitchen and sit by the fire while I get you something to eat." The children scampered off and Michael followed her across polished floors to a tidy kitchen with a large wood table. She motioned to a chair and he sat. A tall, burly man entered, his blond hair brushed off his face and tied in a que at the back. His wife whispered in his ear and he came forward.

Smiling the man held out his hand. "I'm Harry Witt. Welcome to our home." He glanced at Michael and laughed. "I'm not sure that any of my clothes would fit you. But my son, he is your size, tall for his age. Why don't you follow me while the missus gets breakfast ready, and we will find something for you to wear."

"I'd be much obliged," Michael said as he rose to followed Harry into the hall and up the staircase to the second floor and down another corridor. Knocking on a door, a smaller version of his host answered.

"Davey, this man is in need of some clothing. I think he is about your size, can we see what we might spare to help out a stranger?"

"Yes, Father." Turning toward Michael he said, "Won't you come in?"

Both men entered the generous bedroom and

followed the boy to the wardrobe. In short order, Michael was attired from head to toe in dry, clean clothes. Even a freshly starched cravat. The clothing was still a bit more generous in width than his own lean frame, but at least they were the correct length. The boots were a little big for him. An extra pair of stockings helped make up the difference.

"I appreciate your generosity," Michael said, smiling at his host and son.

"It is our pleasure to assist you. Now come. My Clara has prepared us a meal that will help for the journey you have ahead of you."

They returned to the kitchen and sat. Davy and the two younger children, introduced as Cynthia and Anabelle, joined them. Harry sat at the head of the table and Clara seated herself by his side. Michael was granted the seat at the opposite end. Harry reached for his wife's hand and the children all linked hands, the two youngest reaching for Michael's. "Let us pray," Harry said and bowed his head. The family followed suit.

"Lord, You have graced us with the presence of the visitor You told us to expect and we are grateful for Your provision in allowing us to be available to help a fellow brother in need. Bless our meal and sustain us for the work You have for us this day, and bless Sir Tidley as he continues on his journey. May You protect him through all that is in his path. We humbly give You our hearts and our service this day, in the name of Jesus. Amen."

Everyone chorused, "Amen," and the food was passed around.

"Your prayer indicated that you anticipated my arrival," Michael said as he placed some coddled eggs on his plate.

Harry nodded. "I don't often have dreams, but last night I did and I shared with my wife this morning. We knew you would come and that we were to help."

"May God be praised for leading me to your home. I'm appreciative of everything you've done for me." Michael choked back the emotion.

"Tis our pleasure. We have a horse that you may borrow to get to the Inn at Ashford. You can change horses there and we will pick her up tomorrow."

"You need to shave, or your wife won't kiss you," said the little girl.

"Anabelle, that was not a polite thing to say." Clara turned towards Michael. "My humble apologies."

Michael smiled. "She speaks but the truth. I have been away from civilization too long and do need a shave and haircut. I will find someone along my path to do that for me."

"Mamma does it for Daddy. She could help you look human again." This time, it was the dark-haired cherub on his other side.

"Cynthia." Came her mother's warning.

"But Mamma, that's what Daddy says when you shave him."

Michael fought back a grin, glanced at Harry, and chuckled.

"It's true," the farmer said. "Clara, I'll clean up if you would be gracious enough to help our guest look human. Heaven forbid he returns home to find himself bereft of kisses because of his beard."

Clara gazed at her husband and smiled.

Michael observed the love that existed between them. A cozy cottage, love, children, and a simple life.

This is what he hoped for with Katrina. *If* she would have him.

"Very well. Children, take your dishes to the washbasin and assist your father. When you are finished, you may see to your morning chores."

A chorus of "Yes, ma'am" was followed by the movement of chairs and the withdrawal of plates.

Harry sat down his fork and rose to take his plate and his wife's before heading to the clean-up area.

Clara rose as well. "Enjoy some more coffee, Sir Tidley. I will return shortly with all I need to make you presentable to your wife."

Before he could correct her, she was gone. Michael sipped his coffee and reveled in the warmth of this house God led him to.

When the shaving was done and his hair cut and combed back off his face, Sir Michael was ready to ride out to Ashford. He left generous payment on the fireplace mantle when the Witts's refused it from his hand. The family all stood on the front steps of the cottage to wave him off while Harry held the reins on the horse as Michael mounted.

"God's blessings on you, Sir Tidley."

"And may He bless you and your family richly as well for your kindness this day." Michael waved and was off down the road in the late morning sunshine.

~*~

The days passed in dreary progression at Rose Hill. Katrina's pain was reduced to a dull ache and occasional itch, although the scar would always be there. She favored more modest fashions that did not show the shoulders or great expanse of chest, so other than her future husband, no one would ever need to see them. She shook her head. *Husband?* Who was she fooling? Michael might have spoken bold words, but she would never hold him to promises uttered in the midst of a crisis.

"Josie, Marcus wouldn't force me to marry Michael against my will, would he?"

Josie set down her mending and considered the young woman sitting across from her. "I believe he might exert pressure on you and Michael to do what is right. You have been compromised and if society were to find out you not only went to Michael's rooms alone, traveled in a carriage with him, and posed as husband and wife at an inn, sleeping in the same room together…"

Katrina gasped. "How did he know?"

Josie smiled. "The same way the upper ten-thousand would if they looked too carefully at the gray little companion of Lady Orion. That is why we wait for Michael to return and are putting together a more colorful wardrobe to launch you into society. You will take the *beau monde* by storm and they will have no recollection of the companion who disappeared after a fall injured her shoulder."

Josie's eyes told Katrina that both Josie and Marcus were fully aware of how much of a lie that had been.

Katrina blushed. "I don't want a man to marry me because he has to."

"Didn't Elizabeth tell you her story? She wasn't desirous of a forced marriage either, but now they love each other and have a young son."

"I am glad that Phillip has found a wife who suits him, but that doesn't mean a forced marriage between

Michael and myself would be successful."

"I was under the impression that Michael was eager to wed you. He wrote and asked Marcus to call the banns and even sent a notice to the papers."

"He what?" Katrina rose and began to pace with a little terrier wagging her tail as she followed. "How dare Marcus do that."

"How dare I what, Katrina?" Marcus entered the room, tossing his hat on a table and walking over to his wife who rose to greet him.

Katrina turned her face, embarrassed at watching their embrace. A sadness and longing for the lips of a certain other dark-haired, brown-eyed man haunted her.

"I interrupted something. I am sorry. Katrina, what did I dare to do that you find offensive?"

"Calling the banns and posting them in the paper? How could you?"

"Michael made it clear that he desires your hand in marriage. He requested that I take those steps and I obliged him."

"Without consulting me? I thought I still had a choice in who I marry."

Marcus cleared his throat. "I believe, cousin, you made your preference to Michael clear over the years. Recent activities and participation in his work indicated you desire his company. I would never have expected you to be averse to his suit."

"He's never presented his suit, that's what I'm opposed to. Oh, he spoke the words in the warehouse but he was experiencing guilt over what happened. It wasn't a real proposal. You all assumed I would marry him and he has yet to even *ask* me!" Katrina's hands were fisted and she shook them by her side. "Excuse me." Katrina left the room.

Marcus glanced over at his bride with a raised eyebrow. "Is it that big of an issue that he never asked her?"

Josie walked over to her husband and put her arm around his waist. "A girl wants to believe she is loved and wanted. She doesn't want to be an obligation."

"Well, I love and need you and still want to spend the rest of my life with you."

"Silly man. We're already married."

"I thought it couldn't hurt to tell you. Did it?"

Josie gave a sly smile. "Not at all. Shall we go upstairs? You could use a rest from your journey from London."

"Rest. Yes, that is exactly what I need. I missed you, Josie."

Hand in hand they left the drawing room and were not seen again until supper.

~*~

Katrina seethed in her room as she paced. *Men!* How arrogant to think that a woman would be so desperate that she'd jump at the chance to marry. Well, she was *not* desperate. She had her own small fortune. She could stay with Marcus and Josie or return to Lady Orion. She plopped down in the chair, defeated. Was this all that life had to offer? She grabbed her hat and headed outside to the tall oak that signified much of her relationship with Michael. He was as steady and strong as this tree. Always there. Supportive. She glanced up into the leafy branches. It had been so long ago that she had climbed. Did she dare try it now?

Katrina feared heights since that day. *Be brave. You*

can do it! Michael wasn't here to discourage or rescue her. She was her own master. She smiled. With determination she grabbed the lowest branch and swung herself up. She almost knocked her spectacles off in the process. Adjusting them she reached for the next one and continued her ascent. She reached as far as she could go and settled on a large branch, holding on tight to the core of the tree. She glanced around her. Her vision was restricted by the leaves. She inhaled and let the air out. She leaned her head against the trunk and wept.

Where was Michael? Why couldn't he be here? Life was no fun when he wasn't around. Even with the painful things, breaking her leg, or being branded, there was something joyous about being in his presence, in his arms. Safe. Secure.

The wind rustled the leaves and blew a few stray hairs across her face. It was as if God said "I am always here."

"Are you here, God?" The sun coming through the branches warmed her back and the cooler air blew across her exposed limbs and face. She closed her eyes and listened. And smiled. Yes. He was definitely here. She sat there for the longest time, finally she glanced down. With a swallow of fear she began to descend. She was just about to the branch where she had fallen when she heard him.

"Careful. Marcus will kill me if you break your leg again."

"Michael!" Katrina held on to the tree tightly and looked down.

Michael was on a branch below her.

When she finally reached him she gripped the tree with one arm and reached out to touch his face. She whispered in wonder, "It really is you."

Michael smiled. "How about we finish this descent and have our reunion safe on the solid ground below?"

Katrina nodded and together they made their way down the rest of the tree, Michael leading and speaking encouragement to her. When he was finally on the ground, he caught her waist when she hung from the branch, and he slowly let her feet touch the grass.

Katrina wrapped her arms around Michael and without thinking turned her head so that her lips would meet his.

The kiss was sweet and innocent but soon became urgent. Katrina didn't want to stop.

"Oh!" she said as Michael pushed her away from him, unlatching her arms from around his neck. Shame and heat filled her and she stared at the ground.

Michael lifted her chin so that their eyes would meet. "Don't be ashamed, Mouse, that was a welcome back greeting any man would be happy to receive. It's just, well, I was enjoying it a bit too much and I do not want to anticipate our wedding night." Now it was Michael's turn to blush.

The word wedding hit Katrina like a pail of icy cold water. She gasped and shook her head. She turned and ran as fast as she could to the house and up to her room.

Wedding? He presumed a wedding? How dare he? Katrina punched her pillow. A black and white bundle of fur emerged from under it and clicked at her.

"I'm sorry, Fidget. I hope I didn't hurt you." She reached out to stroke the ferret's back and the animal leaned into the comforting touch.

"Your master has returned. He thinks to marry

me. Ohhhh, I am so vexed!"

She lay back on the bed and the mattress dipped under the force of her collapse. Tears came. She removed her spectacles and got up to put them on the side table. She stretched out with the pillow, with the ferret curled up next to her, and cried herself to sleep.

15

The drawing room was empty when Michael entered it a short time later. He had yet to greet his hosts and anticipated surprising them with his arrival. His skin was darker from his trip abroad and in the elements, but otherwise, he appeared the same as he always did. He wondered what Katrina would say after their misadventure upon his arrival.

He had not been very happy when he had searched for her only to find her up in the tree. Like the cat he was, he managed to climb halfway up, undetected, before she began her descent. He could not have been mistaken in the love in her eyes when she'd discovered him there. And that spontaneous kiss was something wonderful, better than his dreams could have conjured up. England's welcome might have been brutal, but Mouse's more than made up for it.

Michael stood by the fire and waited. The bell announcing dinner in less than a quarter hour rang and he was still alone.

Finally, minutes later, Marcus and Josie entered the room, arm in arm.

"Michael. What a delightful surprise." Josie hurried over to him and gave him a peck on the cheek.

Marcus followed, clapped Michael on the shoulder, and said, "Well met, did you just arrive? Does Katrina know of your return?"

"I arrived a few short hours ago, and yes, Katrina

is aware I am here." Michael looked toward the door as if expecting her to enter any minute.

Instead, a footman entered to announce dinner and that Miss Shepherd was indisposed and would not be joining them.

Michael's shoulders slumped at the news, but he put a smile on his face, straightened up again, and joined his host and hostess to the dining room.

~*~

Michael tried hard to hide his disappointment at Mouse's defection at the dinner table. He kept things light and impersonal with Marcus and Josie even though he could tell they were bursting with curiosity over his recent adventures of which he could not share.

When Josie left the gentlemen to their port, Marcus finally broached the topic that had been avoided.

"What is going on between you and Mouse?" Marcus raised the glass to his lips but his gaze was on his friend.

"Why do you ask?"

"She states that she refuses to marry you, as you have not asked her."

"I asked her, but she refused. I figured it was because of the stress of the circumstances at the time."

"And so you moved ahead with posting the banns and publishing a notice, without consulting her?"

"I needed to protect her reputation after our adventures which have inadvertently compromised her if the truth was exposed to the public. I've made my position clear to Mouse. Her reception of me this afternoon indicated that she was not averse to my suit. But…" Michael ran his thumb up and down the stem of the glass on the table before him.

"But?"

"I mentioned something about the wedding and she took off like a frightened hare with a pack of dogs after it." Michael frowned.

"And she refused to face you over dinner."

Michael nodded. "Any suggestions?"

"Perhaps you should propose?"

"How? She won't see me."

"Maybe Josie can help us figure something out."

"I need all the help I can get it seems. And I am not content to wait much longer to begin my life with her by my side. That dream kept me alive these past weeks."

Marcus smiled. "You are most certainly in love and I remember what that frustration was like. Let us go consult with my bride and see what we can come up with." Marcus rose and Michael did likewise.

The two men exited the dining room to seek out the lovely Viscountess Remington.

~*~

Katrina picked at the dinner Josie sent to her room. She requested some port but she thought perhaps she had drunk too much. It was late and she stared out the window into the early summer moonlight. The tree called out to her again, but dare she?

She shrugged, pulled on her robe and some slippers and tiptoed out into the darkened empty hallways of Rose Hill. She made her way down to a side door letting her out into the rose garden. She walked slowly through there, inhaling the scent of the flowers. She existed in a blissful haze, everything fuzzy around the edges even though she wore her spectacles. Had she ever been drunk before? She couldn't remember a time when she had an opportunity to do so. She giggled to herself, twirled, and made her way to the big tree. She came to the wide trunk and leaned her forehead against the rough bark.

Was it only this afternoon that she had been so foolish as to embrace Michael here, practically begging him to make love to her? Her body grew warm at the thought. She turned and found her favorite spot to sit. Leaning against the trunk she tipped her head back to see the moon. How romantic. A full moon and here she was alone and refusing to be with the one man who professed he loved and wanted her. What was that about? She pulled her knees up to her chest, kicked off her slippers and let her toes wiggle in the cool grass. She folded her arms across her knees and leaned forward.

What did she really desire? At first, she longed for her father's name to be redeemed. She had been willing to give everything to that cause until it possibly meant that Michael would die because of it. So, she had thrown away the precious journal. How little she had known of Michael and his skill and cunning as a spy. She did not regret the action, although she missed reading her father's writing. The book was burned in the fire but many of those words still resonated within her heart.

Tears dripped from her cheeks and she pushed her glasses up into her hair as she wiped her eyes with the sleeve of her nightgown. What would her father advise her to do? She shook her head. She would never really know. What about God? Did God want her to marry Michael? What kind of life would she have married to a spy? Would she spend her days as she had the last several weeks, worrying over him and wondering if he'd be killed?

A shadow crossed the moonlight and Michael stood there gazing up at the sky.

"Every night as I walked, I'd see stars and the moon and knew that somewhere you were under the same sky and in the care of good friends, and I could relax. You would heal and recover, but I couldn't wait to complete my mission to return here—to you." Now he focused on her, his eyes hooded and no smile on his face.

He turned toward her and bent to one knee. He placed one arm across that knee and the other hand reached the ground to help support him. "I think I may have always loved you Katrina, but was too blind to notice it. But you kiss me and all I can think about is living the rest of my life with your love and no other future seems satisfactory. Every time I told you I wanted you for my wife, I was speaking the truth. I still want you if you'll have me. But if for some reason you simply cannot fathom living your life with a retired spy of modest fortune who only desires to love and cherish you and raise a family together, I will accept that and withdraw with as much grace as I can." Michael's eyes appeared dark in the shadows and the moon wreathed his hair in soft, white light.

Like an angel. Her wits scattered with the alcohol singing through her veins at the words he had spoken. Warmth filled her and she had an irresistible urge to touch him. She came to her knees before him, put her hands on his face and kissed him with all the passion that was in her intoxicated little heart.

And then she giggled.

~*~

Michael stood and brought her to her feet. "You're drunk."

Katrina giggled again and put a hand up to her mouth as she made an unladylike sound. Michael let go of her and she swayed. He grabbed her.

Michael groaned and closed his eyes. Taking a deep breath, he drew her close and held her tight. He shook his head and without a word scooped her up in his arms and headed for the house.

"What are you doing?" she asked with a silly smile.

"Taking you to your bed."

"Will you stay with me?" Her voice was coy now and she fluttered her eyelashes.

"No."

"But you want me, don't you?" she mewled.

"Not like this, and only as my wife."

"Oh." She laid her head on his shoulder and he could smell her distinctive scent of vanilla. He groaned.

Reaching her door, he managed to open it and put her in her room. Once on her feet, she swayed again. "Can you make it to bed?" he asked as he reluctantly took his hands off her.

"Only if you come with me." She reached for him.

Michael stepped back and shook his head. "No, Katrina. I hate to disappoint a lady, but no." With that he slipped out the door, shutting it quietly behind him.

When he turned in the hallway he found Marcus there with his arms crossed and one eyebrow raised. "This wasn't quite what we discussed after dinner."

Michael frowned. "I proposed outside by the tree, but soon realized she was three sheets to the wind and brought her back to her room. I did nothing improper." Michael frowned and stood there silently.

The door opened behind him. Katrina stepped out from her room, swayed, and leaned against the frame. "Michael, oh good, you're still here." She squinted into the darkness. "Marcus, is that you? Why are you here?"

"Oh, I don't know, Katrina. I heard strange noises in the hallway, came to investigate, and found Michael exiting your suite."

She giggled. "I'm so bad!" She blushed and reached towards Michael who moved away, a frown still on his face.

"I'll be leaving now, Marcus. Thank you for your hospitality."

"Michael…"

"No, don't you Michael me, Marcus. I don't want to marry a woman who can only bear to even consider marriage to me when she's drunk. I'm done." He turned to Katrina. "Good night, Mouse. You get your wish. I will not be pursuing you further." With that, Michael strode down the hallway to his room.

~*~

Katrina frowned. "I think he's angry."

Marcus nodded but unfolded his arms.

"He did give me a lovely proposal."

"And how did you answer him?"

Katrina brought her hand up to her mouth, hiccupped, and shook her head. Her face flushed and she stumbled back into her room. She found the chamber pot in time.

~*~

Katrina awoke in the morning to a horrible headache. It took a few minutes for the room to stop spinning.

"Good morning!" sang out Lady Remington.

Katrina groaned and rolled over. "Leave me be."

"Seems like you need some help. I've left you be for several weeks as you moped about here. Then you play fast and loose with a dear friend of mine and well, I'm not feeling that charitable this morning. We need to get you dressed as we head to London in under two hours." Josie started giving instructions to a maid who entered behind her.

"London? I never said I was ready for London." Katrina groaned.

"Ready or not, to London you will go. If you intend to rebuff Sir Michael Tidley, you need to find another suitor and fast, lest word of your activities spreads around town. Michael did a wonderful job protecting you from the consequences of your choices. He was even in love with you and willing to marry you, but you made your position clear. So now that this has been decided, we depart for London to launch you amongst the *ton*."

"I don't want to go," Katrina protested.

"Marcus did not give us a choice. Molly will get you ready. Cook is sending up a special remedy for that headache as well. You will have the rest of the day to repent of it in the carriage." With that, Josie sailed out of the room.

Katrina squeezed her eyes shut. How did things

get so crazy all of a sudden? London. She didn't want to go there. Josie was right, she needed to go. Taking a deep breath, she forced herself out of bed.

~*~

The carriage ride east was over rutted roads. Normally she wasn't a poor traveler, but with her being sick from her overindulgence, the trip was pure agony. Josie sat next to her and kept up a steady stream of ideas for Katrina's launch into society.

Marcus was riding on his favorite horse, Cloud. Their daughter was in the next carriage with the nanny and Josie's abigail, Molly.

Katrina closed her eyes and tried to sleep even though her head pounded in time with the horses' hooves.

They arrived at the Remington townhouse in the evening.

Katrina went straight up to bed in the room assigned to her.

~*~

Later, Marcus and Josie relaxed in their sitting room.

"Did she say anything to you about Michael on the journey?" Marcus asked.

"No, she appeared miserable, but it's hard to know if it was her head, her heart, or both."

"I could push the issue."

"If Katrina backs out of this engagement, she will need to face the scandal," Josie said.

"Is there any way we can avoid it?"

"Other than Michael marrying her?"

"Yes," Marcus agreed.

"Probably not. Are you concerned about how this might reflect on your work in the House of Lords?" Josie inquired.

"No. We've weathered the tattling tongues of the *ton* before. She's my cousin, not my child. I'm not even her trustee anymore, although she has asked me to continue to manage her funds. She is an independent woman."

"The worst kind." Josie giggled.

Marcus nuzzled her neck. "You think so?"

"Oh, most definitely. Katrina and Michael need each other. They love each other. They're just being stubborn."

"So what do we do?"

"Pray. Beyond that, nothing."

"You're sure about that?"

"Yes, Marcus, I'm sure." Josie leaned over to kiss her husband and neither of them gave another thought about their friends' dilemma.

~*~

"He's back on English soil. Tristan failed you again, my lord."

The Black Diamond reclined in his chair and looked past the minion who delivered his news. He smiled and nodded his head. "Chip off the ol' block, isn't he?"

"Excuse me?"

"My son, Sir Michael Tidley. He's a lot like his father, which happens to be—me."

"You were trying to eliminate your son?"

"As much as I admire his work, he has, more times than I can count, interfered with my plans. I cannot allow that to continue."

"How will you kill him?"

"I think a little game of *Cat* and *Mouse* will be appropriate, but I think I need some cheese as bait." The Black Diamond rubbed his hands together in glee.

16

Theodore knocked on the door. With no response, he pounded harder. When there continued to be no answer he went around back and managed to gain entrance through a secret door he had used once before. He walked into the dark house but did not try to be quiet. Instead, he whistled. He made his way to the study on the main floor. He opened the door and peered inside. The room stank. There was a low fire in the grate and a boot could be seen, attached to a hidden body.

"Michael, I say, be a good fellow and come out with me to the Bellows' recital tonight." Theo entered and stared down at his friend whose clothing was disheveled. Michael had obviously not shaved or bathed in many a day.

The man sprawled on the couch opened up one eyelid and peeked at the intruder. "Theo. It's you. Get out." The eye closed again.

Theo was able to take in the number of empty bottles laying around the floor. "I don't recall ever having seen you shoot the cat before. The ever-secretive, charming, and disciplined Sir Michael Tidley, has finally lost his edge." Theo stayed where he was and waited.

"Leave. Please." Michael ground out through gritted teeth. His eyes were open slits as he viewed his old friend.

"I came to have you join me. I think you need to get out of here and embrace the world again."

Michael's foot came down off the arm of the chair, the boot hitting the wooden floor with a thud. He struggled to sit up and then leaned forward with his head in his hands. He gave a low throaty groan. "I can't go anywhere. She jilted me. I thought she wanted me all along, but it wasn't true. I was pursuing the wind and she destroyed me."

"Nonsense. Katrina has always adored you. I don't know what happened to the two of you. I am sure you can work it out if you only try."

"She ran from me earlier after a glorious welcome home. Later that night, when she approached me, wanting me, it was only because she was drunk. I do not need a wife who needs a drink to tolerate or desire my company."

"Surely you exaggerate."

"I wish I were. I gave up everything that defined my life to have her, Theo. Worst decision I ever made. Don't do it. Never fall in love. It's miserable. I almost wish I hadn't returned from France alive. Death would have been preferable."

"Now you're talking utter nonsense. Or have you finally embraced Marcus's and Phillip's Jesus? They have talked about how wonderful heaven will be according to the Bible. I haven't completely figured it all out yet."

"Heaven. I thought it would be heaven to own a small estate and raise kids with Mouse. But if I can't have her I couldn't stay around to watch her choose another man. I think I would go mad and be tempted to kill him."

"No, you wouldn't. You are too good a man for

that." Theo sat across from Michael.

"You don't really know me and what I've done in my life. Believe me. I would be more than capable. But to what end? If she were happier with someone else, why wouldn't I desire that for her? Wouldn't love want what's best for the object of desire?" Michael laughed. "I'm not a big enough man for that." He rose to his feet and staggered around to the fireplace to stoke the flames up higher. He squatted down and held his hands to the flame. "So cold. My heart is so cold."

Theo watched closely.

Michael continued. "You asked about Jesus. Yes. I now count myself a Christian and that makes this worse. I cannot act out on my base desires. I struggle to forgive her for the hurt and pain I feel. I go through the motions, but the ache doesn't leave. Why would God lead me to her only to slam the door in my face?" Michael fell to his knees and placed his hands on his knees as he gazed into the flames. "Hell. This has to be what hell is like."

"Describe it to me."

"Hurt. Lonely. A knife in the chest that is twisted and withdrawn. Bloody."

"Yet you choose to stay there. Why?"

"I don't choose it. Hell chooses me."

"I think you are creating your own place of torment. God doesn't ask you to beat yourself up when you stumble and fall. At least not the Jesus I've heard our friends talk about."

"I asked you before to leave, Theo. I'm asking again. Go. Leave me alone."

Theo rose.

"Theo?"

"Yes, Michael?" He started for the door, but turned to look back.

"Thank you for caring."

"That's what friends are for," Theo said as the door closed behind him.

~*~

Michael sat by the fire for a long time. He rose and went to his desk and pulled out a drawer. Inside was a small leather bound book. His mother's journal. He held it in his hands and slowly opened the cover. He slumped into his chair by the desk and started to read.

How could I ever have been so deceived by someone? And now this little man in my arms looks up at me with those same dark eyes as his father. I love him but it hurts to look at him and be reminded of my sin. Will God and my father ever forgive me? Will Michael ever forgive me for being unable to give him a proper heritage? I've lost everything for love. My purity, my reputation, and my future. And for what? For a baby boy whom I struggle to love because he reminds me of what I lost. God, where have You gone? Why have You abandoned me? What good could possibly come of this little boy's life?

Michael put the journal down in his lap. Over the years since his mother's death and his discovery of this journal, he had read these passages and wondered again at why his mother chose to keep him in spite of the ostracism and shame she bore until the day she died. What kind of man deserved that protection? Had she been threatened? Had she been paid to keep him? Why was he really here?

Michael closed his eyes and leaned back in his chair. The world spun between the raw emotions inside and the quantity of alcohol he had consumed. *Mouse.* His memory recalled protecting her precious journal of her father's and then when his own life was threatened, sacrificing her one last treasure to the flames. To save him.

Pain ripped through his heart. He imagined her embrace when he had finally returned. The unmitigated joy in that kiss. Oh, what a kiss! And then she ran at the mention of marriage. He frowned and shook his head. The same girl, hours later after avoiding him, approaching him more forcefully. As drunk as he was at this very moment.

Why had he reacted so strongly? It wasn't the drunkenness. He would be the last person to judge that, although this was not a state he embraced often in his life. A spy could not afford to be inebriated. It could be deadly. Why did he storm away? He could have gotten her to commit. They could have married quickly.

No. He didn't want some hole-in-the-wall affair. He wasn't ashamed of Mouse. He would have gladly taken her to wife even if they had never proven her father's innocence.

So why had he run after sharing his heart with her?

Panic seized him. He dropped the journal to the floor, gripped the arms of the chair tightly and struggled to breathe. Something was terribly wrong, but what was it? He did want to marry her. Didn't he? So why did he all of a sudden feel so shaken? Why did the hair begin to stand up on the back of his head? He heard a click and his eyes slowly opened to look into a pistol aimed closely at his head.

Oh, Lord.

~*~

Katrina fidgeted as she waited with the other young ladies at the Stanford ball. Her dress was the requisite white with pink trim and pink ribbon woven into her hair that had been crimped and curled, but was slowly straightening in the stifling heat of the crowded ballroom. The orchestra sounded slightly out of tune and she winced whenever the violin squeaked. Her head hurt and she squinted to see as she had been instructed to leave off her spectacles. She was tempted to pull them out of her reticule anyway. Why should a man consider her as a potential bride but not realize she was basically blind without her glasses?

She was bumped from behind and a deep voice said, "Pardon me, miss," as an arm reached out to grab her to keep her from falling forward. She spun to discover who had been so clumsy, although it would be hard not to bump into someone in this crowd.

She turned around to glance at the other young ladies standing near her. All silently watched the dancing. Katrina saw more of a kaleidoscope of colors twirling together. Faceless men and women. Dark suits and some brighter colors mixed in with the whites. Candlelight reflecting off mirrors around the room magnified the brightness and made the space appear larger than it was.

Why did they think she belonged here? Why did Marcus insist that if she refused Michael she needed to secure her future with someone? Why would she want anyone other than Michael? She grew warm with embarrassment as she remembered throwing herself at him. Putting her hand up to her mouth she cleared her throat, excused herself to no one in particular, and went to seek the ladies withdrawing room.

After taking care of her needs and trying to do something with the long strands that were no longer curling so beautifully, she pulled out her spectacles and put them on. She needed to be more assertive with Josie and insist on wearing them. Something crinkled in her reticule and peering inside again, she found a piece of paper. She turned to read it and paled. She sat down for a few moments and prayed.

How she managed to get through the dances and the supper that evening, she couldn't remember. All she could think of was that Lord Hughes had another assignment and she needed to be at her designated place by two of the clock. She only hoped she could convince Lord Remington to leave the ball before then.

Feigning fatigue wasn't far from the truth. Katrina stifled yawns even in the carriage ride home and wearily did go to her room, longing for her pillow. Dismissing the maid, she waited a brief amount of time before changing once again into a disguise for her mission. The dark cloak stuck to her overheated skin. Even though London was cooler at night, there was still a mugginess in the air that was uncomfortable. She shoved her spectacles in her reticule and departed. As much as she preferred wearing them, they didn't go with this particular costume. She knew her way around Michael's house well enough to not bump into things.

Staying to the shadows, she moved through the back alleys and gained entrance to Sir Tidley's townhouse, and as quiet as the mouse she was, found her way to his study. She slipped in and was confronted with the awful smell of vomit. The door to the garden was open and she tiptoed across the room to close it. She turned to discover two things. One, she'd not been careful enough as a large strong hand clamped over her mouth and another wrapped around her, immobilizing her. The second was the prone body of Michael, unconscious on the floor at her feet, blood pooling from a wound in the back of his head.

A trap.

17

Foul smelling breath washed across her cheek as the assailant whispered in her ear, "There is no one to hear you. Do as I say or the same fate will befall you. Do you understand?"

Katrina nodded.

The grip loosened and she was shoved forward, almost tripping over Michael. She quickly knelt by his side and felt for his pulse.

"He's alive. For now. Bind his wound if you wish. The Black Diamond would not want blood to sully his coach."

Very little moonlight entered the room. Katrina could not make out the features of the man holding the pistol trained on her.

"I need bandages and my spectacles so I can see."

"You cannot leave the room."

"The spectacles are in my reticule."

"No fancy moves or he will die." The gun shifted to aim at Sir Michael's chest.

Katrina shook her head. She pulled out her bag and put her glasses on. She shoved back her cloak but did not remove it. "I need to rip my petticoat to make a bandage."

"Get on with it."

Katrina turned and ripped the fabric. She spied a red book and suspected it was important so she shoved it into her bag. Turning back to Michael she wound the fabric around his head. It wasn't enough. She untied his cravat and gently removed it, exposing the upper part of his chest and the dark hair there. She shook her head. There was no time to be dreaming of anything more than the moment's crisis. She wrapped Michael's head and tied off the linen. She moved his upper body so he wasn't lying in the pool of blood.

Michael groaned.

Katrina looked up at the burly man still aiming a gun at them both. "Now what? You have us in your power. Do you take us somewhere or kill us now?"

"We will take a journey. Someone wants to walk down memory lane and desires company."

Another man stepped out of the darkness to pull Katrina up. She was shoved toward the first man. The second built like a boxer, lifted up Michael and threw him over his shoulder as if he were a sack of potatoes. Silently the four of them headed out to the back alley.

Only Katrina noticed Fidget managing to come along for the ride.

~*~

The rhythm of the horses' hooves and the bumps in the road jarred Michael and he moaned. He didn't know where he was, only that something soft cushioned him. He dared to open his eyes and was surprised to see a vaguely familiar blonde. There was something he couldn't seem to remember. He instantly wished he could kiss her.

"Beautiful." He croaked out, suddenly feeling the reality of how incapable he was of following through on any amorous intentions that had fleetingly raced through his mind.

The woman peered down at him, her brow

furrowed as she frowned. Her hand lay on his chest and he reached up to clasp it.

"Whatever it is, it will be all right," he assured.

She shook her head in response and looked away. The windows were shuttered and little light came in.

"What's your name?" he asked.

Her gaze snapped back to his quickly and she studied his face in silence. "You don't know who I am?"

"Not unless you tell me. But I can keep calling you beautiful if you prefer."

Was that a look of sadness that flickered in her eyes? She pulled back her hood and yanked off the blonde wig, loosening the pins holding her long brown hair in place. Locks unfolded. He reached his hand up to touch one and wrap it around his finger as if it were a hidden treasure. "I always did prefer brunettes." He must be losing his touch. Why couldn't he charm her? "You look familiar, but I still cannot place you."

"Perhaps I resemble someone close to you."

"There is no one close to me. At least I don't think so." It hit him. He had no recollection of this beautiful woman who held his head in her lap, cushioning him against the roughness of the carriage ride. He couldn't remember how he had gotten here or even what he did. His family, his home, his past. It was a blank wall.

He let the hair go and groaned. "I don't know. I can't…"

"Michael." Her hand came up to sooth his face with a loving caress.

"Is that my name?"

She nodded.

"Are we well acquainted?"

"Yes." Her lips were pursed together and tears

formed in her eyes.

His heart raced. "Are we—married?"

She shook her head and looked away.

A tremor shook his body. "Am I married to anyone?"

"No." She refused to look at him.

"Where are we going? What happened?" He struggled to rise but pain created a strong dizziness and this woman gently held him down.

"Don't move. Someone injured your head. I don't know where we are going or why, only that someone desires you and possibly me, dead."

"Dead? What did I do to deserve that?"

"Michael, you did your job and you did it well. You were a successful spy for the British government and aided in our war against France. My suspicion is that somehow your cover was blown and—" She gave a big sigh.

"—and, now they seek to eliminate me."

She nodded.

"So how do you come into this?"

Her eyes searched his face again. She was not telling him everything.

"I was your partner on an assignment. We succeeded in our mission."

"Did I fall in love with you then?" He grinned.

"Only you could tell me that and you don't remember." Her tone was flat, emotionless.

He sensed a tension inside her.

"I wish I could. I can't believe I'd ever forget someone as lovely as you." His eyes closed and he drifted back to sleep.

~*~

Loneliness filled Katrina's heart. She ached for the man lying in her lap. She feared for his life and now, she feared even more because he couldn't remember. How long would it last? With Michael injured and lacking his memory, how much help would he be in trying to escape the clutches of the Black Diamond? Would they be killed outright? No. Probably not. They could have easily done that already. So, was it only being delayed? And why? Why did he need them both? Did he think that they could torture her again to get him to crack? She gave a quiet laugh. A lot of good that would do when he didn't even know who she was. She still hadn't given him her name, either.

She pulled out the journal that had been on the floor next to Michael. She felt a little guilty trying to read it in the darkened carriage but she wondered why he had it. She realized within a page or two that this was a series of entries by his mother.

Katrina remembered only meeting Miss Tidley once or twice and that she had been a graceful but timid woman, almost afraid of her own shadow. She had never conversed much with her but now, reflecting back, she remembered how this lovely young woman seemed to care deeply about her son. She died many years ago. Katrina wasn't quite sure when. Her passing had been as quiet and withdrawn as her life. Did anyone other than her father and son attend her funeral, she wondered? How sad to have gone through life so lonely. Set aside. Abandoned.

Katrina swallowed a lump in her throat as she fought to take a breath. Michael had run away from her the last time. She couldn't let his current state of need and dependence stir any affection she had for him.

Foolish girl. Your heart is already lost to this man, even if he doesn't know you. Maybe that would make it easier to bear? She thought not.

Would he love her now? But what would happen when he came to his senses? He'd feel tricked. She couldn't do it. She needed to give the appearance of being as uninterested in him as possible, even as her heart broke. She would provide him the necessary care but that was it. She gazed down at him. Blood had soaked through the linen wrap but had not spread further in the last few hours.

She relished his hand holding hers, although the grip was relaxed now. Rough calloused hands. Scarred in places. She watched the rise and fall of the muscles not very well hidden beneath the shirt and waistcoat. He had been coatless. She was tempted to touch the hair peeking out of his shirt. What did it feel like? It was brown and curly. Was it soft? She admired the muscles in his arms and legs and the calves encased in his custom boots. Made by Hoby, she suspected, but what did she know? They didn't look as polished as they usually did, but then he probably didn't have time to find a replacement for his valet, Tristan.

Katrina set the journal aside. It was too dark to read. The best she could tell was that they were heading west. She leaned her head back and tried to sleep. Who knew when she would need to be alert and ready for whatever was ahead?

~*~

Her kisses were sweet. Michael loved the feel of the skin on her heart-shaped face. So petite and beautiful. Hair like a chocolate waterfall. He liked chocolate, didn't he? He couldn't remember. Gray eyes with flecks of green that reminded him of a stormy sea. Sea. He felt a rocking. Was he at sea? He inhaled. No. he couldn't smell the water. Horses, dust. Where was he? He looked to her face again and peace overwhelmed him. She was here. He would be all right. Somehow, he knew that as long as she was there, he could handle anything that came his way. He must love her. Something inside told him he did. So why had he not married her? She was too beautiful, too precious, to still be unwed.

God was here too. He knew God. He was certain of it. "For God so loved the world…" he remembered that one. Any others? Something about the enemy being like a prowling lion and to be on the alert lest he be devoured. Was that why this woman looked frightened? Were they in danger? She spoke of his work. Had he made an enemy? It sounded as though he had and she was scared for them both. Someone knocked. Was someone at the door? No. It was only his head pounding. He really wished it would stop. And then for a while it did.

~*~

Michael had been restless. He moaned, squinted, and frowned even as he slept. She "shushed" him, squeezed his hand, and spoke softly to him. He relaxed again, limp in her lap, a heavy but welcome weight. Katrina glanced down at his face. The bloody linen. The bruising forming near one eye that was beginning to swell. The unshaven chin. She reached up and touched the prickly beard. What had been going on that he had found himself in such a state? He was the Cat. Sly, capable, and rarely taken by surprise. His reputation as a spy was stellar. How had this star fallen so far? She kept her palm against his cheek and chin, just to touch and hold him. His skin was abnormally warm. The carriage was unbearably stuffy even in the dark of the summer night. She was sweating under the heat of his body, her long dress, and the cloak she still wore.

She reached up to untie the ribbons of her cloak with her other hand to pry it off her shoulders. Her outfit was looser than a normal gown. Dressed as a lady of the night had some advantages. No tight corset or stays to restrict her. She could feel the stagnant air settle on her exposed skin, even the diamond scar on her back. She frowned. The Black Diamond once again had her and Michael in his power, and with her companion injured how could they ever hope to escape? Tears welled in her eyes and she let them fall as she gazed on the face of the one man she'd always admired. Her hero. Her friend. The only man she loved. Hopelessness threatened to suffocate her more than the heat ever could. He lay so still now. What if he never awoke again to smile at her, to tease her, or to give her that conspiratorial wink?

The tempo of the horses changed as the coach slowed. Soon the door to the carriage would unlock. Then what?

~*~

The door opened and a gruff voice could be heard. "You have five minutes to take care of your needs before we leave. You will be under guard. Don't try anything foolish."

"I would be delighted to comply if you could help me move Sir Tidley."

The head peeked inside. "Still out, is he?"

"Yes," Was all she replied. She managed to wiggle out from under Michael and place his head gently on her cloak for a pillow.

~*~

When she had finished, and had inhaled deeply of the early morning dawn, she was shoved back into the coach and the door slammed soundly behind her. She could hear the lock turn as she struggled to pick herself up off the filthy floor. The coach took off in a jerk that threw her on top of Sir Michael. An arm came to clasp her close and she found herself gazing into his coffee-colored eyes.

"Hello, beautiful. I missed you."

He stunk of stale alcohol, but even so, she found she did not really want to move from his embrace. She wished he had not been injured because she longed to lean on his strong shoulders to find comfort and strength for what lie ahead. Suddenly weariness overtook her. She dropped her head down on his chest and wept.

~*~

He rubbed her back. Confound it. What was he to do now? He lifted his head up enough to plant a kiss on the top of her hair. He inhaled deeply. Vanilla. Something deep inside him stirred in response to that scent. Vanilla. It reminded him of love. Home.

Comfort. Happiness. He sniffed again and grinned. He didn't know who this woman was, but one thing he did recognize was this—she belonged to him and he would fight with every fibre of his being to ensure her safety.

18

The hours wore on and Michael drifted in and out of sleep. Somehow, Katrina managed to sit upright again and position Michael's head on her lap. Her legs went numb as she tried to rest and pray. She thought about what she'd read in Scripture. Jesus had warned about fathers turning against sons. Was this more than a political battle between Michael and his father, the Black Diamond, and the nations they fought for? Could there also be a spiritual battle being waged? How did one fight that? She really didn't understand. She hadn't read that far in the Bible. She believed God was with Michael and her. Surely those stories from church when she was a child, were true. God saving the three men out of the fiery furnace. Daniel, in the lion's den, unscathed. Death was not the worst possible scenario—hell was. She'd been saved from that.

~*~

The carriage slowed and took a trajectory down a rough road. Michael was awakened by the jostling. Katrina had all she could do to keep them from falling off the seat. When it came to a halt he struggled to sit up, groggy but awake.

"How are you?" Katrina asked with concern. The carriage was fairly dim, although it would be late morning by now.

"I suspect I've had better days." He groaned.

"I'm certain you have."

Before Katrina could continue her inquiry, the carriage door was unbolted and opened. A rough looking character peered inside. "Out whicha now, an no funny biznous or I'll pop you one." He waved a gun at them.

Katrina grabbed her cloak and reticule before she alighted from the carriage and turned to assist Michael who could barely stand. The sun blinded but the fresh air and breeze were welcome after the stifling heat of the closed-in carriage. Katrina's hair was plastered to her head from perspiration. Michael, leaning heavily against her, was also drenched in sweat. Katrina struggled to keep him upright in the heat.

The man pointed to a small hunter's lodge a few feet away. Waving his gun, he followed as Katrina struggled to help Michael to the door. Once inside the one room hut, the heat from the closed-up room suffocated. The gun pushing into her backside propelled her forward and she managed to get Michael to the one pallet bed on the far side of the small room. He collapsed unceremoniously and lay still, his eyes open, beseeching her for answers.

Before she could inquire of her captor, the door was slammed and bolted from the outside. Katrina ran to the windows to see if she could open any, but they were sealed shut. She leaned against the wall in frustration and slid to the floor, resting her arms on her knees. She leaned her head forward, feeling utterly hopeless.

"We're trapped?" Michael's voice was soft.

Katrina nodded.

"At least it's not moving. And they did not

separate us. Those are two things to be thankful for."

Katrina lifted her head.

He smiled at her, and moved over to make room on the pallet. He patted the thin mattress. "You need to rest."

"It's the middle of the day," she protested.

"You had other plans I was unaware of? Perhaps an appointment to keep? Maybe a modiste to visit? Or is this your 'at home' day? Are we expecting guests?" He gave a cheeky grin.

"This situation isn't funny, Michael."

"I'm sure it isn't, and while I would like to understand what is behind all of this, I suspect the information will do me no good. Rest will enable us to think more clearly when the time comes." He patted the pallet again.

Katrina's eyes felt like sand and the makeshift bed looked tempting. She struggled to her feet, kicked off her slippers, and stretched herself out next to Michael, with her face to the door. Michael rubbed her back. "Rest, beautiful, we are not alone, God is with us."

"I will never leave you or forsake you."

"What?" Michael asked.

"I read that in the Bible somewhere."

"It sounds familiar."

"You read the Bible?" Katrina closed her eyes.

"I must have." Michael yawned and let his hand rest on her hip. "Rest, beautiful. Worrying will gain us nothing at this point."

"You never worry?"

"How would I know? It doesn't seem to be a profitable thing to do in this case. We may feel helpless right now, but the danger is not imminent. We need to rest and be ready for whatever and whenever something occurs."

Katrina was silent.

"Beautiful? You are tense. Relax."

"I've never slept with a man before," she whispered.

"I'll not ravish you. Your virtue is safe with me."

"I know it is, Michael. Still, I wish…"

"You wish what?"

She rolled over on the narrow pallet to face him. Her hand came up to rest on his chest. He was so warm. The hand that had been dislodged from her hip came to clasp hers, moving it to the tiny space between them. They slept.

~*~

Michael didn't sleep long. He spent time admiring the woman next to him. Dusk was beginning to settle so it was probably getting close to eight-of-the-clock in the evening. His stomach growled. He wondered when he'd last eaten, and if their captors planned to starve them.

He gently pushed a few strands of hair off of this woman's face. Such a powerful personality in a pint-sized package. She obviously knew him well, or she wouldn't have allowed him this close. He wished he could remember who she was. Right now, she was his only link to the world. He tried to imagine his past and found the exercise frustrating. He chafed at the bandage around his head but figured it might be helping with his mammoth headache. He rose to find a place to relieve himself. Not many options in the tiny enclosed space, but a makeshift screen served for some privacy in the event this fellow prisoner should awaken.

When he finished, he searched the small space for any signs of food. He was able to look out the window and saw where guards were posted. Only one window, however, did not give much information about where they all were, and how many of them might be out there.

Something furry appeared in the glass. Long and thin, it stared at Michael, tilted its head, and tapped at the window. Michael could have sworn it smiled and winked at him. How on earth did a ferret get to be out here, in the middle of nowhere?

A short time later Michael heard a small thud coming from the chimney. He went over there and found a branch with some grapes on them. A tad on the bitter side, they were still edible. Michael wiped them off on Beautiful's cloak as it seemed the cleanest thing available and ate a few, saving the majority for his partner. Silently he thanked God for sending a small animal to provide them with food.

Eventually, he went to recline on the pallet as there were no chairs. Soon he was drifting back to a dreamless sleep praying silently for God's wisdom and guidance. It seemed they were hopelessly dependent upon Him for any rescue.

~*~

The moon was high in the sky. Katrina had been awoke for a short time, enjoying the grapes that appeared and trying again to read the journal. Michael tossed and turned but relaxed when she touched him or whispered. Then he would stop and smile. She longed to trace that smile with her fingers or to taste it with her lips. She shook her head. She was hopeless. Why, even in the direst circumstances, would she even think about kissing him? He didn't even know who she was. Beautiful, indeed! When he woke up she would…

The bolt creaked and groaned outside the door and Katrina shook Michael. "Wake up. Someone is here," she hissed at him. She rose to stand, tucking the journal back into her reticule.

~*~

One of their burly captors entered. His presence filled the cabin and sucked the remaining air out of it.

"Yous come wit' me." He waved a pistol at Katrina. "'elp 'im up."

Katrina nodded, threw her cloak around her shoulders, grabbed the bag, and assisted Michael to his feet. She shoved the remaining few grapes in his hand. "Eat," she whispered.

Upon gaining the outside they both stood and inhaled deeply of the cooler, fresh night air. The prod of a muzzle in her back forced her to abandon this momentary delight and move forward with Michael. The carriage was before them again. They were bundled inside, the door locked, and the horses took off.

Michael offered her a grape, but Katrina's stomach was in knots. Was this it? Would these be her last moments with Michael? She turned to look at him as he rested against the squabs. His eyes met hers and her heart melted. If these were her last moments, she could…

Without even realizing she had done so, Katrina leaned into Michael, raised her head to his and sought his lips.

He groaned deep in his throat as he wrapped his arms around her and accepted her offering. The carriage slowed and they broke the embrace.

"Always remember that I loved you."

"Past? Not present tense?" he asked.

"I anticipate the present to end soon."

"Not if I have any say in the matter."

"Michael." Her voice held a warning.

"Listen, beautiful, your name, finally. Please."

"Katrina. Katrina Shepherd."

"Katrina. It sounds like royalty. Beautiful royalty to whom I owe my allegiance and life."

"Now you're being dramatic."

"You're the one predicting our doom here, not me. That's dramatic."

The argument was broken when the carriage stopped and the door flew open. A dark shadowy figure, tall and lean, peered in.

"Ah, Cat and Mouse, indeed, you are both here. Fine. Very fine. Please, be my guests and exit." The deep voice ended this speech with a chuckle.

"The Black Diamond," Katrina whispered to Michael as she moved to the door.

"I'm a Mouse?"

"You're the Cat, silly. I'm known as Mouse."

~*~

Michael's head spun with all that seemed to take place against the black backdrop of his memory. Kisses that stirred up feelings for this woman he couldn't remember but that his brain searched feverishly for. Cat and Mouse. Katrina. Death? The Black Diamond.

None of it made sense. He fought dizziness as he exited the carriage, only to lean heavily against Beautiful. *Katrina. Mouse?*

The fresh air was reviving, however, and he struggled to pull himself to his full height which still fell several inches shorter than the debonair man standing in front of them in a mask and domino.

~*~

"You will forgive me for being hesitant to reveal myself, even if you will never make it back to share what you know. However, Michael, my son, I wanted to share a moment with you. Kind of a family thing, as it were." The man turned and moved towards a graveyard.

The gaoler's gun motioned Katrina and Michael forward.

The Black Diamond came to stand beside a small gravestone and the man behind Michael pushed him forward, causing him to fall on his knees with Katrina beside him, having been thrown off balance. Michael stared at the stone in front of him.

Marietta Tidley

Beloved daughter and mother

1766 – 1804

Something ached behind his eyes and dropped his head forward.

Katrina put her arm around him. "I'm so sorry, Michael."

"Who is it?" he whispered back. The pain was deafening. Blackness closed in.

Before Katrina could answer, the Black Diamond spoke again.

"Moving, isn't it? Dear little Marietta. Did I tell you that I was fond of her? She was a fool, though. She really thought I loved her and would marry her. It was her father I was out to destroy. And I succeeded better than I ever hoped. You were the death knell to his aspiration in the Home Office. Worth it to know that he would not be able to uncover my plans. But Michael, where are her journals? I cannot afford to have them fall into the wrong hands and possibly reveal, even accidently, my identity. The only one who would have access to them would have been you. So, tell me where they are and when I find them, you will be free."

Michael struggled to hold on to consciousness and listen to the man who spoke. None of it made sense. He couldn't grasp what this was about. Marietta had to be important but the name meant nothing to him. Katrina's hand rested on his back, rubbing, almost petting him to offer comfort.

"Michael?" she said.

"I don't know what you are talking about, my lord," he said.

"I suspected that would be your response." The dark lord stepped forward, clasped Katrina by her arm and drew her to her feet.

Michael leaned back on his heels.

The Black Diamond untied Katrina's cloak, let it fall to the ground and then shoved her blouse off her right shoulder revealing the brand of a diamond. "My men did beautiful work, didn't they?" His finger traced the diamond.

Katrina stood still with her head turned away from Michael.

Michael did not respond.

The Black Diamond continued. "I branded her and

expected her to die, but she is a bit of a tasty morsel, wouldn't you agree, Sir Tidley?"

Michael looked around to see who the man referred to. The guards were spread out but not close, with weapons in their arms. He counted four men, but there could be more hidden behind tombstones and trees.

"Are you looking for rescue, my noble knight? You won't be finding it. But maybe I'll let you think about that book while I enjoy the favors of your woman. Only appropriate that we share her, don't you think? After all, we are family." The Black Diamond pulled Katrina close, wrapped both arms around her and kissed her. She struggled against his grip and his assault as his hands moved.

The blackness around Michael's vision was now tinged with red. If only he had the strength to move. He needed to protect Katrina.

~*~

Katrina wanted to vomit as the Black Diamond pulled her close and the scent of his cloying perfume choked her. When he bent to kiss her she was shocked and angry. Catching her mouth open his tongue sought entry so she bit down hard. At that moment, something furry slid by her neck with a clicking noise. *Fidget!* He jumped to the shoulders of the Black Diamond, bit his neck, and emitted a noxious odor.

~*~

Michael watched as the elongated rat climbed up Katrina's clothing and jumped up to the Black

Diamond. The evil man yelled an obscenity while at the same time a stench filled the air. Katrina was pushed back as the Black Diamond screamed for the men to help pull the animal off him. Before they could do that, the animal bit the man in the ear, jumped off, and scurried into hiding.

Michael managed to stand and held Katrina to himself. He had watched the animal in disbelief. In the moonlight, the whites of the Black Diamond's eyes glinted at Michael as the man slowly backed away.

"You think you have defeated me," he coughed as he tried to cover his mouth with a monogrammed handkerchief to obscure the noxious smell that was all over him, "but you have not. This is far from over." With that, the man ran for his horse, and the carriage that had carried them to this place also departed, leaving them standing in the middle of the graveyard.

Michael hugged Katrina to himself. The odor from the animal still hung heavy in the air so they stumbled over the hedgerow, and settled on a stone bench that was there by the entrance to the cemetery.

Together they sat in silence, each holding the other.

~*~

Katrina burrowed into Michael's shoulder. Her tears turned to laughter.

"Beautiful, what's so humorous? You don't smell good and we are in the middle of nowhere with no food, money, shelter, or horses. And yet you are laughing."

Katrina looked up at him with tears in her eyes. She snorted and laughed some more and then began to cry again. "Oh, Michael…"

"I'm not even sure what happened here."

Katrina used her cloak to dry her eyes and then wrapped it further around her as she shivered even though the night air was still warm. "I'm not sure I can explain it all to you."

"What was it that attacked that man? It was the same animal that brought us food."

"Fidget? He is your pet ferret, Michael. He seems to have adopted me though and this is the second time he's saved our lives." She clicked her tongue and soon the furry rodent was in her lap, reaching up to give her kisses.

"I think that rodent—and us—all need baths."

Katrina laughed as she stroked and cooed at Fidget. "You may be right."

Michael searched the stars that shone through the trees. "Do you have any idea of where we are?"

Katrina glanced around. "I suspect we are on what was your grandfather's property which adjoins Lord Remington's Rose Hill estate. It will be a hike. Do you think you can manage?"

Michael sighed deeply. "If it might provide me with fresh food, water, a bath, and perhaps some cleaner clothes? I'm not fast right now, but I will try, even if I have to make the journey on my knees."

"Hopefully it will not come to that. We can rest often. Shall we start out before our tormentor returns to finish the job he started?"

"Lead the way, beautiful."

~*~

They began their walk in silence, with Michael

trying hard to not lean on Katrina whose own steps were slow. They bent to drink at a riverbank while Fidget took a swim. They rested for a bit before returning to their journey.

"Katrina?"

"Hmmm?"

"Why was I *Cat* and you *Mouse*?"

"Your trademark was your ability to move silently like a cat. I believe that was how you got that code name."

"And you, Mouse?"

"I'm kind of invisible. I'm small, quiet, and usually unnoticed. I blend into crowds. You always called me a little mouse when we were young."

"I hope you slapped me for doing so."

"Why? It was true. It has served me well to be the Mouse. Well. Most of the time anyway. The Mouse has retired, though."

"A bit young for that, aren't you?"

"For what?"

"Retirement."

Katrina shook her head. "I'm too old for the marriage mart, and I accomplished the mission I set out to do. Now I just want…"

Michael's voice was soft. "What do you want, Katrina?"

She frowned and stepped ahead of him on the path.

"Wait for me, beautiful."

"Please stop calling me that." Katrina stopped and turned toward him as he caught up to her.

"Calling you what?"

"Beautiful."

"Why? You are beautiful. Why would you think

otherwise?"

"You may have forgotten many things, but lying to charm a lady was not one of them." She turned to go but Michael stalled her with his hand on her arm.

"I don't know what I have said or done in the past to cause you to mistrust me, but I am telling you the truth as I see it now. You are beautiful."

"In the dark with no competition, maybe you could be right. Put me in a ballroom with the diamonds of the *beau monde* and I would be invisible."

"I doubt I could ever overlook you."

Katrina pulled out her spectacles and put them on. She pulled back her hair that was falling freely about her face and twisted it into a tight knot in the back of her head. Michael's eyebrow rose.

"So? You still have the same face and figure and smile, when you choose to use it. Your eyes seem bigger now and still as cloudy as the sea during a storm. I read your heart in them. You want to deny you care for me, but your eyes tell me something else."

"You don't know anything about me."

"I know enough. I know that I'm attracted to you. I know that something in my mind stirs at the scent of you, well before that ferret unleashed his stench anyway. I know you care for me. And while I may not remember my past, I can imagine a future spent kissing your lips."

Katrina began walking again. "Life is more than kissing, Michael."

Michael struggled to keep pace, but he grinned. "I know it is, there are many more delights beyond kissing, but it's a good starting place."

"You speak nonsense. I think that whack on the head addled your brain."

"I think a beautiful woman has addled my heart."

"Really? Do I know her?"

"Maybe not," Michael said quietly as they continued to walk.

19

When they reached Rose Hill by dawn, Michael leaned heavily on Katrina. She took them through the garden to the door to the kitchen. After consulting with the cook and butler, a bath was ordered set up in the adjoining room and Michael and Katrina fought over which one was to bathe first. Katrina finally was given first honors. One of the footmen helped Michael maneuver up the stairs to the room he often occupied when at Rose Hill and where some of his clothes were stored for visits at the estate. Katrina had clothes left from her previous visit to the house.

~*~

Michael awoke late in the day. He struggled to eat earlier but with Katrina urging him on he managed to put away some of the food served by Lord Remington's staff. The room he was in was comfortable—almost familiar. As he awoke from a dreamless sleep his head pounded and he winced as he tried to move. He stretched his arms and realized that he was wearing pants and a loose shirt. His bare feet were cool against the sheet and the light blanket that covered him. Birds sang outside the open windows. He glanced around the room with various shades of blue and cream and heavy oak furniture. His gaze fell on the figure of the young woman who was his lifeline to reality.

She sat reading in a chair not far from the bed. She had her feet curled up in a most unladylike fashion underneath her. The ferret was wound up in a ball on her lap. Katrina was absorbed in the book and he was able to observe her for a few moments. Her hair was pulled back in a loose braid in which many strands somehow escaped. She was wearing her spectacles and they had slid down her nose.

Michael struggled to rise and let out a moan. *Yes*. Now he had her attention.

"Michael, how are you?" Katrina set the book on the bedside table and struggled to put her feet down. Michael was dismayed to see she had slippers on. He wouldn't have minded glimpsing one of her toes or her ankles, but for a woman sitting in a man's bedroom, she was being quite proper. He found that frustrating. The ferret jumped onto the bed.

"My head continues to pound, making me dizzy when I try to rise."

"I wonder if we should consult the local doctor."

"I would rather you didn't."

Katrina didn't say a word.

"How long did I sleep?"

"About ten hours. It is late afternoon on the day we arrived here."

"Any sign of our tormentors?"

"None."

"So, what do we do now?"

"I sent a message to Lord Remington to let him know where we both are."

"Who is Lord Remington again?"

"One of your closest friends, the owner of this fine estate, and also my cousin."

"Will there be a lot of people I don't remember descending on us?" His heart clenched in fear.

"I doubt it. I told them of your injury, that I thought we needed to rest here, and begged them to not worry or come after us for the time being."

"I hear a 'but' in that."

"Knowing Marcus, he will be here post-haste."

"Why?"

"Because I am a single woman in a house with a single man, and nary a chaperone in sight."

"Marry me."

"What did you say?"

"You heard me, marry me."

"You don't even remember who you are. What if you come to your senses and find yourself trapped in a marriage you resent?"

"Why would I resent you?"

"I don't know. I don't live inside your head."

"Well, apparently, I don't live there either because I can't remember anything. All I understand is that I love and need you." Michael threw back the covers and sat up. He gripped the side of the bed to fight off the dizziness. He rose slowly and dropped to a knee in front of Katrina.

"Miss Katrina Shepherd, will you do me the honor of being my wife? Would you walk beside me, leading and guiding and loving me as I struggle to learn who I am? I desperately need you." He clasped her hand.

The ferret lifted his head and clicked at Michael before settling back down again.

"Apparently, the rodent has no objections. We've seen what he can do when he doesn't approve."

Katrina chuckled at that and petted Fidget.

"Katrina? I'm on my knee here. I'm serious. Why

have I never proposed to you before? I must have been an idiot."

"Well, you kind of did."

"And?"

"I got scared and ran away."

"Did that deter me?"

"No. But I did offend you and then you left me."

"And now? Will you run away from me now?" His gaze searched her face.

Katrina sighed. She lifted a hand to touch the rough whiskers that were still there. "This is highly improper."

"Why? Did I do it wrong?"

"We are in your bedroom."

"If you marry me you will have the right to be here."

"Michael, what if you never remember me?"

"Maybe I won't remember the past but we can build new memories together."

"I would like that."

"You're attracted to me."

"What makes you think that?" Katrina smiled.

"That kiss in the carriage before we got to the graveyard. You were trying to express all the passion you have denied, just to have a taste of it as you thought you would die. And you wanted that with me."

"I used you. Doesn't that bother you?"

"Not at all. I quite enjoyed it."

"You are too bold, sir."

He rose to his feet with her assistance. "Am I? I wonder if I haven't been bold enough." Michael placed one hand behind her neck drawing her face to his until their lips met. The kiss was soft and tentative. Michael did not want to scare her away. "Marry me," he whispered.

"As soon as possible, please." Katrina leaned forward and putting a hand on either side of his face, drew him close again for a more thorough kiss.

~*~

Katrina broke the kiss and stood up quickly. "Michael? Do you really want to marry right away?"

"Sure, but how?"

"You already posted the banns. We don't need a Special License—we can go to the church here and wed."

"Are you saying we could do this right now?"

Katrina nodded and smiled.

"Are you sure, beautiful?"

"I thought I would lose you. I was miserable when you went to France and I was overjoyed when you returned. I have loved you for so long that the only future that appeals to me is one where you are by my side."

"You won't regret this?"

"I would be more concerned about you regretting choosing me, Michael. I have always loved you, but you—"

"—were obviously a blind idiot."

Katrina planted a kiss on his nose. "Let's get changed and I'll call for a carriage to take us to the church. We'll see what we can do." She skipped out of his room and before closing the door gave this parting salvo, "Last one downstairs has to bathe Fidget!"

Michael laughed and went to get dressed. As he stood tying his cravat he noticed a box on the dresser.

Supposedly this room contained his personal belongings. He opened the box and found a beautiful opal ring with diamonds. Modest, but stunning for its simplicity. Underneath the box was a small piece of paper that must have been his reminder to purchase the ring. In his own terrible scrawl was "get a ring for Mouse."

He wanted to kick himself for ever referring to her as Mouse and how that had led her to believe she wasn't beautiful. He took the ring and put it in his pocket. Obviously, he was following through on his original intentions. This had to be the right thing. He smiled and brushed his hair back over the lump on his head. His eyes sported a lovely shade of yellow and purple, but he didn't care. Katrina loved him and that was enough.

They both reached the bottom of the stairs at the same time and enjoyed a laugh over that. Katrina bespoke a simple meal for their return.

They headed out the door together to the carriage hooked up for their use, to ride into town to the local rectory.

~*~

Reverend Hall answered the door. He was an elderly man who had retired several years back and had been replaced by a much younger curate who lived in a newer abode on the other side of the churchyard.

"Sir Tidley, Miss Shepherd. How good to see you both again. How can I help you?"

"We tried the curate but he is out of town, and well, we'd like to get married. Would you be so kind as to perform the service for us?" Michael asked.

"You posted the banns. There is nothing to bar me from doing so, but right this minute? You don't want to plan a nice wedding and invite your friends?"

"Reverend Hall, Michael has been away for so long and we have been anxious for his return and we, well, we don't want to wait."

"I see." The older man smiled and nodded. "I remember being young and in love. Come on in and let's see what Mrs. Hall and I can do to help you out."

~*~

The ceremony was simple. In the humble parlor with Reverend Hall and his wife and their maid-of-all-work, Sally, the vows were spoken.

Reverend Hall cleared his throat and whispered to Sir Tidley, "Do you by chance have a ring for the bride?"

Michael grinned and nodded as he pulled out the ring. He reached for Katrina's left hand and slipped the band on. "With this ring, I thee wed. With my body, I thee worship. I promise to love you and be faithful to you all the days of my life."

Katrina looked at her finger in awe. "It's beautiful, Michael."

"Not as beautiful as you are to me."

After signing the church registry, the newlyweds returned to Rose Hill and enjoyed a simple repast before heading up to Michael's suite. Upon learning that the couple had wed, the staff in the house moved quickly to move Katrina's belongings to the room and left extra candles burning. A maid came to assist Katrina as she readied for bed.

"Thank you, Maria, I think that will be all for now."

"Are you sure you don't want your hair braided, ma'am?"

"Not tonight."

~*~

Katrina waited nervously for Michael to come to her. What did a woman do while she waited for her husband? At a loss, she grabbed the first book she could find and was surprised it was a Bible, apparently, a gift from Marcus to Michael many years before. She sat down to read and her face grew warm when her husband entered the room.

She saw him enter and shut the book quickly. "Did I interrupt something?" Michael stalked her as smoothly as the cat he was famed for being.

"It was nothing. Really."

"Do tell." He reached down and grabbed the book. One eyebrow rose. "A Bible? What would be in here that would cause you to blush so beautifully?"

"There's just a book in there that I didn't know about and well…"

Michael opened to where some pages were slightly bent from her rush to hide what she read. He skimmed the pages. "Whoa. I didn't realize this was in here either." He glanced up from the words to his bride who avoided his eyes. "Did this disturb you? Nothing in here is out of place within the bonds of marriage."

"No. It's just that, well, it seems so explicit. I never heard about the Song of Solomon before."

"No, but now that you have, we should possibly

make use of this."

Katrina stood, covered shoulder to toe in virginal white muslin with her long dark hair flowing around her. She reached up for his cravat and began to untie it. "My beloved is mine and I am his." The cravat came loose and was dropped to the floor.

Michael glanced at the Bible in his hands while Katrina was unbuttoning his shirt. "Thou hast ravaged my heart." He set the book down and stilled Katrina's hands and placed them on his bare chest. "I love you."

"And I, you."

They left any further biblical instructions to be discovered for a later time.

~*~

"Marcus, I assure you, there is nothing to fear. Rushing to Rose Hill will not undo any damage to Katrina's reputation." Josie tried to calm her agitated spouse as he strode across the bedroom, throwing a few items into a bag for travel by horseback to his country estate.

"She is my relative. I must have a care for her. He will marry her now. There can be no more delays. The wedding must be planned forthwith. Will you assist with that?"

"Of course. But you need to remain calm. Katrina's letter says that Michael was injured and that they'd been kidnapped and escaped. This was not a run for the border. There was no intention on their part of doing anything that would even appear wrong."

"No intention? They were avoiding each other. Theo said Michael had drunk himself into a stupor over her and then all of a sudden, they are together at

Rose Hill with no one but a handful of servants in residence? Doesn't that seem suspicious to you?"

"I agree that it doesn't make sense, but suspicious? Come on, Marcus, be reasonable. You cannot force love." She stopped him in his tracks and placed a hand up alongside his strong jaw. "Wait till morning to ride out, when it is safer. We can travel by carriage together."

Marcus put his arms around his wife's waist. "Normally I would be swayed to stay here and spend the night with you, but I am compelled to go."

"You like to meddle in the lives of others." Josie stepped out of his embrace and walked around the bed.

"Like you thought I had interfered with Phillip and Beth?"

Josie sat on the edge of the bed but nodded her head.

"Well, that didn't turn out so bad, did it?"

"No, I will admit…"

"Josie, the proprieties are there to protect innocent women from predatory men."

"You certainly don't place Michael in that category. Plus, she said he'd been injured. I would be very surprised if he were to attempt to ravage her under your roof. He has too much respect for you and cares too deeply for Katrina."

Marcus ran his open palm down his face in weariness. "I understand all that. But the sooner I get there the sooner they can be married with no hint of scandal."

"Is reputation everything?"

"It certainly makes a difference. I almost lost you due to a misunderstanding over my conduct."

"True. I was so foolish not to have trusted in your integrity."

"You were human, my love."

"And the rest of the *beau monde* will not be so easily swayed to another opinion."

"Exactly."

"Ride on then, Marcus. I will journey out tomorrow and join you by evening."

Marcus strode over to his wife and gave her a lingering kiss. "I do adore you."

"And I you."

With that, Marcus grabbed his bag and left the room.

~*~

Katrina reveled in the warmth of the body she was tangled up with under the covers. The night before had been a revelation. Pain, yes, but the wonder and passion left her wanting more. Michael slept beneath her as she rested her head on his shoulder with his arm around her. Her husband. She smiled and wondered what other treasures the Song of Solomon would add to this aspect of their married life.

She snuggled in deeper and dozed off. She was startled awake an hour later upon hearing a horse galloping up the driveway. The shout sounded familiar. Someone had arrived but that needn't concern them for now. The servants were instructed to stay away unless summoned. However, the pounding of boots on the stairs made her aware that someone was in a rush. Had the Black Diamond tracked them here? Much to her surprise, the bedroom door swung open.

It was not the Black Diamond or any of his thugs,

but her cousin Marcus, in full riding attire, his crop still in his hand tapping nervously against his thigh.

"Marcus? What are you doing here?"

"I thought I owned the place." His chest heaved as he tried to catch his breath.

Katrina wrapped the blankets more tightly around her. "You do, but why are you barging into our room at this hour of the morning? It's barely dawn."

"I got your note and posted here as quickly as I could to avoid the hint of scandal. I see I'm too late."

"No. If you would let me explain."

Michael's eyes opened with the exchange going on around him and he glanced to the door. "Darling wife, who is that man standing in the door looking as though he's about to challenge me to a duel?"

"Don't play with me, Michael," Marcus growled. "I'm in no mood for any of your teasing today. I'm tired and hungry."

"Michael, the man at the door is one of your dearest friends, Viscount Remington, also known by you all as Marcus or Remy. You went to school together and he has welcomed you as family for many years."

Michael propped himself up on one elbow and the sheet slid down exposing more of his bare chest while at the same time hiding more of his wife. "Glad to meet you, Marcus. I wish I could remember more but, well, there it is."

"There what is? Will you get out of that bed and tell me why you are sleeping with my cousin?"

"I would rise, but well, I'm in the altogether, having just enjoyed my wedding night with my bride. Your cousin, you say? Yes, well it seems that we got married yesterday so all is proper and you can leave us in peace."

"There has rarely been peace where you are concerned lately, Michael. Married? You wed Katrina, is this true?"

"Go to the church and check the registry. We married yesterday," Katrina said.

Marcus let out a sigh and closed his eyes. Shaking his head, his eyes opened again and the crop stopped dancing at his side. "Then congratulations are in order and my humble apologies for interrupting you on your first day of wedded bliss. Welcome to the family, Michael. Again, I'm sorry for this intrusion. I'm glad you made things right."

"Before you had to force us to?" Katrina asked.

Marcus blushed. "Mouse, you know me too well."

"Please, let's not call my beautiful wife Mouse anymore?"

"Excuse me?" Both Katrina and Marcus spoke.

"I don't want her called Mouse anymore."

"You came up with the moniker," Marcus defended.

"Then I can ban it. Katrina is a much more fitting name for my wife." Michael looked at his bride. "She deserves a name that describes her beauty, not one that would diminish it."

Marcus cleared his throat and backed out of the door. "Well, then. I'll be leaving."

The door shut and Katrina pushed her husband back onto the pillow. "I don't mind being called Mouse."

"I do."

"Have I told you today that I love you, husband?"

"I think you just did."

"Let me show you as well."

"I could get to liking this marriage business," Michael said as he submitted to his wife's ministrations.

20

Marcus slept until late afternoon. He discovered from the staff that Michael and Katrina had indeed married after arriving in a disreputable state. He was glad for them and longed for his own wife to be by his side. He paced in his study awaiting her arrival.

When she finally did arrive, it was in the company of Lord Harrow.

He sent a note up to the newlyweds begging their presence at the evening meal. He was surprised to see them appearing as the dinner bell rang. They were walking holding hands. Marcus shook his head. Would wonders never cease?

Josie rushed forward to greet the new bride. "Marcus told me the news. Congratulations, Katrina. Michael." She looked at Michael. "What happened to you?"

Katrina spoke first. "Michael, this is Lady Remington, you call her Josie as you are good friends."

Michael nodded and turned to Josie. "Josie, thank you for your kind hospitality. I was injured somehow in an attack two days past."

"He lost his memory, which is frustrating for him."

Josie stepped back, her brows knitted together. "Lost his memory? Yet he remembered you?"

"I didn't remember her, only that she was important to me. I fell instantly in love and asked her to marry me. She told me a little about our past. Obviously, I wasn't opposed to marrying her before the accident as I posted the banns and already purchased her ring, so we decided not to delay."

"I see," Josie said slowly indicating she was still struggling to grasp what had happened.

"Don't worry, Lady Remington, I don't understand half of it myself. The only thing that makes sense to me is the woman by my side." Michael drew Katrina closer and kissed her hair.

Josie smiled. "Well, we've seen challenges befall our friends before and God work out beautiful things from those tangles. I'm sure He will do likewise for you."

Theo stepped forward after hovering on the edge of the conversation. "Michael, glad to see you sober and happy for a change."

"Michael, this is Lord Harrow, also known as Theodore or Theo. Another member of your merry band of friends."

"Nice to meet you, Lord Harrow," Michael said with all propriety.

Theo stood there momentarily stunned at the reply. "You really have forgotten, haven't you? This is not some kind of practical joke."

Michael frowned. "I wish it were. Attempts to remember only make my head pound more."

Theo looked at Katrina. "Have you consulted with Dr. Miller?"

She shook her head. "We've been a bit busy." A flush of heat rose in her cheeks at this and she averted her gaze.

"I'll send a message to him to see if he can come in the morning." Marcus nodded to Michael. "If that's all right with you, of course."

Michael shrugged. "Couldn't hurt more than it already does. Let him come."

~*~

Conversation at dinner was difficult. Michael couldn't remember any of the events that the others referred to and he didn't even recall ever knowing these people. They were strangers. He felt very much the outsider and it gnawed at him. He wanted to head back to his room to the comfort of Katrina's arms and her soft voice and assurances that he was loved. Beyond that, the world was a blank and he grew increasingly frustrated.

"I will beg you to forgive me the after-dinner drink."

"Michael, please stay for a little, there are some things I don't understand." Marcus smiled as he motioned for the footman to fill Michael's glass.

"It will be fine," Katrina whispered in his ear. "I won't be far away and these are your friends. They care about you. You are safe with them."

Michael nodded to his wife and sank back in his chair, tugging at his cravat to loosen it. He grew warm. His heart rate sped up and it took all of his willpower to stay seated with these two strangers. He trusted Katrina. She wouldn't steer him wrong. He sipped the port and waited as the women left and the door closed. The interrogation would begin.

"Last I saw you, Michael, you were laid out on your furniture drunker than I have ever seen you," Theo started.

"When was that?" Michael asked.

"Two days ago, apparently, the night you said you were kidnapped." Theodore continued. "I asked you to come to a party with me. You refused and rudely told me to mind my own business. You were moaning about Katrina and a broken heart."

"Really?"

Theo nodded.

"Where does your memory start?" Marcus asked as he leaned back in his own chair and swirled his wine in his glass, but kept his gaze on his friend.

"I remember my head pounding and a soft warm pillow. I opened my eyes to see a gorgeous blonde looking down at me. She smelled like vanilla. I thought I knew her."

"A blonde?" Theo and Marcus exchanged glances.

"It was Katrina in a disguise. She took off the wig and, and I felt like I should know her. I couldn't figure out who she was."

"Did you know who kidnapped you?" Marcus asked.

"Some guy called the Black Diamond."

Marcus stared. "Isn't that your father?"

"My father would kidnap me, attempt to torture me by attacking Katrina, and then abandon me?"

"He pretty much did all of that to your mother—at least the last two parts," Theo commented.

"Despicable. Who is he, really?"

"That's just it," Theo said. "We don't know anything other than he is among the aristocracy and is suspected of being in league with Napoleon."

"Who is Napoleon?"

"The Little Emperor of France, and England's enemy." Marcus took a sip of his wine.

"Who am I to him? To any of this?"

"That's what we'd like to know," Marcus said. "You disappear for weeks at a time and then resurface. You have an income, but you never share how you have earned it. You don't talk about what you do to occupy yourself when you are not with us. We know you are not involved with women or gambling. You don't spend your money on material things. You live simply. You gladly help out a friend when in need even at the risk of your own safety. You are an enigma, Michael. The only one who seems to fully understand you is the woman you married."

Michael glanced at the door, longing to be with her. "She's wonderful."

Theo and Marcus grinned.

Michael caught their look. "What? Can't a husband admire and long to be with the woman he loves?"

Marcus laughed. "Go to her, Michael. It's nice to see you so happily in love with your wife. You both deserve that kind of joy after all you've been through."

"The inquisition is over?" Michael started to rise.

"For now," Marcus said with a grin.

Michael made good his escape. He found Katrina and managed to extricate her from Josie who was attempting a similar inquisition with equally frustrating results.

~*~

Marcus, Josie, and Theodore sat in the drawing room having tea and talking.

"I think that tomorrow I will send a notice to the papers announcing Michael and Katrina's marriage." Marcus held Josie's hand lightly between them on the love seat.

"That will fend off any ugly rumors," Theo riposted.

"How soon can we get them back in London? They need to be seen together, in love, and happy," Josie asked.

Theo shook his head. "We need to find out what Dr. Miller says first. It might not be a good idea to be putting Michael in a situation where he doesn't remember anything or anyone. He looked panicked when we wanted to talk to him. I've never seen him in such a state of anxiety before."

Marcus nodded. "Michael has always been calm, collected, and in control. It has to be frightening to know someone is out to kill you but you cannot remember who or why."

"At least he's safe with Katrina, and she would do anything to protect him," Josie said.

"Should be the man protecting the woman," responded Marcus. "He may chafe at his dependence on her after a time."

"True," said Theo. "And she may soon struggle with a man who cannot share with her the memories they have together."

"Let's pray his memory returns. Someone is out to kill our friend and we are at a loss to help him if he cannot give us more of the information that is needed here." Marcus rubbed his jaw with this hand. "I think we need to summon Phillip."

"The more the merrier?" Theo queried.

"Why not?" Josie said as she rose to pull her husband up beside her. "Good night, Theo. I'm going to steal my husband away from you now, but I promise you can spend time with him tomorrow without his wife interfering."

Theo grinned. "Go on, then. I'll be heading up soon too."

~*~

Katrina tried to comfort Michael. He returned to their room only to cast up his accounts. He lay on the bed and moaned in pain. Katrina tried to massage his shoulders but he shoved her away. She fought tears. She had finally won the heart of the man she adored for years, but she didn't have all of him because a large part of who he was continued to be locked away from them both. A fission of fear rippled through her that when he did remember it might not be to her benefit. She was determined to make his memories of their time together now make up for whatever had, on his part, kept him from marrying her before. She did not want him to regret having taken this step. If he rejected her, she didn't know if she could bear it.

She walked into the marriage realizing a change in his memory could jeopardize her happiness, but her desire to have something of Michael, even for a short while, was so strong she'd decided to risk her heart. Now questions as to the wisdom of that assailed her. As her husband pushed her away in his pain and emotional agony at not remembering, she was shut out. Katrina didn't know what to do. She offered him medicine and was declined. He didn't want her touch or words.

She blew out the candles and climbed into bed next to him, trying to not touch him even though everything within her longed for his embrace. How could they have come to this pass so quickly? She almost wished that Marcus and Theo had stayed away longer as it seemed the more Michael was pushed to remember, the less of her he could tolerate. Her pillow was wet as she drifted off to sleep.

~*~

Images swirled through Michael's mind. A tall tree. That tombstone. A woman with a small red leather book in her hands, writing. Laughter. Fishing. Being tossed in the sea and drowning. Someone lunging at him with a knife. Hearing a woman scream in pain and the smell of burning flesh. Trapped and helpless. The images taunted and tortured him mercilessly all while his head pounded a steady rhythm of pain.

He awoke with a cry to find Katrina there, concern etched across her face. His gaze searched hers for comfort and he reached for her. The only safety he knew was found in her arms. Only then could he really rest.

~*~

Dr. Bruce Miller sat down with Marcus in his study after examining his patient.

"Marcus, I will be honest. The head injury has done nothing to diminish Sir Tidley's intelligence and reasoning, but it has definitely impaired his memory."

"Any hope of it returning?"

"It's possible. He could slowly regain memories or it could come back all at once. Either way, it can be emotionally traumatic. If pressed too hard, too fast, it could cause extreme emotional duress. I don't know what any long-term consequences of that could be."

"If he regains his memories of the past, will he lose the ones he is making now?"

"Hard to say, but if there is a discontinuity in the way he is behaving now compared to prior to the incident, it could make things especially difficult when he remembers."

"Sounds like our friend is in for a challenging time."

Bruce nodded. "Hopefully the headaches will decrease. I'll be honest, Marcus, he's a frightened man. Frightened of what he can't remember that lies just beyond his reach. He wants to know but is afraid to at the same time. There is a conflict going on inside of him right now. It might make him volatile."

"Are you saying Michael could be dangerous?"

"If pushed too far, possibly."

"Do you think he would hurt Katrina?"

"Not intentionally. He is genuinely fond of her."

"So…"

"So, what I am trying to tell you is don't force it. Don't push him to do anything beyond what he is comfortable with. Let him rest and heal." Bruce leaned forward, "and pray."

~*~

The days were frustrating for Michael. He found solace in the Bible and enjoyed reading it with Katrina and discussing it with her. They especially enjoyed exploring the Song of Solomon but saved that for their evenings alone. Michael grew restless and struggled against the wall of blocked memories that he couldn't breach. Dr. Miller had told him to relax and not force things. But someone had been out to kill him and Katrina. He needed to know why. If they had tried once, they might try again.

Something was wrong with his wife. He couldn't put his finger on what it was. He struggled every time he saw that diamond brand on her shoulder. Shivers of horror would rumble through him for which he could not explain. When he asked about how it had happened she refused to say, but a sadness filled her eyes and he felt helpless to remove it.

He resented how desperately he needed her. She was his one link to life. To happiness. To any semblance of peace. If she left him for longer than an hour he became adrift at sea. Lost. He would pace and fidget and by the time she would return he would almost be in a rage. He despised himself for the way he would lash out at her.

~*~

"Where were you?" Michael asked as Katrina came in that afternoon.

"I was with Josie, walking in the garden and talking."

"How was I to know that?"

"I told you I needed some fresh air. I always come back. You should be able to trust me."

Michael paced the room with his hand clenched at his sides. "I need you with me. I cannot handle it when you go."

"I can't live like a prisoner, Michael. You may be imprisoned by your memory, but I am not so restrained. I willingly chose to be your wife, but I cannot be your slave."

Michael stopped pacing and glared at her.

Katrina placed her hand over her heart as if doing so would protect her from the venom coming from him. They silently did battle. Katrina's heartbeat accelerated. Everything inside her told her to flee. There was a battle inside Michael she was powerless to help. He needed her and she was suffocating from that. With a big sigh, Katrina walked towards the door.

Michael was there before her, his arm blocking her from opening it.

"Where are you going?" he seethed.

"I think we need a bit of space from each other."

"You weren't listening. You cannot leave me." His other hand came up to rest alongside her throat before tightening.

~*~

Michael saw the fear flash through his wife's eyes. His hand clasped around her neck as he held her against the door. He shook his head. "Lord help me, Katrina. I am so sorry." He dropped his hands, walked to the chair by the window, threw himself into it, and stared blankly outside. "What kind of monster have I become?"

Katrina stifled a sob. "I'm going to the tree." She opened the door and ran down the hallway.

~*~

Katrina reached the tree out of breath. She hugged her arms around herself. When had she ever been afraid of Michael? She loved him. She grieved for the agony he suffered with. She had tried to accommodate him in his fears. She shook her head. Could she possibly continue like this? What would become of their marriage? Would Michael ever be able to relax and start a fresh new life, or would he always be trapped in this fight to remember? Why couldn't they forge a new life together?

Her neck throbbed. She touched the place where he strong hands had been. Pain traveled up to her head as much as it seeped into her heart.

Katrina looked up at the tree, into the large branches filled with leaves, the sun dappling through the foliage. Memories washed over her. She had wrongly thought of Michael as her hero. He helped her down from this very tree when she had broken her leg. But when she had been branded, he'd been tied up. She saw him react in horror when it occurred. Even now she thought she saw revulsion in his eyes when he saw or touched her scar. At the graveyard, it had been Fidget who had saved her. Michael had been too weak from his injury.

He was no longer weak. His strength had returned, but so had a restlessness and a rage she'd never witnessed in all her years of knowing him. But much of that time he had been at war. He'd killed people in battle. Josie told her about how he had helped Marcus fight for her. Beth had mentioned how vital he had been in rescuing Phillip. But now Michael was trapped in his own hell and no one could save him. Not even her. Her love for him wasn't enough. She leaned her head against the rough bark and her hair pulled as it caught on the wood. Her neck experienced sharp pain where he'd almost choked her. She prayed that her husband would find his memory again and be free from the prison he was in.

~*~

Michael waited till the last dinner bell, but Katrina had not returned. He watched her go to the big tree. He wasn't certain but thought she still might be out there. Did he dare go to her?

Entering the drawing room, Michael surveyed the people he had been told were his friends. They had assured him of their concern. Still, a barrier existed between them. Had it always been there? Had he perhaps always kept people at a distance?

"Marcus, Josie, Theo, I need to search for Katrina. She went out earlier and hasn't returned. Start dinner without us."

"Do you need help?" Marcus asked as he started forward, concern etched on his features.

"I don't think so. Thank you." Michael left the room, exited out the front door of the mansion and walked around the house in the cut grass to find his wife.

He came to the large tree and lay a hand on it, feeling the rough bark against his palm. Walking around he saw his wife's slumped form on the ground.

"Katrina?"

Silence.

"Come on, beautiful. Look at me. Speak. Please?" Panic rose inside him.

"Michael?" A male voice called closer to the house. It was Theo. "Is there a problem?"

"Something is wrong. I can't get her to wake up."

"I'll be right there."

Michael knelt, caressing Katrina's cheek. "Come on, beautiful. You can't leave me now. I'm sorry for how awful I was before. You don't deserve a man like me. Maybe that's why I had hesitated to marry you before. I don't know. I will try to be worthy of your love. Just don't leave me."

Michael insisted on carrying his wife to their room and set her down carefully on the counterpane. Soon the doctor was there and Michael was relegated to the corner of the room while Dr. Bruce Miller and Lady Remington hovered around his unconscious wife.

"I'm sorry, Michael, I cannot figure out why she is in this state. There's no evidence of injury other than some bruising on the side of her neck back to her spine. Her pulse is steady. Try getting fluids into her."

Michael flinched at the mention of her bruise. "Thank you, doctor."

Dr. Miller left.

Josie came to stand by Michael and gently laid her hand on his arm. "The bruise?"

"I did that. We had a fight and I lost control and she fled from me." Tears welled up in his eyes. "I don't deserve her. She deserves far better than a shell of a man trapped in the present."

Josie's eyes held warmth and compassion. "Michael, you are both under unusual pressures. She loves you and has for the longest time. Don't let your failures get in the way of building a future together that can be beautiful. God can make this all work out in the end."

"I can't lose her, Josie. I would be lost without her. She is my anchor."

"We all understand that. Now love her and get her well. We will all be praying and helping."

"Thank you, Josie. You show me far more grace than I deserve."

"Isn't that the whole point of grace? Getting what we don't deserve?"

Michael nodded. Josie patted his arm and walked to the door. "I'll have some broth sent up for you to try to spoon into her. Let me know if there is anything else you need." She slipped from the room.

Fidget climbed up on the bed, clicked at Katrina and gave her kisses before snuggling himself around the side of her head.

Michael grinned. "So I am not the only one who needs you, dear wife." He reached over to stroke the ferret's fur as he watched his wife's face, relaxed and peaceful in sleep.

A day passed with no change in Katrina's state of being.

Michael paced. He would reposition her to massage her back. He talked to her and prayed over her and read her Scriptures. Anything to try to get her to wake up. At night, he held her close to him and cried.

~*~

Michael talked, cajoled, read, even sang in his off-key tenor voice. He really shouldn't sing. It made Katrina want to giggle but she couldn't respond. Trapped in darkness and a body that wouldn't wake up. She tried to call out with her heart to her husband. *I'm here! I love you. Yes, I forgive you. I don't want to leave you. Hold me. Touch me. Don't leave me.* The hours when he slept next to her she longed to touch him but she couldn't. She wanted to touch his face and reassure him. But her arms wouldn't respond. What had happened to her? Last she remembered, she'd gone out by the tree after they had fought. Now she was stuck in the dark, helpless, painless, motionless darkness. She wrapped her mind around the promises she heard her husband read from Scripture and his prayers for her recovery. *He does love me. Thank you, Lord, for giving me this man to be my husband.*

~*~

Michael barely ate, and his sleep was fretful. He was tortured with fear and anxiety as his wife lay so still next to him. "Katrina, darling, please wake up and speak to me. I need to hear your voice."

Hazel-gray eyes slowly fluttered open. "Michael." The eyes closed again and she was gone.

"Katrina. Come on, beautiful. Come back to me." He was up on his elbow with one hand alongside her face caressing her cheek.

A slow smile spread across her lips. "I love you." Her eyes opened again and held his gaze.

"Where have you been, sweetheart?"

"Here. Next to you. Where I belong." Her voice was scratchy and soft.

"Can you move?"

He felt her fingers wiggle and her toes. A wide smile spread across his features. He brought her to himself in a bear hug. "Thank you, Lord, for giving me my wife back."

For several days, Katrina was weak and tired easily.

Michael catered to her every need. Within two weeks she was up and taking walks in the garden again with Josie, while Michael hovered nearby.

~*~

"I'm so relieved you recovered, Katrina. We were all worried for you and praying for you."

"Thank you, Josie. I think I understand better how Michael feels now trapped by his mind as I was trapped by my body. I just wish we could move beyond where we are right now."

"What do you mean? Are you not content?"

"No. I love my husband and I appreciate the sanctuary you and Marcus have provided here at Rose Hill. But there is an enemy out there waiting to pounce. And Michael is only living a fraction of the life he used to have. He has no purpose. There is no future or plan for us or a family. We need a life of our own outside of this prison of amnesia. I just wish I understood how to get us there."

"Maybe it's not your role. Seek God for that. He is the One with the key to Michael's memory."

"I pray but am afraid of the answer."

"Afraid of what?"

"Afraid Michael will regret he married me."

"He adores you. How would he regret your marriage? He's never happier than when he is in your presence."

"That's because he needs me right now. With his memory will come his independence, his past, his dreams for the future that may or may not include me."

"He bought you a ring. He posted the banns while away. He proposed before he lost his memory. I think it would be safe to say his future included you. Why would that change?"

"I don't know. I long for his healing, yet I fear

what that might bring as well."

"We pray that God gives you the grace and strength to deal with it and fight for the love of your husband if your fears become reality."

"Thank you, Josie. Maybe someday I will have a marriage like yours."

"And how is our marriage?" Josie asked with one eyebrow arched and a half-smile.

"Happy. You disagree but you serve each other, adore and encourage each other, and you don't live in each other's pockets."

Josie nodded. "Marriage takes work, but it's worth fighting for the love. You and Michael have love and you have God. You could not have a better foundation to build a life together on."

"Thanks, Josie." Katrina looked and saw Michael pacing in the gazebo, awaiting her. "I had better go to him now."

"Go. Enjoy your husband and what you have today. I'll pray for your contentment while you wait."

"Thank you, Josie. You are a true friend." With that, Katrina walked toward her husband who stood watching her hungrily from the gazebo. She smiled in return and realized at least there was one blessing to being married to a man so utterly devoted to her. Passion sizzled between them unabated and it was a delight to explore that. She skipped up the three steps to the white marble building, launched herself into his embrace, and gave herself fully to his kisses. Yes, there may be problems but God provided comfort in the middle of that.

21

Michael woke early and sensed instantly that something was different. He was in his room at Rose Hill. How did he get here? There was an arm around his waist and long brown hair obscuring the face of the woman snuggled up to him. Fear clutched his heart. He was in Marcus's home with a naked woman in his bed? He was in so much trouble.

He carefully eased himself from her embrace and threw on his clothing. He scanned the room. This woman had obviously made herself at home here. She gave a soft whimper as she moved, her face now becoming visible. Mouse. How did Mouse get to be in his bed? What kind of cad was he to sleep with an innocent? He had made it clear to her he would not do that unless they were wed.

They had planned to marry, hadn't they? What happened with that? He couldn't quite remember. He remembered France and longing to be back by her side. He remembered crashing disappointment and a feeling of rejection. Why was he even back at Rose Hill? Hadn't he traveled to London? So many things didn't make sense.

He quietly left the room and sought out the breakfast parlor. No one was there but he was able to get some food and a cup of coffee. He paced by the window looking outside. Late summer? What had been going on here? He inquired of a footman if Lord

Remington was in residence. Upon hearing that he was, he sent a message to him. He set his cup down, walked down the hall to Marcus's study, entered, closed the door, and sat down to wait. Maybe his friend would have some answers.

~*~

Marcus appeared a short time later. "Michael, I got your message. What was so urgent that you needed me this early?" Marcus yawned.

"I'm sorry if I disturbed your rest." Michael glanced at the clock. It was barely seven of the clock. Michael rose and started to pace. "Something isn't making sense to me. I have a confession to make and you will probably want to call me out, but I promise that however this came to be, I will do what is honorable."

Marcus sat down in his chair behind his desk and smiled. "This should be interesting, Michael. What kind of mayhem have you gotten into that you think I might desire to shoot you over?"

"I don't know how it happened, but when I awoke this morning." He looked up at the ceiling and sighed deeply. "Mouse was in bed next to me." Before Marcus could respond Michael rushed on. "I don't remember anything. I never intended to ruin her, Marcus. You must believe me. I read the Bible you gave me." He pulled it out of his coat. "This book even saved my life in France." He stood and threw it down in front of his friend on the desk. "I gave my heart to Christ and longed to follow Him. I don't understand any of this. I would never have done anything to hurt Mouse or her reputation. You need to believe me on that."

Michael awaited Marcus's rage.

Marcus smiled and stood. "You must have regained your memory. This is wonderful news."

"Excuse me? No pistols at dawn?"

Marcus rounded the desk to put his arm around his friend's shoulder. Standing taller than him this was easily done. "No, Michael. You suffered an injury and had lost your memory. Amnesia. You and Katrina married shortly after that. Before I found that out I was ready to put a bullet through you if you had not taken those vows. You already did the honorable thing about two months hence."

Michael broke the embrace of his friend. "I'm married? To Mouse?"

"Up to this point, it seemed to be a state of being that agreed with you. You have been thoroughly enchanted with your bride."

Michael sat down. With elbows on his knees, he leaned forward to put his face in his hands and began to rock. "No. Something is wrong here. This can't be."

Marcus came to sit across from him. "Michael. I've never lied to you, have I?"

Michael shook his head.

"Good. Trust me. You and Katrina were set upon. It was a trap by the Black Diamond. You took a conk on the head and suffered memory loss. You and Katrina ended up here at Rose Hill and because she had been compromised and you loved her, even though you couldn't remember your history together, you married her that day. I came upon you both here a day later and you were blissfully happy."

Michael looked up. "If I loved my wife so much how could I wake today and not remember any of this? Why would I feel such horror and revulsion?"

"My guess is that while you have regained your memory of what happened prior to the attack, you lost the memories of the past two months, which is most unfortunate because I don't know when I have ever seen you so content, but when you are with her."

"I have a difficult time believing you."

"You are a married man. Go to the church and read the ledger. Look at the ring on her finger. Kiss her and see if you still feel that revulsion you spoke of."

Michael nodded his head. "I'll ride to the church right now."

"Michael?" Marcus started. "Be careful. You still have an enemy out there."

"Which is worse, the enemy out there or the enemy of my mind that seems to be keeping me from some deeper truths?" With that Michael strode out of the room and the front door, bespeaking a horse from the stable.

~*~

Michael read the marriage registry in the church with dismay. He married Katrina and had no memory of his wedding day or night. Confused, he rode the horse for over an hour around the Rose Hill estate. He returned to the stable with a horse covered in foam. He stayed to rub down the mare himself, finding the exertion helpful as he tried to puzzle out what happened and how he was to greet the woman who apparently was now his wife.

~*~

Katrina awakened to find the bed empty and her

husband gone. Strange. He rarely ever left her side without telling her. The night before had been wonderful. She felt blessed to find such joy in her husband's arms. She summoned a maid to assist her in her morning ablutions and selected a lemon-yellow walking dress for this late August day. Her hair was styled and put up in a simple chignon that would probably not last for more than a few hours. That never seemed to bother her husband. He delighted in playing with the loose strands of her hair. She smiled as she thought of him. She wondered where he had disappeared to.

She skipped down the stairs to the breakfast parlor and found Marcus and Josie seated there in quiet conversation. Their tone sounded serious.

"I hope I'm not interrupting anything?" Katrina slowed as she entered, hesitating before she helped herself at the buffet table.

"No. Come in, Katrina." Marcus motioned for her to help herself to the food.

Katrina filled her plate and sat across from Josie and to the left of Marcus. "You seemed deep in conversation when I came in..."

"Katrina, I'm afraid we have some disturbing news for you," Josie started.

Katrina heard the tone of voice and laid her fork back down. She glanced from Josie to Marcus. "It's Michael."

They both nodded.

"He regained his memory. Am I right?" Anxiety welled up inside.

"Yes. He awoke me this morning and was greatly disturbed. He remembers prior to your kidnapping, but nothing since. He was shocked to find you in bed with him. He thought I was going to shoot him at dawn for stealing your virtue. He was startled to find you were actually married."

Katrina looked down at her plate of food. Her appetite gone, she shoved the plate away. Glancing up she whispered, "What am I to do now? He's obviously repulsed to find he had me as a wife. It was as I feared it would be."

Marcus lay a hand on her arm. "Katrina, he loves you. He loved you before the accident and after he was not restricted by whatever was keeping him from fully loving you before. You have had two months to see the depths of affection for you untainted by his past. That was real. He just has to fight to get back there."

Katrina gave a shuddering breath. "Where is he now?"

"He rode to the church to check the registry. He's been gone for quite a while. I assume he's been riding around the estate."

Katrina nodded. "So now I wait for him to come to me."

"And we pray," Josie said. Bending their heads, they did just that.

~*~

Katrina wandered into the garden and returned to the tree. The tree that had been the scene of so many significant encounters between her and Michael. A solid strong tree that had withstood the years and storms. Could her love for Michael be sturdy and last like this tree had? Would her children have a legacy of strength and perseverance to climb to new heights from?

She rested a hand on her stomach. Would that she were pregnant. Even if she lost the affection of her husband she'd have a memory of their time in a child who was part of them.

Michael came striding from the stables, across the lawn to where she stood. She leaned her back against the rough bark, biting into her skin. She welcomed the pain.

"What is it with you and this tree? No climbing today, Mouse?"

Katrina flinched at the nickname. Two months of no Mouse and it was back. It stung.

"I'm sure you already realize I regained my memory." Michael's voice was edged with ice. He cleared his throat.

"And lost the ones we made," she whispered.

He nodded. "It is of little importance, really, except that somehow I acquired a wife during that time." He picked up her left hand and his thumb touched the opal ring there. "At least the ring I selected fit." He dropped her arm.

She waited. Michael took a few steps back and ran a hand through his hair. When he looked up his brown eyes were penetrating and held her to the tree. "Why?"

"Why?"

"Why did you marry me?"

"I love you. I've loved you for as long as I can remember."

"Did I want to marry you or did I feel obligated?"

"You wanted it."

"Marcus says I was blissfully happy."

"I had thought we were mostly happy."

"Mostly?"

"You struggled with not having any memories of

our past."

"And you didn't share them with me?"

"Would it have been fair to give you memories that were mine and not yours?"

Michael looked up the tree and shook his head. "Did it occur to you that I might resent being married?"

"It did. You assured me you wouldn't and I desperately wanted to believe that was true. You posted banns and bought a ring. I took a risk and said yes."

"And now?"

"I guess the future of our marriage is up to you, Michael." She swallowed. "I will remove my belongings from your room if you are uncomfortable with me being there."

He stared at her with a frown on his face. "Do as you wish. I'm departing for London within the hour."

"You're leaving?"

"Someone attacked and kidnapped us."

"The Black Diamond."

"Do you want to explain what happened after that and how we escaped with our lives?"

Katrina told him the bare bones of their escape. She left out the kisses and sleeping in the hut together. Michael laughed at Fidget's coming to her defense and did not seem disturbed that she'd been assaulted.

"The journal he was after, Katrina. Have you seen it?"

Katrina nodded and averted her gaze.

"He didn't get it, did he?" Michael asked with an edge of a threat to his voice.

"No. It is in the drawer to the left of the bed. I found it beside you when we were taken and I had hidden it in my bag."

Michael sighed. "Good girl. You have been an invaluable partner. Thank you." He stepped forward and touched her cheek with his finger. He shook his head slightly and walked away.

Katrina hugged her arms around herself and let the tears fall.

~*~

Michael had a fresh mount, a bag with the journal, and a few belongings packed. He pulled up his horse before departing through the gates of the estate and saw Katrina beneath the tree, sitting now. *My wife*. He still wasn't sure what to do about that. He turned the horse and galloped out of the yard.

Michael stopped at his townhouse after he bolted from Rose Hill and Katrina. The house was in tatters. He grabbed a few belongings and went underground, disappearing into the Rookery where many of his contacts were. He needed to discover the identity of the Black Diamond. Only then would he try to figure out what to do with his wife.

He struggled to accept that they had been happily married. That he had slept with her. Not that he hadn't wanted to all along. He used to dream of the day when he would wake up with her by his side. But the reality of doing so without remembering going to bed with her, disconcerted him. Had he hurt her feelings? But what about his? Would she ever begin to understand how unworthy he was to be her husband? What had those two months been like? There was a corner of his mind that remembered and fought against that truth being revealed. The Black Diamond was his goal.

Eliminate that threat and he might consider the possibility of marriage to Katrina.

Except he already was married. He could petition for an annulment. Katrina should be free to marry someone more worthy. He shook his head. Could he imagine anyone else loving her? The thought made him furious.

~*~

Several weeks later, Katrina found herself in a ballroom flanked by Lord and Lady Westcombe on one side and Lord and Lady Remington on the other. She was wearing a gown of the finest silk and tulle that possessed a modest neckline to hide her brand and yet made the most of her curves. Her hair was swept up and anchored with what felt like a thousand hairpins and her face was one of serene aloofness. If anyone amongst the *beau monde* had ought to say against the marriage of Sir Tidley to Lord Remington's cousin, they would be loathe to do so now with the wall of unity they presented. Of Sir Tidley himself, there was no word. No one had seen him at any public event since his bride emerged on the scene.

Other men, however, swarmed around Mrs. Tidley like bees to honey. The Mouse that so easily used to hide in the background was unable to do so anymore. Titled or not, they begged for her favors and sought her to dance.

By the end of the evening, Katrina's feet were sore, her slippers worn, and her toes bruised from being stepped on by young men. She lay her head back against the squabs of the Remington carriage. "I'm exhausted. How many more of these do we need to attend?"

Josie chuckled. "You were the belle of the ball, Katrina, we wouldn't want to wear you out though. Tomorrow night we will be home."

Marcus sat across from the ladies and grinned, his white teeth showing clearly in the dark of the carriage. "You really did shine tonight, Katrina, and have developed quite a bevy of admirers."

"Yes." Katrina's voice was flat. "A lot of admirers." She yawned.

~*~

The next morning Katrina stayed in bed late. She was sore from all the dancing, night after night. She had cried herself to sleep, so lonely by herself after two months of wonderful closeness with Michael. He had not contacted her and no one had heard from him. He had not been at his home either, which had been ransacked.

Katrina sat up quickly and hopped out of bed. *Lord Hughes!* Of course. She needed to see him. He might be able to give her insight into why the Black Diamond was after her husband and maybe, just maybe, she could be valuable to him again. He could help save Michael. She changed into a modest, dark blue walking dress. Sneaking out the back gate was easy and she hired a carriage to take her to Whitehall.

She waited, pacing in the waiting area outside Lord Hughes's office at the Ministry of Defense. When she was admitted, she was enfolded in a warm embrace.

"Katrina!" Lord Hughes stepped back and blushed a little at his faux pas. "Pardon me, Mrs. Tidley, but I'm so pleased to see you well. You positively are glowing. Marriage must agree with you, although why you would choose someone like Michael…" He laughed as he sat down and motioned for her to do likewise.

"Lord Hughes, have you been in contact with my husband?"

The smile disappeared from his face. "Not since he resigned his commission about four months past."

Katrina fidgeted with the strap of her reticule. "Lord Hughes, I was set up and Michael ambushed. We were kidnapped and transported by the Black Diamond's cohorts. Michael suffered amnesia in the process. By some miracle, we escaped but only after the Black Diamond indicated he wanted a journal from Michael's mother. By all rights, we should both be dead now." She took a deep breath and continued. "We escaped and ended up at Rose Hill. We married. Several weeks ago, Michael regained his memory, but lost all recollection of our time together during the past two months. He left and has not been seen since."

Lord Hughes leaned back in his chair. His brow was furrowed and he scowled and shook his head. "If you came here looking to see if he has taken an assignment again, he hasn't."

"I fear for his life, Lord Hughes. Is there any way you can help us?"

"The Black Diamond has eluded us for many years, but it sounds like this battle is now personal and not political. What could his mother's journal have to do with our war with France?"

"I don't know. I read through the journal and there are no names or dates or anything incriminating of anyone amongst the *beau monde*. Miss Tidley did nothing to expose the man if that is what he fears. And with Michael not serving the crown anymore, he shouldn't be perceived as a threat either. There is nothing you can do to help me?"

"My staff is all on assignment. I have no one available who could assist you. Because this is personal, it would be inappropriate for me to do so even though my concern over the disappearance of your husband is great. You might consider going to Bow Street."

Katrina nodded and swallowed hard. "Thank you for your time, Lord Hughes."

Lord Hughes rose as she did and escorted her to the door. "I wish I could help."

Katrina left.

~*~

Katrina walked slowly down the street, opting to forgo the carriage although the walk home was long and she was unaccompanied. She stopped at a small park and plopped herself down on a bench. People passed by walking dogs, and nannies were out with their charges. She lay her hand on her stomach. Over three months since their marriage and she had not had her monthly courses. She tired easily but had no other symptoms. Was it possible she would be with child? How could she do that without a father?

Miss Tidley had done it. If Michael's mother managed to raise a son alone, Katrina could do it too. She had the resources. Her income was sufficient. She would live a humbler life than she did right now, but she would be content. She'd have the title of "Mrs." that Michael's mom lacked. She'd be lonely but comforted by two months of memories to last her a lifetime. She inhaled deeply and smiled. Nodding to herself she rose and walked the rest of the way home.

Entering the front door, she surprised Marcus as he walked across the foyer to his study.

"Katrina? Where have you been?" He stood there much like her father would have. She smiled.

"I've been out searching for my errant husband and I have come to a decision that I wish to discuss with you and Josie."

"I'll have her summoned and we can talk in my study."

"Thank you, Marcus."

Entering the study, she came upon the local newspaper, the *London Times.* The gossip column was laying there open and she spied her name.

A certain Mrs. T, the wife of Sir T, has been seen around town on the arms of various men. But not a sign has been seen of her husband. Has the hen flown the coop? Where is the rooster? And which one of her cisibos is warming her nest at night?

Katrina set the paper down with a thud. "Well, that seals it."

"Seals what?" Josie had entered, followed by her husband.

Katrina turned to her dear friends. "I've come to a decision about my future."

~*~

Katrina packed her belongings and planned for a ride back to Rose Hill. She had told all of her admirers that she was retiring to the country on a repairing lease. She deflected all questions about the whereabouts of her husband and begged off any more invitations to balls and soirees. She looked at the ring on her finger. Deep pain stabbed her heart as she fingered the pale milky stone. She reminded herself. *He loved me.* For two wonderful months. Wonderful for whom? She remembered his frustration and how imprisoned he was by his lack of memory. Now he had his memory and she was the one lost and moorless, her anchor gone. God would be with her. She comforted herself with that.

She entrusted Michael to God's care as well.

Entering the carriage, the next morning, she gave Marcus a peck on the cheek and a hug to Josie. A maid would journey with her. Fidget was in a basket at her feet.

The carriage ride back to Rose Hill was uneventful. Katrina enjoyed the quiet and spent some time reading her Bible. So often she set it down and brushed away a tear as she remembered the moments spent reading it with Michael. She slept in her old room at Rose Hill and arose early the next morning to take a gig over to a smaller Tudor style home with several bedrooms upstairs, all fully furnished from the previous owners.

Katrina walked through the manor, gently touching the furniture and gazing at old photographs of the families that had previously resided there. But now, the house was hers. It was also Michael's, should he choose to exert his rights. Maybe it was a whimsy that made her purchase this home with its particular ghosts. Those were not her ghosts and she feared nothing. But if she was to bring their child into the world it would only make sense that she gave that child a warm home filled with love. Even if only from her.

She selected a room to make her own. She compiled a list of the help she needed and any other items she could ask Josie to purchase for her to send to her new home. She found an old rocking chair in the nursery and sat down. How many babies had been rocked in this very chair? She took out a red leather bound journal and jotted down her first letter to her unborn child.

Hi Little One,

You are not even here yet and I feel compelled to tell you that you were conceived in love and you are a wanted and desired blessing. Your father doesn't know about you, but hopefully, he will soon and be as thrilled as I am at your impending arrival. Grow now and delight my heart with your presence. I love you,

Your Mother

The next day, Katrina moved into her new home with a handful of servants from the local village of Didcot. She began to settle into a routine with her days of rearranging furniture and cleaning the house from top to bottom, taking breaks for naps. She brought furniture out of storage in the attics and put other items away. Fall had come in full force and many nights found her sitting by the fireplace, embroidering, and humming a tune.

Several weeks after she moved in, a letter arrived with a distinctive scrawl. It had been forwarded from the Remington home in London.

Mouse,

Rumors have reached me of your wonton behavior in town. As long as you are my wife, even if in name only, I would appreciate you acting in a more circumspect manner.

Michael

No return address. No news on how to contact

him. But at least her husband was alive. She touched the paper and a tear ran down her cheek. Mouse. During their two months of marriage he had banned the use of that name. He had called her beautiful or Katrina then. She sighed and put the paper away in the desk. He was alive. God could knit her broken family back together again.

~*~

Michael grew irritable. The Black Diamond proved elusive. Michael lived in the slums and his only consolation in all of this was his Bible. He still carried the little book Marcus gave him in his bag, but had a new one with him to read as the bullet had made most of the other book unusable. He carried that close to his heart, almost as an act of superstition. As if God was obligated to protect him again should the need arise. That was not really the case, however, he still drew comfort having that book near him at all times and so he kept it there.

Two months had passed and it was now October. Michael wore a beard and his hair was unfashionably long. He'd been working at the docks in an effort to glean more information. He had developed more muscle. His hands were calloused, and he sported a few more scars from those who dared tangle with him. He doubted his friends would even recognize him now.

One cold October night, he was sitting at the local pub enjoying a pint of brew along with some stew when a rough looking man came to sit down next to him. Michael sized the man up and down, but did not perceive him to be a threat.

"The Cat is no longer playing with the Mouse?" the man said at a voice just above a whisper.

Michael leaned back, took a long drink, and watched the man across from him. "The Cat is history."

"Ah, but the Mouse, she lives and grows larger."

"I know naught of what you speak."

The man nodded and rose to leave.

Michael finished his ale. He slowly meandered to the back of the pub where the man awaited.

"What news have you for me?"

"Bow Street is looking for you."

"Who hired them?"

"Remington."

One eyebrow shot up. Of course, Marcus would search for him. He had abandoned his wife. The thought caused him to cringe.

"And Mouse?"

"Country Mouse grows fat with child."

Michael's eyebrow shot up. So, his wife was pregnant. Did she play fast and loose while in London? He closed his eyes to hide his pain. When they opened again they were clear and cold. He paid his informer and slithered into the night to his hiding place.

~*~

Finally, after months of waiting, his break came. Word filtered to him that he would find the Black Diamond by a warehouse down by the wharf, not too far from where Mouse and he had been held captive. Michael went to survey the area.

22

Katrina shivered in the cold. The journey to London had terrified her. Why had they taken her? Didn't they realize that Michael no longer loved her? If they were using her for bait they would be sorely disappointed. The Black Diamond erred greatly this time. Now she was trapped in a warehouse similar to where she had been branded. She was hungry and cold. She would die here and so would the child in her womb. Locked away in a tiny dark closet, all hope gone, she curled up on the floor praying that death would come soon and that somehow God would protect Michael.

~*~

Michael spied the men. He suspected that a trap had been set for him. He managed to find a way up to a nearby rooftop and crawled silently in the dark night across to where the chasm was between that building and the warehouse. What was stored in there? Contraband to go to France? Smuggled goods? He stretched flat on the roof and listened closely to the men below.

"Sam, I not be likn' this. She's a sweet thing and wit' child. Wat's Diamond goin' do wit her?"

"Tain't no a yous bizness, Walt. We doos wat he

sez and wez get coin."

"I'z know. Grab dis Tidley bloke, scrabble the book, and kill 'em."

"Toss 'im in wit her and torch the place."

"But wat 'bout the book she 'ad on 'er?"

"Yous think that's the one?"

"Shoulda asked."

"Yous go do dat, Walt, but no playin' wit da mice."

"We'z got time 'n she is rather purty."

"Diamond 'ill slit your throat if'n he finds you been messin' wit her."

"Probly wants 'er for 'imself."

"Get the book, Walt."

The man named Walt disappeared into the warehouse, which left only one man visible. So they had Mouse. He experienced a twinge of regret that she was again caught in his troubles. Or did she push herself into them like before? He groaned inwardly as he lay flat and surveyed the area. If he took a run, he could jump to the warehouse, but even so, how would he get in? The night was so quiet with the exception of the waves of the Thames lapping muddy water on the side of the channel. But he was the Cat. He could do this. Pushing himself away from the edge, he stood up and taking a good run, he leapt the span between buildings—just barely making it.

The man below looked up at hearing something. "Probably just an alley cat."

Michael sighed in relief.

The man returned to paring his nails with a knife while he awaited his companion.

~*~

Katrina was surprised when a man entered the room and kicked her in the stomach. She reflexively curled around her baby. The lantern made the man appear sinister.

"Yous got a book? Diamond is lookin' fer one."

"Do you mean Miss Tidley's journal? A red leather bound book?"

The man's face lit up. "Dat be da one. Where is it?"

Maybe it would work to give him her journal. Would the Black Diamond be fooled? She had carried the book around with her as she wrote notes to her baby and prayers for Michael. If she gave it up, perhaps it would save Michael. "It's in the pocket of my cloak." How fortuitous that she brought it with her when she went out walking in the garden yesterday.

The man rifled through her cloak. He was about to try to give her a kiss when a throat cleared behind him. "Best leave her to me and get back to your post."

The tall dark man that was in the doorway was wreathed in shadow, but she recognized the voice. The Black Diamond. As the lackey rose to leave the room, the aristocrat grabbed the book from him and motioned for the lantern to be left. He gave the hireling a backhanded slap on the cheek. "Do what I've promised to pay you for."

"Just tryn to be 'elpful, goven'r." The man scurried into the dark.

"So, Sir Tidley entrusted the journal into your care after all while leading me on a merry chase through the slums of London."

Michael had been in London all this time? The thought pained her more than she expected. She reminded herself that this was not the same Michael she'd married, but a more complex man who had rejected her. She sniffed.

Have courage. Be brave. You can do this. It was as if words from her father's journal, long burned, called to her.

The Black Diamond leaned against the wall where he had hung the lantern on a post and opened the journal to read. He scanned the pages. His eyes narrowed and frowned. He was once again wearing a domino and mask to conceal his identity. He slapped the book shut and deposited it in an inner pocket of his coat. He approached and lifted her to her feet. She barely stood up to his shoulder. His hand clasped her behind her neck. His fist grabbed her long hair and he yanked her neck back. She forced herself to meet his gaze and was paralyzed by the evil she witnessed there.

Yea, though I walk through the valley of the shadow of death, I shall fear no evil for Thou art with me.

The words came unbidden to her mind and she clung to them like a lifeline. She was not alone.

"Where is your husband?"

"I know not."

"You lie." The Black Diamond's gazed raked down her body sending a shiver of fear through her. He sensed it and his mouth curled in a wicked smile.

"Seems like the boy is as virile as his father. Too bad the line has to end here."

"Does it? Have to end?"

"Ah, but my dear. You have proven too valuable to Sir Tidley. You ruined a plan put in motion many years ago. You and my illegitimate son must pay as my losses have been great. Never fear, I will come about in time, however, I cannot allow any further chances of interference."

"Sir Tidley resigned his commission before you took him last time."

"Ah, yes. Our last encounter." His head lowered and he whispered to her, "I believe we have some unfinished business, you and I."

"I'd rather die."

The Black Diamond's eyes flashed. He jerked her head and thrust her away from him. She hit the wall hard and was dazed. "That can be arranged." Grabbing the lantern, he stalked from the room. The door slammed shut behind him and the bolt slid home. She pulled her hood up over her throbbing head and sprawled out on her side. She closed her eyes and silently prayed Michael would escape the trap the Black Diamond had set. She hummed to herself a hymn she had heard that past Sunday in church and prayed for a quick death.

I'm so sorry, baby…

~*~

Michael watched the Black Diamond enter the warehouse and later exit. The man had a red bound journal in his hands. He overheard a man brag about finding it before the aristocrat had joined them.

"Torch the place. I have what I came for." The Black Diamond strode off into the dark. Carriage wheels moved in the distance.

The men below were arguing but eventually went inside the building. Somewhere inside was Mouse. His wife. He wondered how she had come to possess a journal? He'd destroyed it. Did she find another one? Where?

He had a memory of her throwing a similar journal into a fire to save him. He shook that off. There was not time for sentiment. Wife or not, he could not let her be burned alive. He found a ladder off to one side of the building, out of sight, and a cracked window. He slowly broke the glass, trying to be as quiet as possible. He saw nothing inside the warehouse, but heard the men moving around talking to each other. He spied the flash of light. The door opened and closed as flames started spreading across dry straw soaked in oil.

The men scampered away down another alley.

Michael smashed the rest of the glass with no concern for noise. He squeezed into the window and began yelling over the sound of the flames starting to lick up the wooden walls.

"Mouse? Mouse? Where are you?" He hoped she was not unconscious. He ran around until he found a room that was bolted shut. He struggled in the heat of the growing fire to move the bolt. "Mouse? Are you in there?"

What if they had already killed her? With a surge of energy, the bolt moved. He flung the door open and saw her on the ground with her eyes closed. "Mouse? Mouse!" He felt for her pulse. It was there. He shook her and she opened heavy-lidded eyes.

"Michael? I must be having a wonderful dream." Her lids fell shut.

She was cold. Too cold. He struggled to get her to rise and she grinned at him. "I'm tired. Just let me be, Michael. I'm content here."

"You will die. Come on, Mouse. You need to help me." He slapped her face and her eyes went wide with shock. "We need to run. The warehouse is aflame."

Into the inferno they emerged and struggled to find the door. Instead, they ended up by another window. Michael pushed her up and out and followed suit. She lay on the ground coughing, gasping for breath, and held her ankle. He pulled her up.

Katrina shook her head. "No, Michael. You go before he finds you. I cannot run. I can barely feel my feet and I think I twisted my ankle when I fell. I'll only hold you back."

Michael lifted her to her feet, picked her up, and began to move as quickly as he could away from the fire. Through the smell of smoke that covered both of them he still detected vanilla. He inhaled deeply and tramped down the emotions that arose at having her in his arms. Several blocks away he set her down in an alley. Smoke billowed. Michael shielded her with his body as the warehouse exploded. Fragments of wood sailed through the night air, and ashes fell around them.

Lifting his head a few minutes later, he found that there had been no outcry or response to the fire. He listened as he regained his breath. Nothing. He glanced down at the woman laying beneath him. Something stirred in his heart. He shoved the feelings down. There was no time for that now. He needed to get her to safety. He lifted her to her feet again and began to make his way, half-carrying, half-dragging her to where he could finally find a cab.

The hackney he hired stank of vomit and Katrina huddled herself up in the corner. She spoke not a word. He disembarked a block away from the Remington townhouse and carried her through the alley to the garden by the mews into the back of the house. It was about one of the clock in the morning now and he suspected his hosts slept. He crept up the stairs to the room Katrina used to occupy, brought her in there, and set her on the bed.

She looked up at him as he struggled to remove her cloak and pull back the counterpane.

"Your ankle? Still sore?"

She nodded. He removed her half boots and felt her ankle.

"The other one."

He reached for the other ankle and she winced but said nothing. "I think it's just a sprain, Mouse." He removed his hands, gently put her legs under the blankets, and covered her up. He strode over to the fireplace and lit the fire until it was warming the room.

"I'll leave a message for someone to come and tend you in the morning. Rest now."

"Michael?"

"Yes, Mouse?"

"Thank you."

He nodded and left the room. He went to the study, jotted a note to Marcus and left it at the breakfast table for him to find. He slipped out the back-garden gate and disappeared into the dark of the night.

Michael arrived at his own lodging in the Rookery to find his room occupied. He slowly closed the door and reached for the pistol in his coat pocket.

"No need to shoot me, my friend." A candle was lit and the glow revealed that the visitor was none other than Captain Jared Allendale, Marcus's younger brother.

"I'm surprised to find you here."

"Sorry for that, but I obtained something that I believe is yours and wanted to make sure it was returned." Jared pulled out a small red book from his pocket and rose to bring it to Michael.

"How?"

"How did I find you or how did I get this book?" He went back to start the fire in the grate. "Lord Hughes summoned me to locate you as it seems your lovely wife expressed concern for your well-being and begged for help. I've been in town for a month now tracking you. You covered your tracks well and definitely did not make my job easy."

"The book?"

"I followed you this evening and when the man left I was able to filch the book from him before he got to the carriage." Jared shrugged. "It's a gift."

Michael laughed and opened the book. He walked over to the lamp and began to read the page he had thumbed to.

Lord, as the baby moves within me I ask that you would be with his father. Protect and guide Michael. Thank You for the love we shared even if it was for only two short months. I rejoice that You answered our prayers to restore his memory and free him from the prison of amnesia. What a gift for him. Help me to let this child understand how wonderful his father is. Give me the grace to live the life You have given me now as I rest in Your provision and care. Forgive me for my heart that so longs for my husband's love and affection. Fill that void, Lord, and sustain me by Your magnificent grace. Be my comfort in my loneliness and give Michael all that he needs to be happy. I worship and adore only You,

Katrina

Michael sat down on the bed with a thump. This was not his mother's journal. But it was *a* mother's journal. The mother of his child. A woman he'd abandoned just as his father had done. He thumbed through a few more pages and read of the love and affection she continued to hold for him and for the child she carried.

His child. He was to be a father. Marcus told him he had been blissfully happy with his marriage. Why would he run from that? Why, if marriage was so wonderful, had he been unable to remember? Would Mouse even be willing to take him back? His heart started to race and panic took over.

"Michael? You look as though you've seen a ghost. Are you well?" Jared stood by the fire, concern etched on this features.

"I've been such a fool."

"We're men, that seems to be our forte quite often when it comes to women."

"What do you know about my wife, Jared? What have you discovered since you began your investigation?"

"Your wife? Mrs. Katrina Tidley. Lovely woman, but she is my cousin after all so that would make me biased. She is with child, and after a few weeks in London after your defection, she was extremely popular with the men, but chose to instead purchase a small property bordering Rose Hill. She moved in and set up house and has been there ever since. At least until she was abducted two days ago.

"She attends church on Sundays, helps out in the parish by visiting many who are lonely, especially the widows. Her staff adore her. In other words, she has settled down to domestic life and has given up climbing trees or playing at espionage."

Jared sat down by the fire, put his booted feet out in front of him and crossed them at the ankles. His blue eyes held Michael's. Jared had similar rough attire for someone living in the Rookery of London. His blond hair was long and face unshaven.

Michael sighed. "This wasn't even the journal the Black Diamond sought."

"It's not?"

"No."

"Where is the other journal?"

"I destroyed it myself. I burned it to keep warm one night."

"The Black Diamond still seeks it?"

Michael nodded. He held up the book in his hand. "It looked a lot like this one, Jared. And if we are smart, we could dupe him again, only this time to our advantage."

"He is looking for a woman's penmanship."

"We just happen to know a few of those, one of whom I believe we can trust to bury in her words a code for him to break that would lead him on a wild goose chase."

"You are going to ask Katrina to help?"

Michael nodded. "You in?"

"I'll give you one week, Michael. You get me a journal and I'll see it gets into the Black Diamond's hands."

"Do you know who the man is?"

Jared shook his head.

"And even if you did, you wouldn't be telling me, would you?"

"Probably not. I have a job to do. One week, Michael. I will be in contact with you. No need to seek me out. My presence in London is a secret. Marcus cannot be told."

Michael nodded. "I have serious work to do if I'm to get Mouse to agree to help me."

"Do you really not remember your marriage to

her?"

"I wish I did. I heard it was wonderful."

"But you were too afraid to stay and find out?"

Michael turned to glance out the window and avoid the piercing eyes of his cohort. "I'll admit to fear. But I'm not sure of what. What I did was unpardonable."

"Well, use your charm and wit to win her back and get me that journal by next week. I'm off to the Continent again on another assignment."

Michael stood and crossed the room to shake Jared's hand. "Thank you."

Jared rose to leave, but before he did he turned. "You might want to start with a bath and a shave. You've truly adapted to the slums for too long, my good man." With a smile and a wink, Jared disappeared into the night.

Michael returned to his townhouse in the wee hours of the morning and managed to bathe and shave himself. He slept for a few hours in his own comfortable bed, free of bugs, and tried to figure out how he would convince Katrina to cooperate with him.

23

Marcus saw the note on the kitchen table when he came to breakfast.

Mouse is in her usual room. She sprained her ankle. See that she is cared for. Michael.

"Michael was here? Katrina?" He threw the note on the table and was about to quit the room when his wife walked in.

"Marcus? What is it?" Josie asked.

Marcus pointed to the note and waited for his wife. "Michael has been found?"

"I still don't know where he is. However, Katrina is upstairs, injured, and delivered here during the night by her missing husband."

"I thought she was at her country home?"

"She was." Marcus started for the door again, but Josie came up to him and placed her hand on his arm, forestalling him.

"Let me go to her, Marcus. I'll see what I can discover."

Marcus let out a breath of air he didn't realize he held. He nodded and bent over to give his wife a kiss on the cheek. "Thank you, Josie."

She smiled up at him, nodded, and left the room.

~*~

Katrina heard the knock on the door. She rested on

her side, fully clothed, but much warmer than when Michael deposited her there. She dreamt of him again. She marveled at how she still knew him even given his altered appearance. His eyes seemed to speak to her soul in a way she couldn't describe. Her husband was alive and she needed to be content with that. Her hand ran over her protruding stomach and the baby moved. In spite of the roughness of the past two days, their child seemed to fare well. Now if only her ankle didn't throb.

Josie came sailing into the room. "Katrina, Michael left a cryptic note apprising us of your arrival and I must say I am quite curious as to what has happened to bring you to our home in the middle of the night." Josie sat down on the side of the bed and Katrina winced. Josie jumped up. "Oh, I am so sorry. You hurt your ankle and how quickly I forgot. The doctor has been summoned and will arrive here shortly." Josie went to pull up a chair next to the bed. "I did request a breakfast for you."

Katrina smiled. It was so much like Marcus and Josie to swoop in to make one comfortable and take control when life became chaotic. "Thank you, Josie. I'm sorry for the imposition. I had not planned a trip to London. My arrival was entirely against my will."

"Did Michael bring you?"

"Michael rescued me and brought me here." Katrina's eyes were pools of water. Her glasses had been smashed in the carriage when she had been taken and now the world was even blurrier than before. Katrina rubbed her eye.

"Thank God he is alive."

"I have been thanking God for that. And fighting off my anger that I thought I was over his abandonment of me and his child."

"He knows you are with child?"

"He carried me up here. How could he not?" She rested her hand on her stomach.

"Well. We will pray he returns to you now. You will take him back, won't you?"

"He's not the Michael I married, and he's not the Michael from before his accident. I don't know this man, but I'm still married to him."

"God can do the impossible for you both. Don't fret, Katrina." Josie patted Katrina's shoulder and rose to leave. "I will let Marcus interrogate you further later. Rest for now."

"Josie?"

"Yes?"

"I smell like smoke. I need a bath and then to go home. Today. Please?"

~*~

"No. I will not allow it," Marcus said in a quiet voice.

"You won't allow it? May I remind you that you are not Katrina's husband or father? If she wants to return to Hart Manor now, we should assist her." Josie came around Marcus's desk and stood by his side, forcing him to look up from where he sat.

"I am her next of kin."

"And she is a grown woman and able to make her own decisions."

Marcus sighed. "Fine. Once the doctor has tended her ankle we will send her on her way home. But with a full complement of armed footmen."

"Surely the Black Diamond will not be after her

anymore? From what she told me, he probably assumes her dead. She should be safe enough."

"Regardless, I will arrange for extra protection out at her estate," Marcus insisted.

Josie leaned forward to give her husband a kiss. "I always knew you were the best of men."

Marcus smiled and pulled his wife into his lap for a passionate embrace before setting her aside and rising.

"That's it?" Josie pouted.

"I thought I was supposed to summon a carriage and arrange for horses and guards to leave as quickly as possible?"

Josie smiled. "Well then, we will finish this later." With a sly smile, she twirled out the door to go tend her guest.

~*~

Michael procured a blank book like the one Katrina had written in. He labored for a few hours over what information to bury in the journal and what kind of coding could be used. It was late afternoon before he presented himself at the front door of the Remington townhouse.

Shown into the study, he waited a short time before Marcus came in to greet him, locking the door behind him.

Michael raised one brow.

"I'm assuming that given your disappearance for months and your clandestine activities of the previous night, that the conversation we are about to have is private." Marcus motioned for Michael to be seated.

"Are you sure you don't want to scold me for

abandoning your cousin?"

"Your words, not mine. No. I will leave you in God's hands. What goes on between Katrina and yourself in your marriage is your business and I have no right to interfere."

"Even though you're angry with me?"

"Would you feel better if we pummeled each other at Gentleman Jackson's? Or do you prefer to dance with the swords?" Marcus's words were laced with an edge of ice.

"If it would break down the barrier that lies between us? Yes."

"Michael. Where have you been? We searched everywhere. We were afraid for you."

"Thank you for your concern, but as you can tell, I am well."

"You appear ten years older than you did during the summer on your honeymoon."

"Ah, yes. Always promoting the wonders of marriage." Michael sighed deeply. "Speaking of which, I would like to see Mouse."

"I'm sorry, that will not be possible."

"You said you would not interfere in our marriage."

"I meant it. I won't interfere. Your wife left late this morning for home."

"But she couldn't walk. Surely she needed to rest."

"Apparently, she desired to do so from the comforts of her home. I took it upon myself to have armed guards protecting her on the journey."

Michael tipped his head back. He'd lose two days out of the six remaining, just on travel. He prayed he wouldn't need too much time getting Mouse to agree to help. He stood up. "Thank you, Marcus, you are a good friend. I must depart from town without delay. It is imperative I see Mouse at once." He started for the door.

"You cannot bring yourself to calling her your wife even once? During your two months together you forbade anyone to call her Mouse. Katrina is right. You are a different man than you were before the accident and after you lost your memory. I'm sorry to say that I'm not sure I like the change. Have a safe journey."

Thus dismissed, Michael strode out the door without another word. Upon arriving home, he threw together a bag of clothes and changed into riding attire. Mounting his horse, he headed for the home his wife purchased. He racked his brain as to what estate that would be but came up empty.

Wife. She was his wife. He read the registry. She wore his ring. She carried his child. Why would he even think that she would sleep with anyone other than him? She had always been so pure and devoted to him. Why would he doubt her now? Why would he question her motives in marrying him just because he couldn't remember such a significant event? Was that her fault? No. Then why was he punishing her?

He felt robbed. He was angry with himself and his fickle mind. He wanted to remember nights of pleasure in his wife's arms. He was afraid to touch her now. Would he be the same lover she had known? He laughed at himself as night fell. He was jealous of himself, the part of him that knew Katrina in a biblical sense when he didn't. He was jealous that he had two months of freedom from the past, and only delight in the present with a wife devoted to him. And he recalled none of it.

He arrived at Didcot in the early morning hours

and bespoke a room at the inn where he rested and shaved so that he could present to his wife an impeccable husband instead of the disreputable one she last met.

Michael followed the directions Marcus gave him. He grew puzzled. Surely she hadn't purchased…

He rode his horse down a familiar lane. Bittersweet was climbing a trellis on the south side of the house and was in full bloom with reds, yellows, and oranges. He remembered his mother making wreaths out of the branches to hang on the front door, or on the doors of neighbors. He left his horse at the stable, a modest building, and came to the front door where, just like when he was a child, a bittersweet wreath hung. He knocked and was greeted by a middle-aged man dressed appropriately as a servant should be. Michael handed the man his card and asked to see the mistress of the establishment.

The servant looked at the card and back at Michael. "Sir Tidley, welcome back. Let me show you to your room so you can refresh yourself after your journey while I fetch the lady of the house." The servant bowed and Michael clasped his shoulder before he could depart.

"My good man, I slept in the inn last night to avoid upsetting the household at a late hour. I am adequately refreshed and would like to await your mistress in the drawing room if possible."

The man's mouth dropped open and then shut. "Yes, sir. It shall be as you wish." He led Michael across the foyer to wait.

The house appeared much the same as it did when Michael lived there as a child. There were mild changes but they were all for the better. Rooms were brighter and more welcoming. He was left by himself in the drawing room and he came to stand in front of the fireplace where a low fire was in the grate. He stirred the embers to warm the space. Glancing up he noticed the painting that hung there and it took his breath away. It was a painting of a young woman and a child of about eight years of the age. The woman had sad eyes but her affection for her son was visible in the way the artist portrayed them both. Michael remembered sitting for the picture and how tedious it had been. He wasn't sure he'd ever even seen it. Had his Grandfather hidden it in the attic? He hadn't bothered to search there when the house was sold. Since he was not a legitimate heir, the estate had been sold instead of passed down.

"Your mother was beautiful, Michael. She obviously loved you very much." Katrina hobbled in with a makeshift crutch and sat in the nearest chair.

Michael continued to look at the picture before turning to glance at Mouse. No. Katrina. He stared at her with her hair put up on a loose braid and her characteristic strands coming loose. Hazel eyes glanced at him and then down at her fingers.

"You are well, ma'am?"

Katrina gave a short smile and glanced up. "Please be seated, Michael. We need not stand on ceremony with each other. We are old friends."

"Friends. Are we, Mouse?" He noticed the shudder run through her.

"We were at one time." She motioned to a chair near him.

"Last I heard we were more than 'friends.'" He sat, holding his hat in his hands.

A dreamy look came over her face. She peered at

him. What he saw in her eyes rocked him and would have knocked him over if he had been standing. "We were much more than friends for a time, Michael."

Lord, have mercy. She loves me still.

Michael cleared his throat. "I came to beg a favor of you."

"A favor?" Her eyes widened in surprise. They sparkled gray with tinges of green on this fine morning, reflecting the emerald green of her gown.

"Yes, a favor. One last bit of work with the War Office, if you will."

"Lord Hughes sent you?"

"Not exactly. But someone who works with him. I only have five days to have this back in London."

"Five days? What is it exactly that you require, Michael?"

"Remember how we broke the code with your father's journal?"

Katrina nodded.

"This time I need you to write a journal with code imbedded in it." He pulled out the two journals he had carried in his coat. "And I wanted to return yours to you." He handed her the small book and she took it in her hands.

Katrina opened the book and glanced at a few of the pages. "How?"

"A friend retrieved it. But we need to give a replacement, a falsified one. If it is to look like the one my mother wrote, it needs to be written by a woman. I thought you would be the only one I could trust with the task."

"You want me to fill a journal, similar to your mother's, and embed code in it and have it done in four days for you to take back to London? You ask too much of me, sir!"

Michael stood, took two steps towards her and dropped to his knees. "I know I do, especially after the way I've treated you. But if not for me, will you do it for our country?"

She sighed. "I will do it for our country, Michael. But will also do it for you." She glanced at the blank journal he presented to her. "Do you have the messages to be embedded in the code?"

Michael pulled a sealed envelope out of his pocket and handed it to her. "This must be protected at all costs."

She took the envelope. "And what of you? Where will you be as I labor at this?"

"Wherever you want me. I can stay at Rose Hill and visit. I will be glad to assist in any way you desire."

"Michael. As my lawful husband, this is your home as well as mine. You are welcome to take up residence here as long as you wish. The master bedroom is ready for your occupation."

Michael felt as if he had been punched. She not only was willing to accomplish this mission but also let him into her home. The home that he grew up in.

Michael rose. "Thank you. It would be most convenient to be able to be here to assist you in this task. We worked well together in the past."

"Yes, we have." Her voice was soft.

"Why did your purchase my childhood home?"

"You grew up here. I needed a place to live and raise our child. It was available and close to people I have known all my life. I wanted our son or daughter to have roots and the security of a warm and loving home to grow up in."

"Even if you didn't have a husband to share it with?"

"Your mother didn't do too badly with you and I at least have the benefit of your name. Our child will be legitimate."

Michael glanced at her rounded stomach. "How long have you known?"

"I suspected it before you regained your memory and was waiting to be certain before telling you. Before I could do so, you disappeared."

Michael hung his head. "I have much to atone for."

"Perhaps. We can start over if that is what you want, but I will not force you to be married if you do not wish it." She rose and held on to the books in one hand while reaching for her crutch. "But for now, we have a job to be done. We'd best not waste any more time." She hobbled out of the room and down the hall with Michael following. She issued some directives to her staff for food and tea to be brought.

Once in her study, she sat down behind a desk and motioned for Michael to bring another chair. He did, and side by side, they settled down to work.

~*~

Within a short frame of time, Katrina's hand cramped. She put her quill away and covered the ink pot. She leaned back in her chair and closed her eyes. Emotionally she was wound tight and it took everything within her to not beg Michael to stay and love her and their baby. It needed to be his choice. She fought back the tears and reached up to rub her neck.

Michael had been careful not to touch her while

they worked but she longed to throw herself into his arms as she inhaled his distinctive scent of man and horse. She would discuss what to write with him and loved to hear his voice and watch his smile. Oh, how she had missed him!

"I'm sorry, Michael. I need to take a break."

"I'm the one who should be apologizing. I was so wrapped up in our task that I neglected to realize how hard this was on you." Michael stood and came behind her chair and reached down to lay his hands on her shoulders. "May I?"

Yes! Yes! Oh, please just hold me! She wanted to tell him but instead, she stiffened. "No, thank you, Michael." She rose to stand. "If you don't mind I think I'll go rest in my room for a short time. If you want to bring your stuff from the inn, you can. I already took the liberty of moving your personal effects from Rose Hill to prepare your room for you."

She grabbed for her crutch and stepped away from Michael.

"I could carry you to your room if you would like," Michael offered.

"That won't be necessary, but I appreciate the offer. I'll send word to you when I am ready to begin again." She opened a drawer on the desk, placed the code and journal in there, locked it and pocketed the key. "Until later."

"Until later."

~*~

Michael finally realized why the smell of vanilla aroused such emotion in him. His mother often used that scent. He was transported into a different world as he worked alongside Katrina. He didn't think he would ever tire of her hair escaping its pins or her smile and the beauty of her face. Her intelligence was a delight as well. She was willing to engage and offer suggestions that were often improvements on his own initial jottings. He longed to touch her and when she started rubbing her neck he thought maybe just a little massage there would be his chance.

He experienced a thrill as he laid his hands on her shoulders and extreme disappointment when she refused him. What did he expect? Yes, he could claim the rights of a husband but he had already wounded her enough. He would need to woo her back slowly. He wanted her to come to him willingly. That would take time. He only had four more days. Once this project was done he had no excuse to be in this house, to interact with her, to see her.

He donned his coat and hat in frustration and rode to the inn to collect his belongings. He was not about to turn down the offer of staying under the same roof as her.

Returning to the house he was shown to the master bedroom. Even after his grandfather passed away he only once dared to enter this room. It had been dark and foreboding to him even as a young adult. He did not look forward to being here but if that's where Katrina wanted him, he would survive. He'd slept in much worse quarters. When the door to the sitting room was opened, he was pleasantly surprised. The old wallpaper was gone and fresh paper adorned the walls in his favorite color of green with hints of blue and gold. The furniture was different. It had been in his old room. The four-poster bed boasted fresh curtains and counterpane and was a bright spot in the room. The carpets were new and plush. Everything in the room appealed to his senses in a way that brought him peace and comfort he had been missing for so long. Katrina had done this. For him.

He walked to the dresser and touched briefly the effects that had often been left at Marcus's abode. He found the box that originally carried the wedding ring he had purchased, along with the note he had written for the jeweler. What a fool he had been these past months. Tracking a man when he could have been setting up house with a woman who loved him. He'd even questioned her faithfulness! He cringed at the fact that he only wrote her one note and that was to take her to task for shining like the gem she was amongst the diamonds of the *ton*. Why would he have wanted any less for her?

He flung himself on the bed face down. The mattress must be new. He would be loathe to leave this bed in the morning. Pushing up, he explored the closet and found all his belongings just as he wanted them.

There was a knock on the door and Michael went to open it. There stood a young man, a little taller than Michael, fastidiously dressed in servant's attire.

"Sir Tidley, the mistress has asked me to serve as your valet while you are in residence, if it would please you. I am good with cravats and pressing clothing and shining shoes. I promise to do my best, sir, if you would only give me a chance." The young man blushed to have spoken so boldly to the lord of the manor.

"I would be honored to have you assist me." Michael motioned for him to enter the room. "What did you say your name was?"

"Pennington, sir."

"Pennington, I have a bag of clothes I brought with me from London that needs to be pressed and hung. Could you attend to that?"

"As you wish, sir." The new valet gave a toothy grin and set about his work with calm efficiency.

Michael left the room, headed down the stairs, and out to the gardens. Even that had been transformed back to the way his mother once arranged it. He found a rose blooming and inhaled deeply of the scent. He wandered around unil he found a large tree. Funny, he didn't remember it being that big when he was a child. He glanced up at it and smiled. In a few years, he might be climbing up that tree to rescue a son or daughter if any of them took after their mother.

A flash of a scene came to his mind, of Katrina collapsed beneath the tree and not responding to him. He felt panic, and then saw her laying lifeless on a bed. He stepped away from the tree to try to break the spell. Was it a memory or premonition? His head began to throb and realizing he hadn't eaten much, he went to see if food had been set out for the noon meal.

He found the food on the buffet in the breakfast parlour. The room had a warm welcoming atmosphere. While she had kept some of the items that had been there when he was in residence, it felt more like home. This was his childhood house, but it was nothing like the cold, stiff place he remembered. It was better. Somehow, Katrina made it a home. He wasn't quite sure if it was the way she decorated or if it was the woman herself. But for the first time in his life he felt like he belonged here.

He sat down to eat and was finishing up when a servant came to inform him that Mrs. Tidley was awaiting him in the study. He rose from the table and set off to find his wife.

He stopped. His *wife*. He grinned as hope bloomed.

24

Katrina pushed herself hard for several hours. It was difficult work as her lower back ached from carrying the child, and her shoulders, neck, and hand hurt from bending over to write. She almost relished the pain as it distracted her from other sensations that arose from being seated next to her husband. Or the man who was her husband, just not right now. With the time limit set, there was no opportunity for discussion and she wasn't ready to talk about what would be next for their marriage until they finished the book and it had been safely delivered. They broke for a short time before supper and then worked after the evening meal, on into the night.

Katrina could stifle her yawns no longer. "I'm sorry, Michael, but we need to end for tonight. I cannot do anymore."

"We can return to this in the morning. We are making far greater progress than I had anticipated."

Katrina locked up the papers and book. She rose to grab her crutch and hobble off to her room. "Good night, Michael. I pray you sleep well."

"And you too, Mouse."

Katrina stopped and stared. Her heart sank at the sound of that name. "Thank you." Katrina made her way to her room, shut the door, leaned her head against it, and turned the key in the lock. She already knew that the door adjoining their rooms was locked.

She wasn't ready to have her heart broken again, but feared she was too far gone to avoid that fate.

~*~

Morning brought frost to the windows and a cold biting wind from the north. Katrina shivered as she prepared for the day with the help of her maid. She ate in her room and chose to wear a simpler gown of dark blue. It wasn't the gray or brown of her days as a lady companion, but in style, it was of the same simplicity and as modest. She had her hair braided tighter. Her only jewelry was her wedding ring. She hobbled down the stairs with care, struggling with her balance with her stomach protruding. She managed to make it to her study before Michael made his appearance. She settled behind the desk, hoping that somehow, her stomach would be hidden.

She rubbed her tummy and the baby moved. "Hello, little one. Have you enjoyed hearing your daddy? It is nice to have him home, isn't it?"

~*~

Michael walked into the room with his normal cat stealth and was arrested by the image of his wife caressing her swollen abdomen. His heart swelled. He cleared his throat.

She glanced up and dropped her hand. She readjusted her chair and motioned for him to come in. "I'm ready to begin. Are you?"

"Yes." He came to sit next to her and experienced peace just inhaling her scent. He gazed at her dress that covered more skin but also revealed more generous curves than he remembered. Or was he exaggerating because of his abstinence all these months? He trampled down the questions and urges that kept wanting to rise to the surface and forced himself to focus on the task at hand.

At about ten of the clock, there was a rap on the door. A footman announced that Dr. Miller had come for his appointment with Mrs. Tidley.

"I forgot." Katrina shoved the papers in the drawer and locked it. "I guess we will take a break for a short time. We can return to this after lunch." Grabbing her crutch, she hobbled to the door and made her way upstairs to meet with the doctor.

~*~

Michael waited in the hallway, much to the consternation of the footman assigned to the front door. When Dr. Miller descended the stairs, Michael motioned for him into the study and locked the door behind him.

"How fares my wife, Bruce?"

Dr. Miller considered Michael with a furrowed brow. "Why do you want to know?"

"I am her husband. Doesn't that give me enough reason?"

Bruce frowned and he took a deep breath. "I'm concerned about your wife's health with this pregnancy."

"Why? What is wrong?" Michael stood up straighter now.

"She's been lightheaded and isn't eating enough. Now with her on the crutch with her ankle, I'm not happy with her taking the stairs. If she were to black out..."

"Has she passed out before?"

"Only once, but since we never did figure out why she had been unconscious beneath that tree, I'm perhaps more vigilant."

"What are you talking about? Unconscious? That makes no sense."

Dr. Miller rocked back on his heels. "You don't remember. You had amnesia at the time. And you have it still, only now for the period when you lost your past." He took a deep sigh. "Your wife requires rest. She needs someone to watch over her and pamper her."

"Are you taking me to task as her husband?" Michael's voice held an edge.

"No. But if you are not going to be a husband to her you should let her go. She's a treasure and surely someone will be more than happy to fulfill that role."

"Like you, Dr. Miller?"

"Mrs. Tidley is an attractive and winsome woman. Any man would be insane to pass up a treasure like her."

Michael sized up the doctor. He clenched and released his fist repeatedly. "I could call you out for that."

"But you won't, because you know I speak the truth. Take care of your wife, Michael. She needs you."

Michael nodded and went to unlock the door. Not another word was shared between the men.

~*~

Michael watched Katrina bend over the journal to write the latest entry. Maybe two more to go before the book was filled and ready to be delivered. Katrina had dark shadows under her eyes. Her cheekbones were more pronounced. He looked at her hands as she wrote and they seemed thinner than he remembered. Her ring was loose. She yawned and leaned back in her chair.

"Mouse?"

"Hmmm?"

"Would you like to end now? We are close. We could finish in the morning."

"No. Let's push through and get this done." She sighed and pulled herself back to the desk. "Now, that last bit of code, how about I write it something like this…"

~*~

It was close to midnight when they finally finished and Katrina could barely keep her eyes open. She handed the completed journal to Michael after he had burned their notes in the fireplace.

"You will head to London in the morning?" She moved to sit on the loveseat with her feet out in front of her, little blue slippers peeking out and her ankles exposed.

Michael swallowed as he gazed at his lovely wife. His wife. *The task. Remember the mission.* "I will depart early."

She leaned her head back and closed her eyes. Her neck was long and thin and he longed to press kisses there.

"Will I be welcome back here when my mission is complete?"

Her eyes shot open. "This is your home, Michael."

"No, this is a house. A lovely house, I will grant you. My home is with you. Am I welcome back home?"

Katrina struggled to rise.

Michael rushed to her side. "Allow me." She stopped moving and gazed up at him. She broke eye contact but allowed him to assist her to her feet. "Let me walk you to your room."

"I'm sure I can manage on my own." She yawned and attempted to cover it up but failed.

"Humor me."

Katrina grabbed for her cane but only to carry as Michael put his arm around her and supported her up the stairs to the door of her room. He noted that it was the suite adjoining his own. He released her but brought his hand up to her face. "You are so beautiful." He turned to leave.

~*~

Katrina watched him walk away. She had been certain he would kiss her. She wished he would. But tomorrow he'd leave, taking her heart with him. And when would he return? Ever? She yawned and entered her room. Exhaustion plagued her.

~*~

Michael rode hard the next day. Arriving in town late that night he let himself into his townhouse and up the stairs to his bedroom. He had a day to spare but hoped Jared would find him early. He was eager to return to Hart Manor to pursue his wife. He collapsed into bed without even starting the fire in the grate in spite of the cold.

He awoke to the sound of flames crackling, in the middle of the night. He was startled as it initially reminded him of rescuing Katrina from the fire. He sat bolt upright and scanned the room. A dark figure loomed by the fireplace. Michael reached under his pillow for the knife he kept there.

"Hold your fire," the voice in the darkness called out and hands were held up in surrender.

"Jared?"

"Do you have the book?"

Michael threw back the covers, withdrew the book and handed it to Jared. "She worked hard."

"She fares well?"

"As well as she can be given her low-life husband."

"Redemption is worth pursuing."

Michael nodded. "Just pray that my attempt is well-received."

Jared came and put a hand on Michael's shoulder. "I will definitely be praying for you both." He lifted up the red book and made for the door. "I have a delivery to make and then I'm off to France. You haven't seen me."

"Godspeed, Jared."

Michael was wide awake after Jared left, but his horse would not be ready to depart so soon. He paced his room, prayed, and sat to open his Bible. He noticed that pages were turned down for one book and he began to read.

There, in those pages, he found his memory.

~*~

Hope soared in him as he rode back to Hart Manor. He felt complete and whole as never before. He made it to the house by midafternoon. His horse was lathered, but he let the stable hand take care of him as he ran for the front door. Without knocking, he opened it up and ran inside the foyer.

"Katrina! Where are you? Katrina!"

"I'm here, Michael." Katrina stood by the drawing room door wearing a yellow woolen gown and a blue shawl. Her hair was falling out of its pins and her eyes appeared red.

"Beautiful!" He came to her and dragged her back to the room kicking the door closed behind him. He picked her up and kissed her soundly. Her arms wrapped around his neck and she returned the kiss before pushing him away. Her face was flushed and her lips swollen, her eyes filled with confusion.

"I remembered, Katrina." He pulled out his Bible and opened to the Song of Songs, Solomon. "I am my beloved's and my beloved is mine." He fell to his knees and placed his hands on her abdomen and kissed her stomach. "Our love made this baby. I'm going to be a father. Katrina, I do not deserve you. Please forgive me. Take me back. I need you as much now as I did when I couldn't remember my past. I need you to complete my future."

Katrina hobbled backwards and fell into a chair. Sobs overtook her and she leaned forward covering her face with her hands. Michael was before her, still on his knees, and enfolding her in his strong arms.

"Sweetheart. I adore you. I'm so sorry for the way I've treated you. For the way I abandoned you and our child. I can't blame you if you are not ready to forgive me, but please, give me a chance to earn the right to be your husband again. I missed you."

Katrina dropped her hands from her face. She dried them on her skirt and brought them up to Michael's. She gazed into his eyes and he saw the love reflected there. She spoke no words but leaned forward to kiss him gently. She pushed him back on his heels and rose to stand. She held out her hand to him and drew him to his feet. Without speaking a word, she reached into her pocket and drew out a key. She placed it in his hand.

"What?"

"The door that separates us at night. I never kept it locked to keep you out. I kept it locked to keep me from seeking *your* bed. I love you, Sir Michael Tidley."

"I don't deserve you, Mrs. Katrina Tidley, but I'm definitely glad God saw fit to give me a treasure for my bride."

With that, he swept her up into his arms and headed for the stairs.

~*~

The next morning Michael awoke to find his wife—his *wife*—snuggled up next to him. He brushed her hair away from her face and placed a kiss on her hair. She stirred and a soft smile played on her lips.

"Morning, beautiful," he whispered.

She tilted her head up to him with eyes open and a smile. "Good morning, Michael. I'm so glad you are here, where you really belong."

"Me, too. I was thinking…how about we enjoy a picnic today. There's a tree in the yard that would be a great spot."

Katrina smiled. "I'd like that very much. But it is

too cold out for that now. How about we picnic inside near where the tree is instead."

"That'll work." He hugged her close. "Thanks for waiting for me to regain my memory."

"Oh, Michael, I've been waiting years for you to figure out that we were meant to be together."

His lips met hers for a sweet kiss. "I don't deserve you."

"I know, but you're stuck with me anyway." She winked and kissed him again.

He allowed himself to get lost in the wonder of the love of this woman. A woman who had hid herself from him, rescued him time and again, and gave him a reason to live. God had given him a second chance to have her in his life.

They managed to emerge from their chambers in time for their picnic.

Epilogue

The Black Diamond scanned the book before him. It had disappeared but now it was back. Several of his minions had lost their lives over that. While he'd killed his son's wife, the Cat continued to elude his grasp. He would read it to discover if the boy's mother had exposed him.

"My lord, a message has arrived for you." His valet approached and waited.

He opened the letter.

Your daughter-in-law and grandson departed during the night.

Growling he crumpled it up and tossed it into the fire. His daughter-in-law, Valeria, was gone? With Dartanian, his heir? What was the woman about? Did she think she could escape him?

"We leave in the morning. Pack my bags."

"Yes, my lord."

As the servant departed, the Black Diamond paced. Women were the bane of his existence. A necessary evil to be used only to further his cause. This was one woman who would not be so fortunate in her escape from him. He grinned, imagining the screams of terror of Michael's bride as the fire engulfed her. He'd taken care of her and the baby, snuffing out that line. No. His heir would be legitimate and while his true son had died, the weakling lacked the mettle for this kind of work. He'd do better with his grandson and raise the child to take over his rule when the time came. When he found Valeria—well, she'd regret the day she ever crossed him. She'd denied him a spare and he'd make sure she gave him one—or else.

He grinned as he stared into the dancing flames of the fire. He served a master who allowed him all his heart desired. As for Michael? The boy's end would come in time.

In the meantime, as future Emperor of England, he would enjoy the delights his power granted him. His daughter-in-law wouldn't, but she'd have no choice in the matter and was expendable. She would pay for crossing him. He'd find her.

Acknowledgments

It would be impossible to thank everyone who has helped me on my journey, so I apologize in advance for those I will miss. It doesn't mean you are any less valuable and thankfully, God keeps better track of those things than I do and His "well done, good and faithful servant" has more merit than any thanks written here.

So here it goes. Special thanks to:

Elizabeth Herman – you amaze me. Thanks for all the ways you've invested in me.

Doris Pollard Wichern – another early reader and one of my most faithful cheerleaders in this writing adventure. You will be missed.

Lisa Lickel – thanks for being such a wonderful mentor, friend and shoulder to cry on when the publishing process throws me those curve balls. I don't think I would have ever taken that first step in this journey to publication without your gentle push.

David Mundt and Ken Nabi – for your support and believing in me and the calling God has on my life.

Sally Shupe – my faithful editor. Thank you for finding all those silly errors!

Nicola Martinez – my beloved Editor-in-Chief, who continually supports my writing while allowing me the joy of helping others on their journey to publication. I'm grateful for our partnership and friendship.

Biography

Susan M. Baganz chases after three Hobbits, and is a native of Wisconsin. Susan writes adventurous historical and contemporary romances with a biblical world-view.

This book is the third full-length novel in the Rose Hill Romance series. *The Baron's Blunder,* Henrietta's story, is a novella and prequel. Previous stand-alone novels include: *The Virtuous Viscount* and *Lord Phillip's Folly*. Future novels are: *Lord Harrow's Heart* and *The Captain's Conquest*.

Susan speaks, teaches, and encourages others to follow God in being all He has created them to be. With her seminary degree in counseling psychology, a background in the field of mental health, and years serving in church ministry, she understands the complexities and pain of life as well as its craziness. She serves behind-the-scenes in various capacities at her church and is a member of American Christian Fiction Writers (ACFW), and serves on the board of the southeast chapter. Her favorite pastimes are lazy…snuggling with her dog while reading a good book or sitting with a friend chatting over a cup of spiced chai latte.

You can learn more by following her blog www.susanbaganz.com, Twitter feed @susanbaganz or fan page, www.facebook.com/susanmbaganz

Thank you

We appreciate you reading this Prism title. For other Christian fiction and clean-and-wholesome stories, please visit our on-line bookstore at www.prismbookgroup.com.

For questions or more information, contact us at customer@pelicanbookgroup.com.

Prism is an imprint of
Pelican Book Group
www.PelicanBookGroup.com

Connect with Us
www.facebook.com/Pelicanbookgroup
www.twitter.com/pelicanbookgrp

To receive news and specials, subscribe to our bulletin
http://pelink.us/bulletin

May God's glory shine through
this inspirational work of fiction.

AMDG

You Can Help!

At Pelican Book Group it is our mission to entertain readers with fiction that uplifts the Gospel. It is our privilege to spend time with you awhile as you read our stories.

We believe you can help us to bring Christ into the lives of people across the globe. And you don't have to open your wallet or even leave your house!

Here are 3 simple things you can do to help us bring illuminating fiction™ to people everywhere.

1) If you enjoyed this book, write a positive review. Post it at online retailers and websites where readers gather. And share your review with us at reviews@pelicanbookgroup.com (this does give us permission to reprint your review in whole or in part.)

2) If you enjoyed this book, recommend it to a friend in person, at a book club or on social media.

3) If you have suggestions on how we can improve or expand our selection, let us know. We value your opinion. Use the contact form on our web site or e-mail us at customer@pelicanbookgroup.com

God Can Help!

Are you in need? The Almighty can do great things for you. Holy is His Name! He has mercy in every generation. He can lift up the lowly and accomplish all things. Reach out today.

Do not fear: I am with you; do not be anxious: I am your God. I will strengthen you, I will help you, I will uphold you with my victorious right hand.

~Isaiah 41:10 (NAB)

We pray daily, and we especially pray for everyone connected to Pelican Book Group—that includes you! If you have a specific need, we welcome the opportunity to pray for you. Share your needs or praise reports at http://pelink.us/pray4us

Free Book Offer

We're looking for booklovers like you to partner with us! Join our team of influencers today and periodically receive free eBooks and exclusive offers.

For more information
Visit http://pelicanbookgroup.com/booklovers